PARTY GAMES

THE EROTIC COLLECTION

VICTORIA RUSH

COPYRIGHT

For the uninhibited...

TURN UP THE HEAT IN YOUR LIFE!

To receive more free books and other steamy stuff, sign up for my newsletter.

Victoria Rush Erotica

VOLUME ONE

PARLOR GAMES

1

THE INVITATION

This had to be the strangest party invitation I'd ever received. And the most titillating.

It was from my friend Madison, and the subject heading simply read *Parlor Game*:

You are cordially invited to a special party at Madison's house, Saturday, June 15, at 9:00 p.m. sharp. Dress code is optional. It's a sit-down affair, but I assure you it will be anything but boring. Be prepared to be entertained like you've never been before. Come alone, but come often!

Mad

P.S.: There will be special arrival procedures. Text me five minutes before you get to the door. Please be punctual because the game cannot be interrupted once started. RSVP by Friday, 6:00 p.m.

WTF? I thought upon first reading the invitation. *What kind of parlor game is 'dress code optional'? Did that mean we were free to wear whatever we wanted, or did it mean we were meant to wear no clothing at all? And why couldn't I bring a date?*

But I liked the *come often* idea.

What was Madison up to this time? I knew she had a kinky side, but

I had no idea what she had planned for this event. Who could turn down such an invitation? Her parties always had the most interesting people, the best music, and plenty of unexpected hook-ups.

I picked up the phone and called her as soon as I got the message, dying to get all the dirt on this shindig.

"Whassup, gurl?" Maddie said when she answered my call, recognizing my caller ID.

"You've definitely got my attention now," I said.

"You got my message?"

"Uh–*yeah*. That is one crazy, cryptic invite. What are you getting us into this time?"

"Sorry, I can't provide any more details," she said. "Need to know only. Everything will be explained when you arrive. Are you coming?"

"How could I *not*, with that kind of invitation? But I'm confused about your dress code comment. I have no idea what to wear."

"It doesn't matter what you wear. I assure you no one will be paying attention to any of that."

"Oh, *come on!*" I said. "Now you've really got me squirming in my chair. You have to give me at least a *hint* at what's going to happen. Is it at least *legal*?"

"Of course," she said. "We're all consenting adults. But there will be an opt-out clause for anyone who doesn't feel comfortable participating. I'd never put my friends in a compromising position."

"Okay, you've twisted my arm," I said. "But what's this calling five minutes ahead business? I've never heard of such a thing beyond the usual RSVP."

"It's just to ensure the privacy and confidentiality of our guests. It's the anonymity of the affair that makes this party so special."

Anonymity? I thought. *So I'm not going to know anyone who'll be attending? How does she propose to maintain everyone's privacy?* This thing was getting weirder and more exciting by the moment.

"Fine," I said, shaking my head in frustration. "Your house, your rules. But this better be everything it's cracked up to be. Because now you've seriously raised my expectations."

"I hope that's not the *only* thing I've raised," she purred over the phone. "See you Saturday at nine. Don't be late!"

When I hung up the phone, I could feel my heart pounding in my chest. The call had done nothing to lessen my confusion about the event, only to further arouse my curiosity and excitement. And yes, she'd definitely succeeded in raising more than just my expectations. Feeling my clit hardening in my panties, I opened my blouse and squeezed my erect nipples.

I wasn't sure what I was getting myself into, but my rapidly moistening panties told me this wasn't going to be a party soon forgotten.

2

———

IN THE DARK

On the night of the event, I circled Madison's block at least three times trying to get a better idea about this mysterious game she'd cooked up. But all I could see was a slow procession of strangers approaching her door, one at a time. In each case, she opened the door to greet them, then closed it just as quickly. I had no way of determining how many guests had arrived or what was going on inside. I thought I recognized a few cars parked on the adjoining streets, but there was no way of knowing for sure if they belonged to people I knew.

Note to self. Next time take a pic of my friend's plate and attach it to their contact listing on my phone. You never know when that might come in handy.

On my fourth go-round, I called Maddie from the next street over five minutes before nine. I didn't want to be the first one to break protocol and miss any of the fun.

"I'm here," I said when I heard her pick up.

"Cool," she said. "Find a parking spot close to the house, then come up to the door in five minutes. I'll greet you and get you all set up."

Set up? I thought, hanging up the phone. *What does that mean? And what's with all this careful spacing of guests? Isn't a party supposed to be all about getting to know one another and meeting new faces?*

No matter, I thought, circling around the block and finding a spot on the side of her street four houses down. Judging by the number of cars queued up, it looked like it was going to be an intimate affair. I walked up to her door and tapped the bell. Madison opened the door and after glancing outside to make sure I was alone, she ushered me into her foyer.

"Glad you could make it," she said, smiling at me. "I was afraid I might have scared you off."

"Are you kidding me?" I said. "Wild horses couldn't keep me from coming to this party. If only to see what you've got cooked up."

"I'm glad," she said. "It wouldn't be the same without you."

She pulled a thin black cloth out of a bag resting on the floor and handed it to me. "First up, I need you to put this on."

"A *blindfold*?" I said, widening my eyes. "What for?"

"You'll see," she said. "Maybe not in the *literal* sense, but everything will become apparent soon enough."

She carefully positioned the bandana over my eyes then tied it firmly behind my head.

"No peeking," she said. "That'll ruin all the fun. Not to mention everyone's privacy."

"I couldn't even if I wanted to," I said, feeling the soft fabric wrap snugly over my nose and cheekbones, blocking out my entire field of vision. "Are you going to escort me inside so I don't break a leg?"

"Of course. But you'll have to strip first."

"Say *what*?" I said, cocking my head.

"Oh *please*," she said. "You've never been shy about showing off your amazing body before."

"Well yes, but that was usually with a modicum of cover or around people I know. In this case, I have no idea who'll I be exposing myself to."

"Nor will they. That's why everybody *else* will be blindfolded too."

"Okay," I said, beginning to understand why she'd been so careful not to let anyone see her arriving guests. "But is it safe? I mean, how do I know I'm not going to be accosted by some stranger once I get to the meeting room?"

"You've got nothing to worry about. Everyone will be seated two feet apart on separate chairs. And remember, you can always pull out anytime you feel uncomfortable. I've got your back, girl."

"Jesus, Mad," I sighed. "You are one twisted bitch. I'm just going to have to trust that you know what you're doing."

I started removing my clothes and handed them to Madison and when I was completely naked, she escorted me down a hall into another room where I heard her place my belongings on a table. Then she took my hand and led to me to terrycloth towel-covered chair and eased me down onto it.

"I'll be back after the next guest arrives," she said. "You're welcome to chat with the other guests already here while I'm away. Just don't reveal any names and keep your blindfold in place to maintain the secrecy. The party will get started shortly."

I heard Madison head back to the foyer then for the next few awkward moments, silence filled the room.

"Welcome, new guest," a baritone man's voice said.

I couldn't place him, but he sounded about my age, mid-thirties.

Okay, so at least I know it's a *co-ed* affair.

"Hello," I said timidly, placing my right leg overtop of my knee to protect my modesty.

"It's okay," a woman's voice said. "We were just as freaked out when we got here too."

"Good to know," I nodded, happy to hear another woman's voice in the crowd. The idea of sitting stark naked in a room full of naked strangers was disconcerting to say the least, but strangely arousing. I shifted uncomfortably in my chair, hearing the sound of plastic squeaking underneath me.

"That's a voice I recognize," a familiar-sounding woman said.

It sounded like my friend Lily from last year's camping trip. We'd shared a brief but passionate fling on our one-week excursion into the woods of northern Canada, and suddenly I felt the space between my overlapping thighs become slippery with lubrication.

"Is that–?"

"Sh!" she quickly interrupted me. "No names, remember? You don't want to get kicked out before all the fun starts."

"Mmm," I nodded, squeezing my thighs even tighter together, feeling my clit twitching in excitement between my legs.

I could hear the sound of another guest arriving and quiet murmuring from the other end of the house, then Madison escorted the person into the room and sat him down with the rest of the group. From the minimal smalltalk we'd engaged in during her absence, it sounded like everyone was arranged in a circle roughly twenty feet in diameter. I smiled at Madison's ingenuity concocting such a bold idea, and as I listened to the group of strangers talking around me, my mind began to wander with what she intended to do with us.

When the last guest was seated, I heard her take a seat a few feet to my left as she opened the proceedings.

"First off," she said. "I want to thank everyone for coming. I know it was a pretty vague invitation, and I can't blame any of you if you're wondering what you've gotten yourself into. But I know each of you well enough to know that you're open to new adventures and that you're reasonably uninhibited, if that's the right word."

"If we weren't before, we sure as hell are *now*," the husky-voiced man said.

Everybody chuckled nervously, then Madison continued her briefing.

"Okay, I won't keep you in suspense any longer. What I had in mind was a kind of free association body exploration between willing partners. I thought it might be kind of fun to receive, and then later on, provide some physical stimulation to a chosen partner one at a time, without anyone actually knowing who was doing the giving and who was receiving the stimulation..."

"And by *stimulation* you mean–" I heard Lily enquire.

"Whatever your partner feels comfortable providing. And what you feel comfortable receiving. Because of the blindfolds and the no-name rule, each of the connections will be anonymous. I'll make the initial introductions, and then it's up to each couple to decide how far they wish to proceed. In some cases, you'll be able to guess the gender of your partner, and in some cases you may not. But in all cases, you won't know who it is you're engaging with.

"Unless, that is," Madison said. "You have a prior history with that person and you're specially attuned to your partner's technique and endowments."

"What about–?" someone said, voicing what all of us were thinking.

"For heterosexual combinations, I've put aside a set of condoms on each of your tables to your right. Along with your choice of beer, wine, or cocktails in unspillable containers. Sorry for the sippy cups, but I thought some of you might need a little extra lubrication to get started, and we don't want to make too much of a mess."

"Speaking of–" another woman said.

"You'll also find a tube of lube on each of your tables, should you feel the need. As for cleanliness and diseases, each of you is on your honor to step away or refuse to participate if you have any known issues."

Awkward silence suddenly filled the room.

"Is there some kind of *goal* or *prize* with this parlor game?" I asked. "Or are we just supposed to go with the flow and take everything it as it comes?"

"There will be special prizes later on in the evening for each partner who correctly guesses who received and who provided stimulation. But I suspect the main reward will be enjoyed while you're *living* the experience."

I could hear nervous laughter around the circle as everyone knew exactly what Madison meant.

"Okay," she said. "Now that you understand the rules of engagement, anyone is free to withdraw if you're feeling at all uncomfortable, or abstain from participating once given the choice. I've assembled a small enough group that everyone should have a chance both to receive and give before the evening is over. Does anybody want out?"

Awkward silence filled the room again as I listened to the sound of guests shifting uncomfortably in their chairs. Whether it was because they were nervous or because they were already becoming aroused, I couldn't be sure, but I certainly knew which it was in *my* case.

"Okay then," Madison said. "Let the fun begin. Raise your hand if you want to be the first to give it a try."

I heard the sound of shifting a few chairs away, but I decided to hold back to see how things played out at first.

"Good," Madison said. "I see some of you guys came to play. We've got our first two candidates."

I heard Madison rise from her chair and walk to the other side of the circle, then a pair of footfalls approached a chair a few feet to my right.

"You may proceed at your leisure," Madison said. "If at any time you feel uncomfortable or wish to stop the engagement, simply cross your arms and/or legs and your partner will stop immediately. However, if you're enjoying what you're experiencing, I encourage each of you to let down your guard as much as you feel comfortable and open yourself up to all the possibilities."

"Can we *talk* to our partner while we're engaged in the process?" a man's voice said in front of the chair.

"By all means," Madison said. "Feel free to provide whatever guidance, requests or feedback you feel heightens the experience. The only rule is no revealing of names, and no peeking at any time."

As I listened to the sound of the man kneeling on the carpet in front of the chair, I placed my hands in my lap and pressed my fingers down over the front of my mound. Even before I'd been touched by anyone, I was already feeling more excited and aroused than I'd been in a long time.

3

MF

For the first couple of minutes, I could only hear the sound of the man's hands caressing someone's skin and the subtle squeaking of a chair to my right. I didn't even know if it was a man or a woman who he'd been paired with, and my mind raced with the idea of stretching each of our sexual boundaries. Although I considered myself pansexual, I suspected many of the other guests considered themselves straight who wouldn't under normal circumstances engage in intimate relations with another person of the same sex.

But this was far from typical circumstances. Madison had created a unique, non-judgmental environment for open-minded strangers to explore each other's bodies while focusing only on the sensations they were giving and receiving. It was a brilliant idea, and I could feel the terrycloth towel under my butt already moistening from the stream of juices beginning to run down my vulva. Now I knew why she'd covered each of the chairs with a plastic screen and a towel. I was pretty sure I wasn't the *only* one getting this turned on listening to the two strangers exploring each other's bodies in the dark.

Suddenly, I heard a woman moaning where the man had been placed, and the sound of plastic squeaking under her seat.

Okay, I thought. *So this first pairing is a man giving pleasure to a woman. Madison's playing it safe to start, hoping to ease everybody's nervousness about engaging with an unidentified stranger.* Although I preferred lesbian sex myself, I was not above enjoying other people's intimate relations, especially at a safe distance.

"Mmm," I heard the woman purr, squeaking her chair more loudly.

It was obvious to all of us that whatever the man was doing, she was enjoying his attention while she squirmed her hips on the chair.

"That feels good," she said, encouraging him to continue. "I want to feel your hands on my breasts. Squeeze my tits and pinch my nipples."

"Hmm," the man hummed in acknowledgment, shifting his position closer to her body on the plush carpet below my feet.

"Yes," she hissed, feeling the man's hands caressing her tits. "Whoever you are, I like your touch. Now suck my nipples while I run my fingers through your hair..."

I heard the sound of wet lips smacking on skin as the woman groaned, and I spread my knees apart, circling my clit listening to her getting more and more turned on by the man's ministrations. There was something incredibly sexy about not knowing who was engaged in the veiled sex act or what they looked like.

While the smacking and moaning sounds continued a few chairs away, I began to hear the squeaking of chairs and subtle sighs of *other* people around the circle. It was obvious that many of the other attending guests had become just as aroused as I was from what was going on beside them, and they felt brave enough to touch themselves knowing nobody else was watching.

Nobody except Madison, I smiled. *You scheming bitch. You designed this scenario not only for the enjoyment of your guests, but so you could shamelessly watch everybody while they pleasured one another and themselves.* I could only imagine what she was doing while this was all going down. It must have been a feast for her eyes watching the naked couple exploring each other's bodies, not to mention all the guests touching themselves while they listened in.

"Can you feel how hard my nipples are getting?" the woman said as the man continued sucking her teats.

"Oh yes," the man murmured with his face buried in her cleavage.

"Start licking your way down the front of my stomach. There's something *else* getting hard that needs your attention."

"Mmm," the man purred, kneeling back on the carpet as he lowered his face down her body.

"Yes," she moaned. "Just like that. Rub your rough face over my bare mound. I want to feel your stubble scratching my skin before you fuck me."

Jesus, I thought, spreading my legs further apart while I jilled my clit furiously. I could feel the towel underneath me getting wetter by the moment as I listened to these two strangers ramping up the action. There was a whole extra level of excitement from not being able to see what was going on and only being able to listen to the two lovers as they touched one another. It was true what they said about our other senses being heightened when another one is compromised. My whole body was buzzing like it had an electric current running through it.

I could hear the scratching sound of the man's whiskers rubbing against the woman's skin, and knowing how close his face was to her most sensitive part was driving me crazy with anticipation. And from the sound of the rustling plastic all around me, apparently I wasn't the only one who felt this way.

"Now put your face between my legs and lick my lips up and down," the woman instructed. "I want you to taste my juices while I feel your bristles between my legs."

Holy shit, I thought, placing my palm over my snatch, rubbing my entire vulva with my hand. *I love the way she's bossing him around like he's her slave. It must be driving him crazy not being able to be touched himself. Kind of like the rest of us, except we've got a little more freedom of expression not having other distractions getting in the way.*

"Fuck, yes," the woman groaned. "Your tongue feels so warm on my lips. Now stick it inside me and fuck me while I pull your face into my crotch."

I could hear the sound of wet skin slapping against each other as other voices around the room began to moan and sigh in concert with the woman next to me. Imagining it was me on the receiving end of the man's attention, I stuck my middle finger in my pussy and began fucking myself while I circled my nub with my other hand.

"Deeper," the woman moaned. "I want to feel you probing into my deepest recesses. You're sucking my cunny like a good boy."

"Um-hmm," the man hummed, obviously enjoying the feedback he was getting from his partner while he ate her pussy.

As I listened to the muffled sound of his voice, I imagined her grabbing the back of his hair while she held his face against her cunt. I placed both of my hands between my legs and closed my thighs around them, envisioning it was the man's head pressed against my sex instead of my hands. I could feel my pleasure beginning to rise, but I wanted to hold off coming so I could enjoy the woman's orgasm fully.

"That's it, baby," she growled. "Fuck my pussy with your tongue. I'm getting close now. Lift your head and take my button into your mouth. Suck my clit like you've never sucked on anything before. Make me cum all over your face."

"If you insist," the man murmured with gentle laughter filling the room.

This whole experience was turning out to be even more exciting than I had envisioned. Multi-gender partner swapping with the mystery of not being able to see the couples in action, and even a little humor.

I have got to try this blindfold thing with more of my own partners, I thought. *What a great way to get more attuned to their touch and learn to give better feedback.*

Suddenly, the woman gasped as the plastic on her chair squeaked from the shifting of her ass on the seat. There wasn't much mystery as to what they were doing to each other now. As the licking sounds escalated in volume along with the movement of her hips in her chair, everybody knew he was now sucking on her clit while she pressed his face between her legs.

"Yes," she panted. "Suck my bean and swirl your tongue over it like you're licking a lollypop. I'm going to come in your mouth soon."

"Mmm," the man hummed in assent, not wanting to interrupt the rhythm of his tongue action.

I could only imagine how hard he must have been kneeling between her legs as he sucked her pussy, listening to the sound of her escalating tension. I could almost *see* the cum dripping from the tip of his penis onto the carpet below her chair while he focused on maximizing her pleasure. I nodded at how clever Madison had been in separating the acts of giving and receiving so that each person could enjoy the experience to the fullest without any other distraction.

"That's it, baby," the woman grunted. "Suck me harder. I'm going to come any second."

As I listened to the sound of the woman's chair squeaking and her breath rising in pitch, I spread my legs further apart and pinched my clit between my fingers while I rubbed it up and down. I was ready to come along with the woman, and there was no longer anything holding me back from expressing myself fully. I didn't care if my seat-mates heard what I was doing or how much pleasure I was giving myself. This blind exploration experience had turned out to be more arousing than any explicit porno I'd watched on my computer on lonely nights.

"Yes!" the woman grunted. "Don't stop. Oh God, I'm going to cum! I'm gonna cum so hard in your mouth. *Fuckkk!*"

As I listened to the woman wailing at the top of her lungs, I felt my own orgasm wash over me while I clamped my legs together and gushed all over my hands. After my climax began to ebb, I became more aware of the sounds of the other people in the room as they experienced their own climaxes listening to the sexy couple. With everybody grunting and gasping in collective ecstasy, I turned my head to face Madison, knowing she was watching the whole scene only a few chairs away.

You little fucker, I smiled. *You knew exactly what you were getting us into.* I was so turned on I wanted to jump out of my chair and grind my pussy against her face just like the woman had done with the man.

But I knew that would have to wait. There were still too many *other* possibilities to explore in the meantime.

After a few moments, I heard the sound of the woman's breathing return to normal and the man pull away, wondering what to do next. Although she'd just had a powerful orgasm, there were still many other ways they could connect, and he must have been bursting in anticipation. Sensing his discomfort, the woman sat up in her chair and cleared her throat.

"God damn," she said. "You sure know how to satisfy a woman with your mouth. Can I see what *else* you've got to work with?"

I heard the man rise up from his kneeling position and take a step forward. I could imagine his hard pole dripping in anticipation as he pressed it closer to her face, when Madison, who'd been silent up to now, suddenly interrupted their proceedings.

"Remember the rules," she said. "Each interaction is limited to giving or receiving only. The gentleman will have his opportunity to receive equivalent attention in due course. You can't touch him sexu-ally yet–only *he* can touch *you*."

"That hardly seems fair," the woman huffed. "I'm dying to feel the rest of his package. Can't he touch me with his *cock* also?"

"If that's what you'd like," Madison said. "You just can't touch him in return. At least not *that* way."

"So *other* parts of my body are allowed to touch him, as long as he's taking the lead?"

"Um-hmm," Madison nodded.

"You heard the lady," the woman snarled, shifting her weight in her chair. "Assume the position. I'm ready to feel something *else* in my pussy now."

"If you insist," the man said as the rest of the room chuckled softly.

"But go slow," the woman instructed. "Since I can't touch you with my hands, I want to savor every inch of your cock as you slide inside me. Lift my legs over my shoulders and point your python into my hole."

I heard the sound of the plastic squeaking loudly, then the chair creaked as the woman's weight shifted further back toward her backrest.

"Yes, baby," she purred. "I'm so wet for you. Let me feel the head of your cock pressing into my cunt. Let's savor this moment together."

With the sound of her dirty talk getting me all worked up again, I lifted my feet on top of my chair seat, spreading my knees far apart like I imagined hers were. Suddenly I wished I'd had the foresight to bring one of my favorite dildos to fuck myself at this moment, but I wasn't sure that would be allowed under Madison's rules. Then I remembered that she said each of us had a tube of lube next to us on our side tables. Desperate for anything to put inside me, I reached over and tapped the table gently until I felt a cylinder-shaped object.

Thank God, I thought, running my fingers over the round cap and the tapered end of the tube. *This stuff is going to come in handy in more ways than one.* I picked up the tube and placed the round end against my hole, half expecting her to stop me. Fortunately, her attention seemed to be directed elsewhere, and I groaned as I pressed the tube into my slit.

"Do you need me to–?" the man said, remembering the instructions Madison had given us earlier regarding protection.

"It's already taken care of," the woman purred. "I want to feel your bare skin inside me. I've got my *own* protection."

The man exhaled heavily. I wasn't sure if it was from relief at not having to worry about fumbling with a condom or because he'd reached the limit of his self-control. He lifted the woman's thighs up toward her chest and took a step closer to her. Suddenly both of them groaned as they joined in congress.

"Fuck yes," the woman moaned. "Your dick is so warm. And *thick*. Tease me with your head while I imagine how much more you've got to give me."

The chair began to squeak softly as the man shifted his weight back and forth, lubricating the head of his cock with her juices.

"Mmm," the woman said. "That feels good. "Is it good for you too?"

"Uh-huh," the man grunted.

For a brief moment, I considered lifting my blindfold just enough to see his pole probing her slit, but I dared not be the first to break Madison's rules. I didn't want to interrupt their rhythm with another reprimand from my friend. And besides, she'd put so much forethought and planning into this event, it would be unfair to spoil the fun.

"Okay," the woman continued. "Now slowly push your dick further inside me so I can feel every inch of your burning meat. I want to feel you impale me all the way to the hilt."

"Uhnn," the man groaned as he pressed himself further into her hole.

"God damn," the woman purred. "That's one hell of a joystick. I can feel you spreading me apart the further you go inside me."

"Yes," the man grunted. "You're so tight and wet. Squeeze me while I give you all eight inches."

I heard a few gasps around the room, and smiled imagining how turned on many of the women and some of the men were imagining themselves on the receiving end of his snake.

"Oh God," the woman groaned, feeling him press more and more of his length inside her. "Fill me up, baby. Let me feel all of you inside me now. I want you to pound your meat inside my pussy."

The man grunted as he thrust his full weight against her splayed legs, and she shuddered when he reached the end of her tunnel.

"Holy shit!" she gasped. "You weren't kidding about the size of your cock. I can feel you pressing up against my uterus. Be careful you don't slam me too hard. You might *kill* me with that thing."

"No worries," he said. "I'll be careful. Just let me know if I'm hurting you."

"Ahh," a few women muttered around the room, apparently equally taken by his sexiness as by his concern for his partner.

I pressed the tube of lube as far into my hole as I dared, gripping the tapered end tightly with the fingers of my right hand. The last thing I needed was to lose it inside my pussy and have to go to the hospital to have it removed. Besides, I had *other* purposes I was saving my pussy for. I needed to keep it unoccupied in case Madison decided to hook me up with a man later.

It didn't take long for me to hear the unmistakable sound of the man's penis thrusting in and out of her pussy as their wet bellies slapped together and the woman's chair squeaked loudly next to me.

"Fuck yes," the woman grunted. "Fuck me with that spear. You feel so good. I want to feel you shooting your load inside my pussy."

"Uhnn, uhnn, uhnn," the man groaned as he slammed his cock in and out of her hole. I could hear the sound of his balls flapping against the underside of her vulva as the sloshing sound of her dripping pussy filled the room.

But that wasn't the *only* thing I heard in the room. From almost every direction around the circle, I could hear the grunting and moaning sounds of both men and women pleasuring themselves as they listened to the couple copulating only a few feet away.

I pulled the tube out of my pussy for a moment, then flipped open the cap and squeezed a dollop of lube inside my hole. Then I closed the lid and thrust it back inside me while I trilled my fingers over my burning clit.

"Yes, baby," the woman panted. "I want to feel you come inside me. I'm getting close–"

"Ahem," Madison suddenly interrupted again. "I hate to disturb your fun at this delicate moment. But I want to remind both of you of the rules. Remember, this engagement is designed for the *woman's* pleasure only. Unfortunately, I must ask the gentleman to resist the temptation to consummate the act. Your focus must be on *giving* pleasure for the moment, not receiving."

"Argh," I heard the man groan in frustration.

"Are you *kidding* me?" the woman complained. "If the goal is to give me pleasure, nothing would make me happier than to have my partner experience the penultimate pleasure along with me."

"That may be true," Madison said. "But he'll have to wait his turn.

That's the main attraction, focusing on *one* person's pleasure at a time. If you break the rules, I'm going to have to ask each of you to sit out the rest of the proceedings in a passive role."

"Alright Tiger," the woman said, readjusting her position in her chair. "I'm close. Do you think you can hold off long enough until I climax?"

"I'll try," he said. "Maybe if you take over more of the rocking action. The harder I thrust inside you, the harder it will be not to come."

"Okay," she said. "Just hold steady while I do all the work. Pretend you're a rock while I fuck your magnificent penis. Someone *else* is going to have a wonderful awakening later this evening when they take matters into their own hands."

I heard the woman grip the arms of her chair and begin to rock her hips forward and back as the plastic squeezed under her ass while she fucked the man's pole with her slippery pussy.

"I'm fucking you baby," she panted. "I'm fucking your red-hot poker with my dripping cunt. I'm going to come all over your balls. Are you ready?"

"Uhhh," the man groaned, straining with all his might to resist popping off inside her.

"Here it comes baby," she said. "I'm going to cum all over your big firehose. Oh! Oh! *Uhhhn!*"

As I listened to the sound of the woman grunting in the throes of another orgasm, I pulled my knees together and clamped down over the tube of lube planted inside my pussy while I hissed in ecstasy from the feeling of my own orgasm taking hold of me. This time, there was less reluctance on the part of the rest of the crowd to hold back as they grunted and groaned in orgasmic unison with the woman a few seats over.

While I rocked forward and back in my seat with my entire body quivering in excitement, I couldn't help thinking about the man who'd been forced to contain his pleasure while she rolled her flapping pussy over his giant organ. With any luck, I thought, I'll be the one to finish him off later this evening. I was already beginning to think about how I could make it up to him.

4

———

FF

For a few moments after the woman came, the only thing I could hear in the room was the sound of other people shuffling in their seats and towels rubbing up against bare skin. It was obvious that I wasn't the only one who'd made a mess cumming so hard listening to the sexy man and woman next to me. I envied Madison being able to spy on everybody pleasuring themselves while each couple engaged in their own sexual exploration. It was a brilliant idea on so many levels, and I resolved to hold my *own* blindfold party at the first opportunity.

"So what happens now?" the woman next to me said after she recovered from her orgasm. "My partner is still hard, and I can think of many other ways he can still satisfy me."

"I'm sure he could," Madison said. "But I think it's time to let some of our other guests share in the fun."

As if they haven't already, I grinned under my blindfold as I wiped the dripping tube of lube off with the towel under my seat and placed it back on the table next to me. It felt strangely liberating being able to touch myself with my body on full display, knowing that nobody could actually see me.

"If the gentleman could, um, *extricate* himself now and take his seat," Madison said, seeing the man's cock still impaled in the woman's pussy. "I'd like to ask for a new set of volunteers to continue the entertainment."

I heard the sudden squeaking of plastic all around the circle as everyone threw up their hand.

"Whoa!" Madison exclaimed. "We can't take everybody at once. What do you say we mix it up a little bit this time? If you guys are game to try something a little different, I've got a couple of candidates in mind."

I could almost picture everyone's head nodding as they begged to be chosen next. But knowing Maddie, I knew she'd want to stretch the next couple's boundaries.

"Okay," she said, walking to the other side of the circle. "I think I've identified another interesting pairing. Let me take your hand and escort you to your next partner."

I heard a pair of footfalls crunch across the plush carpet to the opposite side of my circle, three or four chairs away.

"I'll leave you now in the capable hands of your partner," Madison said. "But remember the rules. Only one person at a time can enjoy each coupling. Like the gentleman before, one of you will have to save yourself to receive similar attention later in the evening. Are you guys ready to resume the festivities?"

I heard the shifting of a body in the chair to my left, then the sound of someone kneeling on the carpet in front of the chair. I smiled at how tentative each of the partners were in beginning each engagement, first wanting to identify the other person's sex before deciding to become more actively involved. I still had no idea who'd been paired together, and my pussy throbbed in anticipation as I held my breath dying to find out what Madison had concocted this time. Moments later, I heard the sound of soft hands caressing someone's thighs and a woman purring.

Good, I thought, pressing my hand back down over my dripping mound. At least there's another girl involved. I couldn't place her voice yet, but I was excited to see if it was someone I knew.

"Your hands are so soft," the woman said. I cocked my head recognizing the timbre of her voice. "I like the way you're caressing my thighs."

I recognized the voice instantly. It was my sex therapist friend Hannah, who I'd had more than one sexy rendezvous with myself.

"Mmm," another woman's voice purred between her legs.

Fuck yes, I smiled, feeling my nipples hardening. *This is what I've been waiting for–hearing two women get it on.* I spread my thighs further apart, pressing my fingers against my twitching clit.

"Don't be shy," Hannah said to her hesitant partner. "Feel free to touch me in *other* places."

It seemed obvious that this was the first time her partner had touched another woman this way, and I felt a stream of juices run down the crack of my ass as my pussy twitched in excitement. With nobody else watching, I hoped that the new girl could be encouraged to explore Hannah's body more directly.

I heard the sound of the girl's hands moving further up Hannah's thighs, and she moaned softly.

"Yes," Hannah said. "Press your hands up against the side of my vulva. Can you feel the heat between my legs?"

"Mmm–mmm," the girl hummed.

"Is this your first time touching a woman this way?" Hannah said.

"Mmm–mmm," the girl nodded.

"Feel free to explore at your own pace," Hannah said. "There's no expectations or pressure here. It's just you and me, and nobody else is watching."

"Okay..." the younger woman's voice said.

"Hold your hand over my pussy to see how wet you've made me," Hannah instructed.

I heard the girl shift her body a little closer to Hannah's chair then the sound of wet skin being touched.

"Yes," Hannah moaned. "Your hand feels warm against my cunny. Caress my lips and probe deeper. That feels good."

"Mmm," the girl purred as I heard the smacking sounds grow louder.

"You're making me get all warm and puffy," Hannah sighed. "Can you feel how plump my lips are getting?"

"Yes..." the girl said.

"Press your finger inside me. I want you to see how tight and wet I am."

As I listened to the two women interacting, I suddenly became aware of how quiet the rest of the room had become while everybody strained to listen. Not wanting to interrupt the girls' rhythm, I circled my clit quietly with two fingers while I sat mesmerized on my chair.

Suddenly Hannah groaned as she pressed her body lower in her chair, taking the girl's finger deep inside her pussy.

"Oh God," she panted. "You have no idea what you're doing to me. I love feeling you inside me. Place another finger into my slit and curl your fingers toward the front of my pussy. I want to feel you caress my G-spot."

A few chairs around the room suddenly squeaked as some of the guests adjusted their position uncomfortably. It was obvious I wasn't the only one getting turned on listening to two girls touching each other–especially knowing that for one of them, it was her first lesbian experience.

"Fuck yes," Hannah panted. "Just like that. Can you feel my pussy squeezing your fingers while you caress me inside?"

"Mmm–hmm," the girl hummed shyly.

"That feels incredible the way you're stroking me. Can you see my clit pushing out of its hood?"

"Yes," the girl groaned, becoming aroused watching Hannah's splayed pussy mere inches in front of her face.

"Let me feel your breath on my pearl while you caress me."

"Okay..." the girl said, shifting closer to Hannah's dripping pussy.

"Mmm," Hannah purred. "I feel you so close to me now. Blow on my clit while I imagine you watching me."

I heard a soft blowing sound then Hannah groaned more loudly.

"Oh God," she said. "You're driving me insane. Can I feel your lips on me? Even if for just a brief kiss?"

I smiled at how Hannah was gently coaxing the girl to take

progressively bolder steps exploring her body. She was an experienced therapist who'd had many years of experience bringing similarly uptight women out of their shells.

I heard the girl press her body slowly forward, followed by a wet smacking sound.

"Yes, baby," Hannah purred. "Take my jewel between your lips. Feel how hot and hard I am for you. Let me feel you suck my bean while I squeeze your fingers. Can you see what you're doing to me?"

"Mmm," the girl moaned into Hannah's pussy.

"Swirl your tongue over my button now," Hannah said, continuing to guide the girl. "Show me how a woman is properly made love to."

"*Fuckk,*" Hannah groaned, gripping her chair's armrests tightly with her hands. "Your tongue feels so hot on my clit. Suck me harder into your mouth while you swirl your tongue in circles over my nub."

Suddenly, the familiar sound of squeaking chairs from around the circle filled the room as the rest of the group began to get more and more aroused listening to the two women. I thrust three fingers into my pussy and began pressing them in and out of my hole, trying to imagine what Hannah was feeling.

"Yes baby," she panted more deeply. "Now curl your fingers against the inside of my pussy while you suck and tease my clit. You're doing an amazing job. I haven't felt someone excite me like this in a long time."

I suspected Hannah was stretching the truth a little bit there, knowing how often the two of us had shared a passionate encounter, but I liked how she was continuing to give her partner positive encouragement.

"Are you enjoying this as much as I am?" she said to the girl.

"Mmm-hmm," the girl hummed in agreement.

"Do you want to make me come with your sweet mouth?"

"Mmm–hmm," she hummed even louder.

"Press your fingers deep inside me while you keep caressing the front of my pussy. Maintain the steady action of your tongue over my clit. Flick it from side to side, then roll your tongue over it in figure-eight motions. I want to feel you sucking my whole gland."

I heard the girl shift her weight to get more comfortable between Hannah's legs then Hannah uttered a deep guttural moan.

"Fuck *yes*, baby," she said. "Just like that. God damn, you sure know how to eat a girl's pussy. Suck my clit. I'm going to cum soon. I'm going to cum all over your sweet face."

For the next thirty seconds, all I could hear was the escalating sound of Hannah's breathing and the accelerated squeaking of her chair a few feet to my left. Every so often, I heard the soft moaning and grunting of other guests pleasuring themselves as they listened to the two girls, and I began to jerk my hand harder up against my snatch, feeling my own pleasure beginning to build.

"That's it, baby," Hannah hissed. "Don't stop. That's perfect. I'm going to come soon. Oh God...I'm cumming! *Nnngh!!*"

This time I managed to hold off coming long enough to listen to the sounds of pleasure emanating from all around me in the room. My pussy twitched while I listened to Hannah climaxing in her partner's mouth then the rest of the group coming one after another.

"I'm still cumming baby!" she panted. "Don't take your mouth off me. Can you feel me pulsing on your fingers?"

"Mmm," the girl moaned, thoroughly enjoying how well she'd managed to please her partner.

"*Uhnn, uhnn, uhnn,*" Hannah grunted with each powerful contraction of her pussy.

It seemed to take almost a full minute for her to stop thrashing in her chair before silence filled the room once again.

"Whoever you are," she sighed after finally coming down from her climax. "You're a quick learner. That was amazing. Come up here and kiss me. I want to thank you properly for your amazing performance."

The girl lifted herself up off the carpet and pressed her body closer to Hannah then I heard the sound of the two women kissing.

"Come sit on my lap, baby," Hannah said after a few moments. I want to feel your tits pressing up against me."

I heard Hannah's chair squeak as the girl placed her legs through the open armrests and sat down spread-eagled on her lap.

"Your body feels so hot against my skin," Hannah said, kissing her face softly. "Your tits are nice and full. And your nipples are hard. Do you like it when I squeeze them like this?"

"Yes," the girl panted.

I heard the sound of Hannah's hands roaming over the girl's body, then the familiar sound of someone's fingers pressing into a moist pussy.

"How about *this*?" Hannah said. "Do you like it when I touch you *here*?"

"Fuck, yes," the girl panted.

"Ahem," Madison said, clearing her throat. "Don't forget the rules. This is supposed to be a *one-way* engagement only."

"But she's obviously enjoying this," Hannah protested. "And since it's her first time with another woman, can't we make an exception?"

"She'll have her chance soon enough," Madison said. "If you two can't control yourselves, perhaps it's time to separate..."

"Wait," Hannah said as the girl began to lift herself from the chair. "I'd like to try one more thing. Can you change your position so you're facing the other way, with one of your legs threaded through one side of the armrests? That way we'll be able to touch our pussies together and I can enjoy this connection in a *different* way. That's allowed, right Madison?"

"As long as your partner will be able to contain herself," she said. "But I have my doubts. I'd hate to see her miss out on her own one-on-one opportunity later tonight."

"Just try it for a few seconds," Hannah said to the girl. "I want you to get a taste for what it feels like when two women join together in the most intimate way. Don't worry about making me come again if you find it too hard to continue. Let's just have a little fun together."

"I like the sound of that," the girl said. "But you might have to show me how to position my body correctly. I've never done it like this before."

"Stand up and turn your body around so your ass is facing my hips," Hannah instructed. "Then put your right leg through the armrest on the right side of my chair and sit down on my lap. I'll take care of the rest."

"Okay," the girl said.

I heard her shift her feet on the carpet then the squeaking sound of the chair as the girl sat down over Hannah's hips.

"That's it," Hannah said. "Now lean forward while I tilt my hips up. Can you feel the heat between my legs?"

"Yes," the girl panted.

"Just a couple more inches and–"

"*Uhnn!*" the girl suddenly groaned.

"Can you feel that baby? I'm touching my pussy against yours. Can you feel our wet skin joining together?"

"Oh God," the girl moaned. "That feels incredible. I never even imagined–"

"It only gets better," Hannah purred, grabbing the girl's hips, pulling her harder toward her snatch. "God, you're burning up against me."

"Yes," the girl groaned. "Fuck me with your pussy. Rub your cunt against mine. I want to feel *every* part of you rubbing up against me."

"Mmm," Hannah moaned, as her chair began to squeak rhythmically.

"Does that feel good, baby?" she said.

"Fuck, yes," the girl moaned.

"Lean forward a bit more while I tilt my hips higher..."

"Nnngh," the girl groaned more loudly.

"Do you like that? Can you feel my clit rubbing up against yours?"

"Yes," the girl said. "Don't stop. That feels so good."

As I listened to the two women's breathing rate escalate toward the inevitable tipping point, I knew even before she said anything what was going to happen next.

"You have no idea how much I hate to do this," Madison interrupted again. "But I'm going to have to ask you two to slow down or separate. I don't think your partner is going to be able to hold out much longer."

"You are *so* cruel, Madison!" Hannah huffed. "How can you deny this beautiful creature her chance to enjoy her first lesbian experience to the fullest?"

"I promise I'll give her a chance to consummate the experience later. Why don't you finish up now so we can move on to the next couple? But I suggest you try a different position to avoid putting your partner over the edge."

"Jesus," Hannah said. "I was just about to come. What do you think, baby? Do you mind finishing me off another way then I'll try to make sure you're properly taken care of later?"

"I'll try," the girl said, still breathing heavily. "What do you want me to do?"

Hannah paused for a moment, contemplating the simplest way to get off, then she shifted her position in her chair.

"Can you lift yourself up a few inches and reach between my legs? I'd love to feel you finish me with your hands while I caress your body."

The girl straightened her legs and lifted her body off Hannah a few inches, then I heard her hand moving over Hannah's wet vulva as she began moaning in pleasure again.

"Yes, baby," Hannah said. "That's perfect. Rub your fingers in circles over my hard clit while I squeeze your tits. It won't take long to make me cum this time."

"Mmm," the girl purred as the chair began squeaking from the weight of her hand propping her body up on the side armrest.

"Your nipples are so hard," Hannah moaned. "Next time I want you to fuck me with your tits. I hope this won't be the last time we have a chance to be together."

"Absolutely," the girl said. "This is way better than fucking a man. They're only interested in one thing, and they're always in such a hurry to get it over with. I'm not sure I'll *ever* go back after this."

"That's my girl," Hannah purred. "I'm ready now. Press your fingers harder against my clit and move them around in circles over my shaft. I love the way you're touching me."

"Yes," the girl purred. "I want to feel you come in my hands. Spray your juices all over me."

"Oh *fuckk*!" Hannah suddenly howled, losing control hearing the girl talk dirty to her. "I'm cumming, baby. I'm cumming so hard. *Uhnnn!*"

Suddenly, I heard the whole room erupting in a cacophony of grunts and groans as the other men and women around the circle could no longer contain their pleasure listening to Hannah having another powerful climax. I'd been holding back for the big finish too, and as I listened to Hannah gushing all over the girl's ass perched inches above her flapping pussy, I grunted loudly as I sprayed my own juices all over my seat.

5

MM

"Okay then," Madison said after giving Hannah a few moments to recover. "That certainly was exciting. Who'd like to give it a try next?"

I heard some chairs squeak as a few more guests put up their hands.

"I'm glad to see you're all enjoying this enough to want to participate directly. But I'd like to stretch everyone's horizons a bit this time and test some new combinations."

There was some shuffling sounds a few feet to my left, then a group of footfalls moved across the carpet to the other side of the circle.

"Allow me to escort the lady back to her chair to make sure nobody trips over each other. Now, let's see," Madison paused. "Yes–I think *this* might make for an interesting pairing."

I heard some heavier footsteps being escorted to the opposite side of the circle, then Madison sat back down in her chair.

"Remember," she instructed, "there's no pressure to do anything you don't want to do. That applies to both of you. But you never know how much you might enjoy something until you try it. So I encourage both of you to explore each other at your own pace and open your minds to some new possibilities."

Hmm, I thought, rubbing my slippery thighs together. *This sounds even more interesting than the last two pairings. What has Madison cooked up this time?*

The room was quiet for a few moments, then I heard the sound of someone kneeling on the carpet in front of the designated chair. There was a brief scuffing noise that sounded like hands rubbing against hairy skin, then it stopped almost as abruptly.

The room filled with awkward silence for a few moments, then Madison interjected to break the tension.

"I can see both of you are feeling a little squeamish. Remember, this is all about sharing new experiences and enjoying the attention of different partners without any judgment or preconceptions. I encourage both of you to open yourselves up to try something new. *All* of us have fantasized about exploring new sexual boundaries at one time or another. This is one place where it's completely safe and judgment-free. Am I right, ladies and gentlemen?"

A soft cheer rose from around the circle as the guests clapped quietly.

"See?" Madison said. "Nobody here cares who's connecting with whom, and they'll never know anyway unless you choose to reveal it later. Live in the moment and enjoy yourselves for a while!"

There was another awkward silence then I heard the squeak of a chair and the crinkling of plastic as someone spread their legs further apart. The other person hesitated for another long moment, then I heard the sound of hands moving over rough skin.

Okay, I nodded. *That definitely sounds like a man's thighs this time, unless someone hasn't shaved her legs in quite a while. The only question now is, is his partner a man or a woman?*

The scratching sound seemed to get rougher and rougher until I heard the familiar sound of skin rubbing over stubble.

There we go, I smiled. *At least someone's done some grooming down there.* I could almost see the man's cock slowly inflating as his partner caressed his bristly pubis and private parts.

"Uhnn," a husky-sounding man groaned, shifting his position again in his chair. "That feels good, whoever you are. You're making me hard."

I heard his partner exhale deeply and wondered if it was because they were getting turned on watching the man get aroused or because they were nervous about proceeding.

"If you just want to touch me with your hands, that's cool," the man said, sensing his partner's hesitation. "I've never done it with a man before, but so far it feels just as good as with any woman I've been with."

So it's an all-male coupling this time, I nodded excitedly. I'd always been fascinated watching gay men have sex online, and the thought of two *straight* guys hooking up excited me even more. I spread my legs apart and began stroking the sides of my vulva, trying to imagine what he was feeling.

"Yeah, play with my balls, man," the receiving man groaned. "That feels good. I can never get my girlfriend to give me enough attention down there. They always think it's all about the cock."

"Mmm," his partner hummed in agreement.

Fuck, this is hot, I thought, feeling my juices begin to run down over my slit. Listening to two guys who knew what they liked was utterly fascinating. I wondered how many straight women around the room were making mental notes of how to better please their partners, just like the *guys* were when Hannah and her partner were getting it on.

"Fuck man," the husky-voied man purred. "I'm hard as a rock. My dick is flapping up against my stomach. Grab my shaft and feel how hard I am."

"Uhnn," the other man grunted, his breathing beginning to grow more ragged.

Straight or not, it was apparent he was getting just as excited as his partner feeling another man's hard cock in his hands. I suddenly wished I could lift my blindfold again to see his lengthening cock swinging between his legs while he leaned over to touch his partner. The scene was becoming more exciting by the moment.

"Yeah, man," the first man groaned. "Grab me with two hands. Squeeze my shaft while you stroke me up and down."

As I strained to listen, all I could hear was the sound of both men breathing heavily.

"Fuck, yes, that feels so good. Can you feel my head popping in and out of your hands while you stroke me?"

"Uh–huh," the other man nodded.

"I'm getting sticky on top with precum. Do you mind putting some lube on my dick to make it more slippery? I want to enjoy this handjob properly."

I heard a tapping sound as the other man reached over to the side table, then a pop as he flipped open the lid and squirted some lube over the top of the other man's cock. Seconds later, I heard the familiar slapping sound of skin rubbing against wet skin as the first man began to moan louder.

"Yeah, man," he groaned. "That's so much better. Squeeze me hard while I pump my cock in your hands. Are you getting hard too?"

"Uhnn," the other man grunted, which I took to be a yes. Now I *really* wanted to take my blindfold off to see the two of them getting aroused touching each other.

"God damn, that feels good," the first man moaned. "I like your tight grip on my dick. Can you feel my cum dripping out of the tip and down over your hands?"

"Yeah," the other man spoke for the first time.

I couldn't place either person's voice, but that didn't stop me from enjoying the experience to the fullest. While I listened to both of them grunting and breathing heavily, I circled my clit and moaned softly along with them.

"Play with my balls again," the first man said. "Squeeze them with one hand while you work the head of my dick with the other. Yeah–that's it, squeeze them tighter. Is that the way you like it too?"

"Uh-huh," the other man groaned.

"Listen," the first man said. "I could come any second now, but I'd love to feel your dick before I pop off. Can you stand up and let me touch it for a second? I've never felt another man's hard cock before either."

This is fucking awesome, I smiled, feeling my pussy twitch listening to the two straight men exploring each other's bodies. It's even better than I imagined. Madison must have known when she selected the guests what she had in mind, and I nodded in appreciation at her courage in pairing these two up. Nobody's ever a hundred percent straight. Sometimes they just need a safe place and the right opportunity to explore the other side of their sexuality.

I heard the other man rise up from his kneeling position then take a step forward. Suddenly he groaned, as his partner grasped his cock in front of his face.

"Damn, man," the husky-voiced man said. "That's a pretty impressive piece of equipment you've got there. It feels like you're circumcised like me. And you're dripping, too. Can you do me a favor and touch your cock against mine? Maybe we can *both* have a little fun if that's okay with Madison."

"No problem on my end," Madison chimed in. "As long as your partner doesn't get too carried away."

The other man knelt back down on the carpet as the first man shifted his weight forward on his chair. Then I heard the lube container flip open again while the second man squirted some on top of his own hard-on.

"Yeah, man," the first man said. "I've always wondered what this would feel like. Place the underside of your dick up against mine, then let me hold them together while we jerk our cocks together."

I heard some more shuffling sounds, followed by a rhythmic smacking noise while both men moaned together.

"That feels incredible having your dick rubbing against mine," the deep-voiced man groaned. "Your cock feels so hot. Is this feeling as good for you as it is for me?"

"Yeah," the other man grunted. Whether he was just being shy about revealing his identity or he didn't want to show how much he was enjoying his first man-on-man encounter was unclear.

But *I* was sure as hell enjoying it. And from the sounds of other men and women around the circle, so was everybody else.

God damn, Madison, I thought. *This idea was absolutely fucking brilliant. Not only are you giving everybody a chance to stretch their individual boundaries, you're also giving the rest of us a chance to live out our wildest fantasies listening in on the action.*

"Can you picture our cockheads rubbing together while I grip our shafts with two hands?" the first man said.

"Fuck yeah," the other man grunted.

"I wish I could see it too," the husky-sounding man said. "Maybe Madison will give me a chance to switch positions with you later."

"Maybe..." Madison grinned a few seats away.

"Damn, man. I can feel your *balls* rubbing up against mine too. This is even hotter than I thought it would be. I'm getting close, how about you?"

"Yeah," the other man panted.

"Okay guys," Madison suddenly interrupted. "As much as I'd love to watch the fireworks, I'm going to have to ask you to disengage. Let's focus primarily on stimulating the gentleman in the chair. As you said, your partner will have his chance for reciprocal action soon enough."

"I'm sorry, man," the first man said. "But I promise to make it up to you later. I love the feel of your cock in my hands. I can't wait to watch you spew all over my dick. Do you mind finishing me with your hands?"

"No worries, man," the second man said.

I smiled listening to the dynamic between the two men. If this was how straight guys spoke when they had sex with each other, I found it kind of amusing. There was none of the usual love-talk between regular gay men. For some reason, it was turning me on even *more* listening to them pretending to sound all macho.

I heard the second man shift his position a few inches further away from the chair, then the rhythmic, wet smacking sounds resumed.

"Fuck yeah, man," the first man said. "I can feel your sticky cum coating my dick. Your hands feel so warm around my cock. It won't take long now. Squeeze my balls while you stroke my dick. I'm going to cum hard in your hands."

"Do it, man," the second man spoke up, momentarily forgetting where he was. "This is so hot watching your dick flare in my hands. You seem to be getting even bigger the closer you get to popping off."

"Yeah man," the first man huffed. "I can feel it. I'm gonna cum any second now. Let me cum all over your chest."

Suddenly, I heard the second man shift his position again, and the husky-voiced man let out an unearthly groan.

"Oh my God," he grunted. "Yes, suck my dick into your mouth. Your lips feel so hot on my dick. I'm gonna cum, man. Oh fuck, I'm gonna cum so hard in your mouth."

"Um-hmm," the other man hummed, obviously ready to accept his load.

"Yeah, baby," the first man growled. "Here it comes. Squeeze my balls. Oh *fuckkkkk*!!"

As I listened to the man howl in ecstasy, I could picture him pouring his load into the other man's mouth. It must have felt incredibly exciting for the other man to feel him pulsing in his hands while his partner exploded in his mouth. Whether he was swallowing his cum or letting it drip out of the side of his mouth, I had no way of knowing. But from the sounds of all the other grunting men all around me, it was apparent he wasn't the *only* one spilling his load.

$$6$$

FF

After the two men had their turn, I eagerly awaited Madison's next choice of partners. She once again asked for a show of hands, and when she took my hand and escorted me to the other side of the circle, my pussy throbbed in anticipation to see who she'd paired me with. When I knelt down in front of my partner's chair and placed my hands on her thighs, my heart pounded when I felt the smooth, soft skin of a woman.

It had been weeks since I'd felt another woman's body next to mine, and I smiled at the opportunity to give the mysterious guest some girl-on-girl attention. I still had no idea if she was straight, bi, or lesbian, but it hardly mattered. I was about to give her a sexual experience like nothing she'd ever experienced before.

At least nothing she'd experienced *blindfolded*.

Her breathing began to deepen when she felt my hands on her legs, and I slid them slowly up the outsides of her thighs until I reached her ass. I took a moment to caress the sides of her buttocks, squeezing her muscles as she reflexively contracted them into two tight globes. I still had no idea who I was touching, but one thing was for sure. She hardly had a stitch of fat on her body, and her ass must have been a magnificent thing to see from behind.

The woman still hadn't uttered a single word, not even a moan or a sigh, but I could hear her breathing rate beginning to escalate the further I pressed my hands upward. With my face so close to her pussy, it was tempting to move closer toward her genitals, but with her seeming to hold back, I decided to press further up her body to see if I could get her to open up. I pressed her knees gently apart and pushed my breasts into her gap as I slowly lifted my hands up the side of her stomach toward her chest. When I felt the curvature of her breasts, I cupped them with both hands and pressed my tits against her wet snatch. I smiled feeling the river of juices cascading over my skin, belying her attempt to pretend indifference.

Damn, I thought. *This is one uptight girl. This calls for some more aggressive action.*

I raised myself up from my kneeling position, then threaded each of my legs through the armrests on both sides of her chair and lowered my ass onto her steaming lap. Then I slowly leaned forward until I felt her hard nipples touching my own. Twisting my torso from side-to-side, I flicked her teats with my tips then pressed my tits hard against her as I tilted my sopping pussy toward her quivering stomach.

As I leaned in closer toward her, I turned my face toward the side of her head.

"Do you like what I'm doing so far?" I whispered into her ear.

"Uh-huh," she squeaked softly.

I smiled as I nibbled and sucked on her ear, feeling her hot breath pulsing against my neck. Then I pulled back a few inches and squeezed her firm breasts, kneading her tips between my fingers. When she uttered a deep guttural growl, I leaned forward to kiss her. She pursed her lips, resisting my intrusion at first, and I bit her lower lip gently, sliding my wet tongue under the rim. When she parted her lips unconsciously, I thrust my tongue into her cavity, pressing my face hard against hers.

With my tongue probing her insides and my hands pinching her nipples, she slowly began to surrender herself as she tilted her hips upward, pressing her mound against mine. When she began moaning in my mouth, I grabbed both sides of her head, pulling her harder toward me. She responded by swirling her tongue around mine while rocking her hips, trying to increase the stimulation between her legs.

After a few seconds, I pulled back and smiled at the woman, sensing she was ready for the next stage in my exploration.

"Would you like me to move a little *lower* now?" I asked.

"Yes," she panted.

She still hadn't said enough for me to place her voice, but not knowing who it was turned me on even more. There was something about the idea of intimately touching a stranger–especially a straight woman–that I found insanely exciting.

I pulled my legs out from between the armrests and kneeled back down onto the carpet between her legs, determined to draw her further out of her shell. This time, as I pressed my hands up the insides of her thighs, I found them coated with a slippery film while she parted her legs, inviting me to move closer. When I pressed my hands against the side of her dripping vulva, she groaned softly and placed her hands on top of my head, running her fingers through my hair.

"That feels good," she said softly.

I thought there was something in her voice that sounded familiar, and I moved my face closer to her pussy, encouraging her to provide more verbal feedback. Normally, I would have been inclined to tease her some more with my hands, but I could feel the heat emanating from her pussy and her juices running down over my fingers, and I leaned in to encircle her flaming nub between my lips. When I sucked her clit into my mouth and began rolling my tongue over her exposed bulb, she groaned deeply, pulling my head in harder toward her slit.

"Oh God," she groaned. "That feels so good. Lick my pussy with your tongue."

I paused for a second trying to place the voice, then it suddenly struck me. It was my married neighbor, Valerie, who'd invited me to a pool party a few weeks ago at her house on the opposite side of my yard. We'd ogled each other's bikini-clad bodies for much of the event, but neither of us felt comfortable making a move with her husband and friends milling so close nearby. I was amazed how tight and shapely her figure was for a mother of two teenagers, and I couldn't take my eyes off her shapely ass the whole time I was there. For a long time after, I spied on her whenever she went outside to swim in the pool, masturbating to orgasm many times, wishing I had the courage to approach her directly.

Knowing I finally had my sexy neighbor exactly where I wanted her drove me crazy with desire, and I grabbed her ass with both hands, pulling her pussy hard against my face as I flicked her hard pearl with my lips and tongue.

"Fuck yes," she panted, losing herself in the heat of the moment. "Suck me into your mouth. Your lips feel so hot against my pussy."

"Mmm," I nodded, happily lapping up her juices as she rolled her hips over my face.

Her breathing beginning to quicken and become more ragged, and I knew it wouldn't be long before she came. Whether it was because I was doing such a good job eating her pussy or because she was excited feeling another woman's lips on her clit for the first time, I wasn't sure. All I knew was that I wanted to enjoy her orgasm to the fullest when the moment came.

I held the tips of two fingers against her widening hole, then I pressed them slowly inside her. She gasped when she felt me penetrate her, and as I began to curl my fingers forward caressing the front of her G-spot, she bunched her fingers into a fist, clutching my hair with two hands. While I swirled my wet tongue over her clit, she pulled my hair harder and harder as she unconsciously clenched her hands approaching the peak of her pleasure. When she finally hit the tipping point, she screamed out loud, jerking her hips hard against my face in spastic twitches.

While the walls of her pussy clamped down against my fingers in rhythmic pulses, I held my face against her vulva as I felt my own juices running down the insides of my thighs in sympathetic union. When her contractions finally began to subside, she loosened her grip on my hair, and I pulled away smelling the sweet musk between her legs.

"I'm sorry if I hurt you," she said. "It's just that I haven't felt a woman touch me like that and I guess I got a little carried away."

I wanted to tell her it was no bother, but she still hadn't guessed who I was, and I didn't want to spoil the mystery, so I simply nodded and mumbled *um-hmm* to indicate that I was fine. But I was far from being finished with my sexy neighbor. Before the evening was over, I wanted her to experience the full spectrum of girl-on-girl sex, and I had more plans for her. I leaned forward, pressing my breasts between her thighs, then I grabbed one of my tits and swiped it up and down over her slippery vulva.

"Oh my God," she panted. "Is that your–? Yes, fuck my pussy with your tits. You're so soft. Much softer than my–"

"Husband?" I purred.

"Yes," she said. "And slower and more sensuous. I love the way you tease me with *every* part of your body."

"I'm far from finished teasing you with the rest of my body," I purred.

When I felt Valerie's fingers reach down over her mound and begin to circle her clit above my breast, I reached out and stopped her with my hand.

"I think we might be able to find another way to stimulate you there," I smiled.

"Yes," she panted. "Rub my clit again. I want to come again."

I thrust my arms under her thighs and pulled her closer toward the edge of her chair, then I pushed her knees up toward her chest, placing my legs over the top of her armrests. Grasping the sides of her backrest for support, I lowered my pussy down on top of her flayed legs. When she felt my hot cunt press against her vulva, she groaned loudly in my ear.

"Do you like that, baby?" I said, mashing my tits against hers while rocking my hips against her dripping pussy.

"Fuck yes," she panted in my ear. Then she pulled my head closer to her face, breathing against my neck. "I know who are, Jade. I've fantasized about making love to you ever since you moved in next door. You're even sexier than I imagined. Rub your cunt against me. I want to feel you come against my lips."

"I'm not sure Madison's going to allow that," I whispered back. "But at least I'll be able to feel you coming against me. Until *next* time, that is."

"Oh, there's definitely going to be a next time," she panted.

"Hold on babe," I purred. "Cause I'm going to ride you like a bucking bronco."

As we began to rock our hips back and forth, the loud smacking sound of our two vulvas began to echo around the room, and I wondered how many of the guests knew just how tightly the two of us were pinned together. From the sound of all the moans and sighs around the circle, I guessed their imaginations were already wandering to some interesting places.

As Valerie and I pressed our bodies harder together, I reveled in the feeling of her hot, slippery skin rubbing up against my tits and pussy. It must have been a feast for Madison's eyes being able to watch both of our exposed pussies pushing over the edge of Valerie's chair as we gnashed our cunts together. While I tribbed my clit hard against Valerie's hard nub, we moaned in unison, feeling our passion rising in tandem.

"Hold on ladies," Madison interrupted, right on cue. "Are you going to be able to–"

"I *got* this Maddie," I said, holding out a finger from the side of my body. "Just give me one more minute."

"You're threading the needle here," she said. "I'd hate to stop you before your partner is fully satisfied."

I pulled my arms against the side of Valerie's back rest, drawing my face closer to her ear once again.

"Come all over my pussy, Valerie," I said. "I want to feel your cunt twitching when you come."

"Uhnnn," she groaned into my other ear as I felt a dribble leak out of her slit and down the crack of my ass.

"Yes, baby," I purred. "Come for momma. Grind your cunt against me while I feel you gush into my hole."

"Oh God..." Valerie suddenly grunted. "Yes, I'm coming! I'm going to cum so hard against your hot pussy. Here it comes. *Aieeeee!*"

Listening to Valerie scream in my ear as she clamped her pussy against mine in the throes of another powerful climax took all of my willpower to contain myself from coming along with her. But I knew from Madison's viewing angle that I wouldn't be able to hide my usual flood of waterworks. So I simply held Valerie close to me and purred into her ear, encouraging her to enjoy her orgasm to the fullest.

"Yes, baby," I said. "I feel your pussy pulsing against me. Come all over me, baby. I love feeling your sexy body against mine."

"Oh Christ," she panted. "I'm still coming. I'm still coming against your beautiful, hot pussy. *Uhnn, uhnn, uhnn...*"

I smiled, feeling the contractions of her vulva syncing with her loud grunts in my ear. I hadn't fucked another woman like this for a very long time, and I reveled in every twitch and groan of my newly liberated straight friend. Something told me this wouldn't be the last time we stole a few clandestine meetings away from the prying eyes of our nosy neighbors.

7

FM

For the next hour and a half, Madison continued selecting random participants from around the circle until just about everybody had had a turn both ways. But I'd just had a single turn so far, and I was eagerly looking forward to my next pairing, especially since I'd been prevented from fully enjoying the last episode. But when she grabbed my hand and pulled me out of my chair, indicating that I'd be the giver not the receiver again, I paused and turned my face toward her inquisitively.

"But I thought–"

"Something tells me you'll enjoy being the one in charge of this next encounter," she smiled, leading me to the far side of the circle.

When I kneeled down in front of my partner's chair and placed my hands on their thighs, I hesitated when I felt the telltale bristly skin of a man. I usually preferred making love to women, but in this case I was prepared to make an exception. I'd been biding my time patiently touching myself listening to everybody else get off, but the tube of lube just wasn't cutting it for me any longer. I needed a proper, full-sized cock in my pussy to finish things off.

And besides, I thought. It would be kind of fun to explore a man's body while blindfolded, learning what turned him on without the benefit of any visual cues.

Not knowing the identity of the person she'd coupled me with, I decided I'd have a little fun teasing him with a slow build-up. I placed my hands on top of his legs and gradually slid them up toward his crotch, pressing my fingers into the inside of his thighs.

"Mmm," a husky-sounding voice purred. "This feels a little different than the last time."

My heart raced knowing it was the same deep-voiced man I'd heard earlier in the evening when he'd been paired with another guy. I was excited to feel his organ in my hands and give him a different perspective this time. Knowing he was straight, I suspected he preferred having sex with women, and I planned to give him an experience he wouldn't forget.

As I slowly spread his knees apart with my shoulders, I caressed the inside of his thighs with the tips of my breasts. I could feel his hairs standing on end while my hands slid over the goose bumps on his skin.

"Yes?" I purred. "Do you like feeling my tits against your thighs? Are you ready for a *woman's* touch this time?"

"*Fuck* yes," he panted, spreading his legs further apart.

"Mmm," I smiled, pressing my breasts up against his balls, feeling his cock already pointing straight up at full flagstaff. "Is there anything in particular you'd like me to do with my special endowments?"

"Yes," he moaned. "Rub your tits on my balls. Then tit-fuck me with those nice melons of yours."

I smiled at the crude labels men often used to describe women's lady parts, but it didn't bother me this time because I knew I'd be the one in the driver's seat controlling the action. And before our turn was over, I planned to make him *beg* me to do his bidding.

I grabbed the sides of my tits and lifted myself up a few inches, surrounding his cock in my cleavage. It was hard for me to tell just how big he was without touching him directly with my hands, but there was plenty of dick still poking out from the top of my tits even though I was bustier than most women.

"That feels incredible," he groaned, angling his hips upward, pressing his balls tightly against my chest. "Your tits are so soft and warm..."

"Softer and warmer than a man's hands?" I teased.

"Yes," he grunted. "I far prefer feeling a woman's skin against my body."

"You didn't seem to be complaining too much last time."

"Yeah well, when you're horny, just about anything will do the trick. But chicks turn me on a lot more than men."

"Well you better strap yourself in then," I said. "Because I plan to give you a hell of a ride."

Although I could feel his hard pole burning up between my compressed tits, it was hard to get traction rubbing dry skin on dry skin, so I leaned over toward his side table and grabbed the tube of lube, pouring a generous dollop over the head of his throbbing member.

"Yeah, baby," he said. "Lube me up. I want to fuck your tits and come all over your face."

Fat chance of that, I smiled. Apparently, he still needed to be shown who was in charge here.

I grabbed his dick hard with two hands and slowly pulled them down the length of his shaft, coating his hard-on with the lube.

Jesus, I thought, feeling his thick phallus in my hands. This guy is the real deal. By the time my hands reached the base of his dick, I estimated he was at least nine inches in length. I wasn't even sure if it would fit inside me.

I might need to change up my plan of attack after all.

I wrapped my tits around his shaft, pressing them tightly against his organ, then I began to slide myself up and down his steaming erection.

"Yeah, baby," he moaned. "Fuck me with your tits. Feel my big pole sliding in and out of your pit. Stroke the whole length of my tool."

He sure is full enough of himself, I thought as I slid my breasts over his flagpole. *He knows he's got it and he likes to flaunt it.* But to be honest, I was digging it almost as much as he was. I enjoyed feeling a man's cock from time to time, and this one was far bigger than most.

I tilted my head up, hoping to get a glimpse of his head poking in and out of my slippery breasts, but Madison had tied my blindfold carefully enough to prevent even the slightest peek. As I listened to his dick slurping between my lubricated breasts, I felt the head of his pole poking up against the underside of my chin, and for a moment I was tempted to angle my face down and take him into my mouth.

"Oh God, baby," he groaned. "I want your mouth over my dick so bad. Can you suck the tip while you fuck me with your tits?"

I'd given enough blowjobs in my straight days to know how to satisfy a man, but I wasn't really into that anymore having long since shifted my preferences to women. And besides, I never much cared for the taste and texture of a man's cum, and I wasn't about to let him pop off in my mouth without warning.

On the other hand, I *did* want to drive him crazy with desire before I finished with him.

I pulled away from his beanstalk for a moment and leaned in, slowly licking him from the base of his pole to the flaring crown. I could taste his precum spilling out of his slit and dripping down his shaft while I continued licking him like a giant Popsicle. I was enjoying making him squirm, and I wanted to give him just enough of what he craved so that when we reached the end he'd explode with the biggest orgasm of his life.

"Mmm," I moaned, pretending to worship his giant phallus. "You're so big. I can feel every inch of your python with my tongue."

"Yeah, baby," he grunted. "Lick my dick like an ice cream cone. Make sure you swirl your tongue over the head to catch my drips."

Knowing his most sensitive part was the soft tissue under the ridge of his crown, I pointed my tongue and slowly circled my head around the edge of his rim.

"Oh my God, baby," he panted. "Yes, lick my head with your tongue. You know how to drive a man crazy..."

"As well as another *man*?" I smiled, feeling his dick pulse in my hands as two more drops of precum spilled over his helmet.

"Yes," he said. "Suck my cock, baby. I need you to swallow me. Let me feel my cock in your mouth."

I was prepared to give him a little bit of latitude, just enough to let him think he was still in control. But I had a plan, and it didn't involve him cumming in my mouth.

I lifted myself up a bit further, then I paused with my mouth poised over the tip of his cock. He could feel my hot breath on his cum-coated glans, and he pressed his hips upward, desperate to feel my lips around his shaft. I pursed my lips and emitted a long stream of spit that landed on top of his flaring head with a soft splat.

"Oh, fuck yes," he groaned. "Lube me up with your spit. I want to fuck your mouth so bad."

Feeling temporarily sorry for him, I lowered my mouth to his burning head and spread my lips, feeling his girth stretch me open until I had his full circumference inside me. I was shocked at how thick he was, and I gripped his shaft tightly with both hands to make sure he didn't press himself too much further into my mouth. As I began to bob up and down gently on his pole and swirl my tongue under his ridge, he placed his hands on my head and pushed down gently.

I was glad that I'd had the presence of mind to grip his dick hand-over-hand so there was only two inches or so at the top of his hard-on that he could comfortably insert into me. But that was plenty enough. With his coke-can-sized girth, my jaw soon became sore from being stretched so wide, and after a minute or two of sucking his tip, I pulled away to catch my breath.

"What's the matter, baby?" he said. "Am I too big for you?"

"You *are* pretty fucking huge," I panted, wiping his precum from the sides of my mouth. "Maybe you're better suited for a man's equipment after all."

"I'm sure there are *other* parts of you that can accommodate me more easily," he grinned. "If you can deliver a baby, I'm pretty sure you'll be able to fit my dick in your pussy."

"Maybe," I smiled. "But I'd like to have a little more fun playing with that thing first. I want to feel your joystick throbbing in my hands while I pleasure you. Would you like to see how a woman's handjob compares to a man's?"

"Absolutely," he snarled. "Let's see if your little hands can handle my big poker."

Chuckling at his arrogant attitude, I clasped his dick again with both hands and squeezed it as tightly as I could. He felt hard as a rock, and his manhood burned in my hands.

"Yeah, baby," he grunted. "Squeeze the cum out of my dick. Rub my shaft while I fuck your pretty little hands. Can you feel my cock throbbing?"

"Oh yes," I purred.

"Don't forget to play with my balls. It feels so much better when you stimulate every part of me down there."

I moved my right hand up to his crown then cupped his balls with my other hand, squeezing him tightly.

"Yeah, baby," he groaned. "Squeeze my balls. That feels awesome."

As I squeezed the tip of his cock with the fingers of my right hand, more precum oozed out the top, mingling with the lube, creating a loud smacking sound as the air pocket under his frenulum filled with the sticky mixture. I could hear the sound of other men from around the circle flapping their dicks as they imagined me giving them a similarly dedicated hand job. I was pretty sure every one of them fantasized about a naked woman kneeling in front of them, giving them every bit of her attention while she gazed admiringly at their manhood.

Men are so predictable, I thought. *They really are all about the cock after all.*

"Yeah, just like that, honey," the man grunted. "Work my head while you play with my balls. Do you want to feel me cum all over your tits?"

"Mmm," I said, pretending to play along. "Do you *want* to cum on my tits?"

"Yeah, baby," he hissed. "I just need a little longer, then I'm going to spray all over your pretty breasts."

Seeking to heighten his fantasy cum shot fantasy, I lowered my left hand below his balls, caressing the space between his testicles and his ass. I knew this was another sensitive space for most men, and one his previous partner hadn't explored.

"Yes," he hissed. "Tickle the area below my balls. That feels incredible. I'm getting close..."

"Knowing he was close to cumming and wanting to make him climax on my own terms, I slid my hand lower, pressing my little finger toward his pucker. When I rolled my digit over his sphincter, he groaned and pushed his body lower in the chair, pressing harder against me.

"Oh fuck, baby," he grunted. "Whatever you're doing, don't stop. I've never been touched there before. That feels incredible."

When I heard his breathing begin to escalate and felt his precum pour out of his slit over my hand massaging his head, I knew he was close to the point of no return. With a huge grin on my face, I pressed my little finger harder against his sphincter until it slipped inside.

"Fuck," the man moaned, angling his hips harder against my finger until it was buried two knuckles deep in his anus. "I'm going to cum baby. I'm going to cum all over you face. Fuck me with your finger–"

Suddenly I pulled my finger out of his butthole and pulled back, listening to his dick flap excitedly against his stomach.

"What the *fuck*, man?" the man groaned. "I was just about to come! What are you doing?"

"Don't worry, man," I said, imitating his macho-man language. "I have something even better in mind to finish you off with. You didn't think I was going to let you waste all that hard meat coming in my *hands*, did you?

"You mean–?"

"Yes, baby," I smiled. "I'm going to finish you with my pussy. Would you like to cum inside something a little warmer and wetter?"

"*Fuck*, yes," he growled. "Give me anything you've got. I need to cum so bad."

"Do you think you can hold off long enough for me to have a little fun first? With a weapon like that, I assume you've practiced firing it enough to learn how to properly satisfy a woman."

"I'll try," he said. "But maybe you should hold off stimulating me like that until you're ready. I don't know how much longer I'll be able to hold out."

"Never fear," I said, standing up and turning around with my back facing his chair. "I'll take care of it the rest of the way."

Knowing I'd just finished my period, I wasn't worried about protection. Besides, I wanted to feel his hot flesh inside me when he shot off his cannon. I grabbed his tool between my legs then slowly lowered my hips over his lap as I felt his mammoth organ spread me apart.

"Uhnnn," I groaned, feeling his dick sliding inside me.

"Fuck, baby," the man panted. "Your pussy is so tight. Fuck me with your pretty cunt. I'm going to cum so hard inside you."

"Yes, baby," I purred, flexing the muscles in my legs as I bobbed up and down on his pole, feeling his balls slapping up against my wet vulva.

As much as I wanted to squeeze his testicles rubbing up against me, I didn't want to risk of setting him off. I'd planned this scenario pretty much from the moment Madison had planted me in front of him, and there was no way I was going to let him come before I'd enjoyed myself to the fullest.

The man grabbed the sides of my hips and began pistoning his cock harder inside me, and with his breathing becoming more ragged, I knew I didn't have much time left. I moved my right hand over my clit and began circling my nub furiously. The combination of his big dick filling me up together with my already heightened state of arousal from having him almost cum in my hands had already taken me close to the brink. As the two of us moaned louder and louder ramping up our rocking pace toward the inevitable climax, I suddenly heard Madison clear her throat.

I held up my hand in front of me, pointing it toward her like a traffic cop ordering a driver to stop. There was no way she was going to deny me this last chance to enjoy my orgasm while impaled on this beast of a man. Knowing we were the last pairing of the night, there was no need to save ourselves for anyone else. Signaling that I was ready to let him come, I reached between his legs with my other hand and squeezed his balls tightly.

"I'm ready, baby," I panted. "Let it rip. Let me feel you spray your firehose inside me. I'm going to cum with you."

"Fuck yes," he groaned, pulling my hips tighter over his cock. "I'm going to cum in your tight pussy. Here it comes, baby! *Ngahhh!*"

As the man emptied his gigantic load inside me, I clamped down hard over his dick, gushing like a waterfall all over his tight balls. Between the howling sound the two of us were making and the sound of my waterworks splashing over his testicles, it must have sounded like an erotic symphony for rest of the listening guests. While we wailed together in orgiastic union, I heard an orchestra of squeals and groans coming from all sides of the circle around me. I smiled in blissful delight, knowing that we'd provided a fitting finish to Madison's exciting blindfold game.

8

GUESS WHO

After the man and I recovered from our orgasms, Madison escorted me back to my seat. For a few moments, there was an uncomfortable silence in the room as everyone waited to see what would happen next. She'd mentioned at the beginning of the party that we'd have a chance to guess who we were paired with and that there would be prizes, but it was hard to imagine how we could do that blindfolded. With everybody sitting buck naked facing each other in a circle, the only question now was just how much we'd have to reveal.

"Well I don't know about you guys," Madison said. "But *I* certainly enjoyed this experience."

"Woo-hoo!" isolated cheers came from around the circle as everyone applauded loudly.

"Part of the fun in doing this of course," she said, "was in guessing who your partners were. I know for *some* of you, we stretched a few boundaries, and I'm really glad you opened yourselves up to a new type of sexual exploration. I hope we opened your eyes, figuratively speaking, to the myriad possibilities for sexual expression, even if it only allows you to better understand and appreciate the preferences of our LGBTQ brethren."

"Absolutely," one of the women hollered, with the rest of the group applauding even louder.

"So now, as we approach the end of our little parlor game, the question is—how comfortable do you all feel taking off your blind-folds and revealing yourselves in front of your fellow participants? I promised there'd be prizes for those of you who guessed correctly who your partners were, but we can only do this if we reveal our identities."

There was an awkward silence as Madison paused to let her comments sink in.

"I don't want to make anyone feel pressured to expose themselves to a bunch of strangers if you don't feel comfortable. So, if you'd like to exit now with your modesty intact, there will be no judgment, and I can escort you to the front of the house where you can get dressed and leave quietly. If so, please raise your hand now, and we'll allow you to make a graceful exit."

I cocked my head and listened to the telltale squeaking of seat plastic to see if anyone was raising their hand. But the room stayed pin-drop quiet as everyone held their breath waiting for the next step.

"Okay then," Madison said. "You're welcome to remove your blind-folds then and take a look around the room to see if you can find any clues as to who your partners were."

I pulled off my veil and swiveled my head slowly around the circle, smiling as I recognized a few familiar faces. In addition to Hannah, Valerie, and Lily, whose voices I'd recognized earlier, there were a few other familiar faces in the crowd. There were my friends Bonnie and Emma from last year's camping trip, Cheryl from my favorite sex shop in town, and my friends Dylan and Jake and from my previous job.

But at least half of the group were a mix of people I'd never seen before. As everybody crossed their arms and legs trying to cover up their naked bodies, a few of us chuckled when we recognized some of the obvious suspects. I was surprised to see even *Madison* completely naked, sitting erect in her chair with her firm breasts pointing proudly out from her chest.

"I see some of you know each other already," she said, "while many others are meeting for the first time. And yes, I've *also* been naked this whole time, enjoying the proceedings along with the rest of you. I didn't think it would be fair being the only one covered up, especially since I could see everybody else in the buff."

"Who are you *kidding*, Mad," I huffed. "You just wanted to have as much fun as the rest of us while you watched all of us getting down and dirty."

"You might be right about that," she smiled, being careful to conceal my identity among the other guests who didn't yet know me. "And enjoy it I *did*."

"So," she said. "Who'd like to go first guessing who your partners were?"

"Are we guessing as the *giver* or the *receiver*?" Hannah asked a few seats to my left.

"Both," Madison said. "There will be prizes for each correct guess."

"It might be easier if each of us said something first to help us place the voice," Cheryl suggested. "Or at least uncrossed their arms and legs to give us some more clues about their special endowments."

"Fair enough," Madison nodded. "But for those of you who already know each other, I'm guessing you won't need too many extra clues."

Valerie was the first to raise her hand as she peered at me with a lopsided grin.

"Yes, ma'am," Madison said, giving her permission to proceed.

"Are we allowed to use names, or should we just *point* to our partners?" Valerie asked.

"That's between the two of you. Whatever makes you more comfortable."

Valerie lifted her arm and slowly pointed in my direction, making direct eye contact with me.

"I have to confess that I recognized Jade's voice while she was touching me. And I'd recognize those magnificent breasts anywhere. I've spied on her swimming in her pool from the other side of our yards for quite some time."

"Did you enjoy your first face-to-face, or should I say *body-to-body*, connection this evening?" Madison smiled.

"We'd met previously at a few neighborhood get-togethers, and this wasn't actually the first time we'd touched each other. But somehow it seemed even more exciting not being able to *see* her this time."

"I'm so glad you enjoyed the experience," Madison nodded. "What about when you had *your* turn to provide the stimulation? Do you recognize who that might have been?"

"Well it was obviously another woman," she blushed. "But I didn't recognize the voice."

"Would the recipient like to reveal herself, now that you've heard your partner's voice?"

Everybody sat quietly in their chairs, then Lily raised her hand, smiling shyly at Valerie.

"Ah yes," Madison smiled. "That was a memorable coupling, as I recall. Did you both enjoy your connection?"

"Oh yes," Lily purred. "Valerie has quite a way with her hands, not to mention her talented tongue."

"Well I'm glad you both enjoyed the encounter," Madison said, reaching beside her into a large canvas tote bag on the floor. "Because you answered one of your connections correctly, Valerie, I have a special prize for you."

She lifted a Pocket Rocket vibrator out of the bag and passed it down the circle toward her.

"I hope this little sex toy will keep you entertained on lonely nights when you think back on this experience."

Everybody cheered as Valerie took possession of the toy, pretending to rub it against her vulva.

"How about if we mix it up a bit now?" Madison said, looking around the circle. "Do any of the *men* want to try guessing their partners?"

Everyone paused for another long moment, then a muscular, hairy-chested man raised his hand slowly.

"Yes, Neil," Madison said, nodding in his direction.

"I *also* recognize Jade's voice now that she's spoken," he said, grinning at me sexily.

"As the giver or receiver?"

"Well actually, I think maybe she was one of the lucky ones who experienced it *both* ways we me."

"I think you might be right about that," Madison said, turning her head to smile in my direction. "She *did* break the rules, but we might have to give her a pass since it was the last coupling of the night. And what about your *other* partner, do you have any idea who that might be?"

He glanced around the room at the other men in the circle, pinching his eyebrows suspiciously. Then one of the men on the opposite side slowly parted his legs, gazing him in the eye. Neil glanced down at his swelling equipment and smiled.

"I can't be a hundred percent certain," he said, pointing at the other man. "But based on the size of the gentleman's cock, I'm guessing it might be him."

"What do you say, Ryan?" Madison said. "Do you recognize the gentleman's voice or anything else about him?"

"Ah, *yeah*," he said, glancing down at Neil's semi-tumescent monster. "That's not the *only* thing I recognize."

Everybody around the circle chuckled as they watched the two men's cocks beginning to swell again in recollection of their memorable connection.

"Well, Neil," Madison said, reaching into her prize bag again, this time pulling out a purple silicone ring toy. "For guessing the *lady* half of your equation, I'm passing around this lovely vibrating cock ring. Though I'm not entirely sure you'll be able to fit into it."

Then she reached behind her into a large duffel bag, pulling out a full-size inflatable doll. The round mouth had a large hole with a bright red ring of painted lipstick around it, and between the doll's legs was a large red slit.

"Maybe you'll be able to fit yourself more easily into this lovely inflatable companion?" Then she pulled another doll from the bag, this one with a puffy cock pointing up between its legs. "Or would you'd prefer to have the *male* doll?"

"I'll take the female one, thanks," he smiled as the rest of the group erupted in laughter.

For the next twenty minutes or so, Madison continued around the room until everybody had had a turn to guess and reveal their partners. Once again, she saved me for last, and I cocked my head smiling at her, guessing what she was cooking up.

"So I guess that just leaves Jade without a parting gift," she said. "Each of your partners have already revealed who you were paired with, so it doesn't seem fair to hand out two prizes. But because you've been such a sport saving yourself to the end this evening, I'll let you decide which prize you'd prefer."

She held up each of the inflatable dolls in her separate hands, looking at me with a devilish smile.

"You seemed to have an *equal* amount of fun with each of your partners," she smiled. "Something tells me you'd be able to entertain yourself for hours with either one of these dolls."

Then she reached into her bag and held up one of my favorite sex toys, the two-pronged Osé vibrator.

"Or perhaps you'd prefer this special toy which simulates the movement of *each* sex against your private parts?"

I peered at Madison through narrowed eyelids while I parted my legs slowly.

"*Actually*, Maddie," I said. "I've been thinking about a different kind of prize all evening. After everyone leaves, I'd like to have *you* all to myself."

"Why wait until everybody leaves?" she grinned. "Why don't we get it on right here and now where everybody can see?" She looked around the group and held out her hands, seeking input. "What do you say, guys–would you like to enjoy one last pairing without the restriction of the blindfolds?"

A loud cheer rose from the circle as everybody clapped loudly, egging us on.

"Which would you prefer this time?" Madison asked me. "To give or receive?"

"Fuck that idea," I said, lifting myself out of my chair and lying seductively on the plush carpet in the middle of the circle. "I want to fuck you every way possible. It's time you got some of your own medicine."

"With pleasure," she purred, crawling across the carpet in my direction.

As she moved toward me, I glanced around the circle and noticed many of the men had separated their legs, revealing their hard poles pointing straight up in their laps. Something told me this party was far from being over, and that before the end of the evening there'd be quite a few more connections made among the hot and still-horny guests...

VOLUME TWO

THE TOY PARTY

1

———

"How goes the practice?" I asked my best friend and certified sex therapist, Hannah, over lunch. "Any interesting new cases?"

We were meeting for our weekly catch-up at our favorite restaurant on Chicago's Navy Pier overlooking Lake Michigan. With our busy schedules, it wasn't always easy for us to find time to nurture our longstanding friendship. But I could always count on Hannah to share some juicy tidbits from her private practice during our two-hour break every Wednesday.

"Never a dull moment," she said. "You'd be surprised at the endless variety of dysfunctions people come to me with. Just yesterday, I had a young woman worried about her excessive squirting when she orgasms."

"Is that a problem?" I said. "I mean, isn't that a *good* thing? I squirt sometimes when I come too, but it's usually after a long buildup and during an unusually powerful orgasm. Most of my partners find it to be a huge turn-on."

"That's what I tried to tell her. I explained that it's perfectly natural for many women and that she shouldn't worry about it. She thought she was literally peeing on her partners during sex."

I choked on a salad crouton in mid-swallow and quickly washed it down with a gulp of water.

"Just to be clear, though—it's *not*, right? There's a lot of misconceptions about vaginal squirting. I don't want to feel self-conscious about it—"

"No," Hannah chuckled. "You needn't worry about spraying your lover with an unintended golden shower. Ninety percent of the time, it's just the ejection of your natural lubrication when your vagina contracts during orgasm. As you suggested, whenever it happens it's usually a sign of exceptional internal wetness and/or unusually strong contractions."

"And the other ten percent of the time?"

"Some women expel a secretion from the Skene's glands, located next to the urethra. And yes, in very rare circumstances, one can become temporarily incontinent and expel a small amount of urine. But it's all healthy organic fluid, and in all cases an indicator of a powerful orgasm. Most women should be thrilled to experience that kind of 'dysfunction'. The more common problem is the lack of ability to orgasm at all."

"Really?" I said, watching some dark clouds roll in from the east side of the bay. "I thought that was mostly limited to heterosexual couples where the man doesn't know how to properly stimulate his partner."

"That's common, yes. Most guys can't find a woman's clit with a magnifying glass. But honestly, most of the time it's because the woman has some kind of mental block. Either she grew up learning sex was something to be ashamed of or she had an early traumatic experience. The latest studies show that seventy-five percent of women can't orgasm from intercourse alone and up to fifteen percent can't come at all."

"How do you help them overcome their problem, if you don't mind my little play on words."

"Actually, that boils it down to the core of the problem. They have to learn how to break down the barriers stopping them from achieving climax. First, I teach them that pleasure is a natural part of the sexual experience, designed to encourage procreation. Then I tell them the best way to experience orgasm is to stop trying to orgasm. It's like a guy who can't get it up when the chips are down—they're feeling too much pressure to perform. I encourage them to find a quiet place where they can explore their bodies without any distractions then lose themselves in the journey of discovery without worrying about the destination."

"Alone?"

"At first, yes. There are too many expectations when you bring a partner into the equation. They have to learn how to break down the walls restricting their freedom of expression before they can let others into their intimate space."

I nodded, reflecting back on my own first time experiencing sexual pleasure. It was when I was taking a bath and I discovered how good it felt to let the water from the faucet flow over my pussy. From that day forward, I experimented with endless types of self-stimulation. By the time I had my first fling with a high school boyfriend, all my hang-ups about sex had been thoroughly dispelled.

"What about when they return to their sexual partners? Is there even such a thing as a vaginal orgasm? What happens to the *other* seventy-five percent who can't come with their husbands?"

"That whole vaginal vs. clitoral orgasm concept that Freud first introduced is a total myth," Hannah said. "It wasn't until about twenty years ago that scientists properly mapped the full anatomy of the clitoris. Did you know that over ninety percent of the clitoral structure is actually *inside* the vagina? The tiny glans and shaft on the outside are just the parts that we can see. There's no reason why a woman can't experience a penetrative orgasm if properly aroused and stimulated by a caring partner."

The sun suddenly broke through a hole in the clouds, casting a spotlight over the nearby grounds in Millennium Park. The chrome skin of the famous bean-shaped sculpture glistened in the light, reminding me of my favorite U-shaped vibrator.

"Is that what happens when we stimulate the G-spot?"

"Partly. The G-spot corresponds to the location of the underside of the shaft of the clitoris. It's a bit like the sensitive frenulum on the underside of a man's penis. But the rest of the clitoral structure surrounds much of the vagina, which is why it feels good even when we're having missionary sex. We're all born with the same genital anatomy. It's not until around the third month of prenatal development that the structures deviate into the familiar male and female forms."

My panties began to dampen as I began to think about all the new ways I could explore my pussy with my large collection of vibrating dildos.

"Fascinating," I said, shifting restlessly in my seat. "Do you ever encourage your clients to experiment with *sex toys* to mix things up if they're still having trouble making it work?"

"After a while, yes. But first they have to get in the right frame of mind. It's not an exaggeration to say that the brain is the largest sex organ. A lot of women can actually *think* themselves to orgasm. You've got to be *mentally* aroused before you can achieve physical excitement. I don't want my clients to become too dependent on the artificial stimulation of a sex toy before learning to enjoy sex the natural way. No partner can hope to match the intensely focused stimulation of a sex toy. At its core, sex is designed to be a social activity to ensure procreation."

I slammed my knife and fork on my plate and stared at Hannah in mock indignation.

"Don't tell me you're one of those sexist shrinks who still believes sex is only meant to be enjoyed between a man and a woman under holy matrimony."

"Of course not. We humans have thankfully evolved to the point where we can enjoy sex for its own sake. You know me better than that. I consider myself to be pansexual. I enjoy and encourage all forms of sexual expression. Gay, straight, bi, transgender—whatever turns your crank. Life's too short to be worried about all that hypocrisy about only one proper way to experience sex. So if using toys helps you spice up your sex life and keeps your relationships fresh and exciting, I'm all for it."

"Cheers to that," I said, raising my glass of sangria.

"To *hump day*," Hannah winked, clinking her glass against mine.

"You know, all this discussion has got me thinking. I feel like I've grown so much since my boring marriage ended a few years ago. My sex life is so much more enjoyable now that I'm open to having sex with other women. And my house is a veritable sex toy museum. I've often thought about inviting some of my closest friends over for a toy party. You know—to share the *wealth*, as it were. Would you be willing to give a little talk about some of your insights on sexual health? I'm sure there's a lot of other women who could benefit from your knowledge and experience."

Hannah peered across the table at me with a raised eyebrow.

"Were you intending for this to be a 'hands on' party, or just an educational meeting?"

I paused as a small curl formed at the edge of my lips.

"I was thinking we could start out as an informational forum and see where it goes from there. You could share your knowledge of sexual anatomy and mental health while I demonstrate the latest advances in sex toy development. If some of the ladies want to practice some of their learnings and avail themselves of the available sex aids, I don't see why we should want to stop them. Are you down for that?"

Hannah took another sip of her wine as she peered over the rim of her glass with fluttering eyes.

"Sounds like it could be fun. Knowing you, I have a feeling this little party will soon devolve into a full-blown orgy. But I've never experienced one of those, so count me in."

"Good," I said. "I'll send out the invites later today. Are you available next Saturday?"

Hannah reached into her purse and pulled out her phone. I could tell even before she checked her schedule from the way she was squirming in her chair that she was already committed. She tapped the screen twice then looked up at me and smiled.

"I think I can make that work."

I could barely contain my excitement on the drive home thinking about how I would organize our get-together for maximum enjoyment. Part of me was genuinely looking forward to educating my friends about all the cool sex toys I'd discovered in my journey of sexual exploration since my divorce. But I definitely had another agenda. There were a few girls I'd had my eye on for some time who'd rebuffed my subtle advances. Whether it was because they professed to be 'happily married' or because they just weren't into lesbian sex, I had a feeling this party would tear down whatever remaining walls they might have to expanding their sex lives.

I knew full well that some of the toys I'd be demonstrating would tempt more than one fence-sitter into wanting to try them out right then and there. I just had to create the right atmosphere. By the time I pulled into my driveway, my car seat was soaked in a puddle of wetness under my burning crotch. I raced upstairs and flipped open my laptop, starting a new email message with the subject *Girl's Slumber Party*. With trembling hands, I began composing my message:

Dear friends,

This Saturday, I'll be hosting a most unusual and exciting party. The theme of the gathering is 'sexual health and wellness'. I've invited my good friend and registered sex therapist, Hannah Bristol, to give an informative presentation on the latest developments in the area of women's sexual health.

A big part of this is learning to relax and explore our bodies in a safe and nurturing environment. To this end, I've invited another friend, Cheryl Clifton from the local branch of the Babeland adult emporium chain to demonstrate some of the exciting new sex toys they've recently introduced. You're encouraged to learn, experiment, and dabble to the extent you feel comfortable.

This is a girls-only party. Leave your husbands, boyfriends, and other cockadoodles at home. Dress comfortably—it'll be our own little slumber party. Come one, come all!

RSVP by Friday p.m.

See you all soon,

Jade xo

As I began to fill in the To: field with the email addresses of my friends and associates, I paused after entering the names of the obvious candidates. It went without saying that I would invite the women I'd already shared a private tryst with and those who I knew to be lesbians. But half the fun would be trying to entice my stanch heterosexual friends to drop their britches along with everyone else.

By the time I finished filling in the list of addressees, I'd assembled an eclectic list of twenty friends and acquaintances, all of whom I'd be happy to fuck at the slightest provocation. I paused for only a millisecond before tapping the Send button. Then I tore off my pants and plunged my favorite rabbit vibrator dildo deep into my pussy. As I slid down in my chair spreading my legs wide apart, I closed my eyes imagining what it would be like to watch twenty sexy women pleasuring themselves while the rest of us looked on.

2

———

By Saturday afternoon, I was already dripping in anticipation of the coming festivities. Almost everyone I'd invited had RSVP'd that they were planning to attend. The only person I still hadn't heard from was the hot housewife who lived on the opposite side of my back yard. I'd caught Alana stealing lingering glances at me from her upper deck whenever I lay around my pool in my bikini. But her needy husband always seemed to be hanging about, and we'd never managed to find any private time together. Tonight, I had a special plan for how I might entice her over to my place.

I'd arranged the guest chairs in a semicircle in the middle of my family room, with two additional chairs in front of the arc, facing the backyard window. One of the chairs would be reserved for the official presenter—first Hannah, then Cheryl. I would sit in the second chair providing color commentary. But most of the 'commentary' I was planning to provide would be more *visual* than verbal. I knew the only way I was likely to get the rest of the women to sample the vibrators would be if I demonstrated how some of them worked myself.

There wouldn't be enough replicas of each vibrator for every participant to try them at the same time, but between the many different types we were planning to show, there'd be more than enough to keep everyone entertained. And unlike most other sex toy shops' policy of offering no returns of purchased products for hygienic reasons, each woman at *our* party would be welcome to share and pass along their toys for the pleasure of the other participants.

Beside each chair, I'd placed a container of alcohol wipes and a fresh towelette so everyone could safely clean each device before reuse. I didn't want anything stopping the ladies from being willing to experiment and enjoying themselves to the fullest. The last thing I did to set the mood was draw the drapes and turn the dimmer switch down. I wanted just enough light to create a playful atmosphere while still providing enough visibility for everyone to watch one another.

In front of my own chair, I left the curtains parted a small crack with a direct line of sight to Alana's balcony. There wouldn't be enough space for someone outside my fenced yard to make out what was going inside with an unaided eye. But using the spyglass I'd often caught Alana using behind her kitchen window, she'd be able to zoom in on the action all she wanted. After dusk, the light from inside my house would create the effect of an illuminated stage in a darkened theater. Everybody else's privacy would be safely protected facing away from the window. But Alana would have a bird's-eye view of me displaying all of my favorite toys.

As my friends began to arrive, we shared some wine and cheese and made small talk about the latest developments in our work and personal lives. Nobody wanted to broach the subject of our planned activities for later in the evening, but by the time the last attendee arrived, everybody was nicely loosened up by the free-flowing alcohol. I invited everyone to take a seat in the semicircle, while Hannah and I took adjacent chairs facing the group. Hannah had brought a small case with her that she placed it on the floor beside her chair.

"Good evening everyone and welcome to our little get-together," I said. "It's great to see all my close friends together once again. We seem to find it more and more difficult these days to make time to commune with our busy schedules. We've got an interesting theme for tonight's gathering, and I've invited two close friends to make a presentation in the context of women's sexual health. I think you'll find the planned festivities will be both mentally and physically stimulating."

As I began to make eye contact with the women around the room, they smiled nervously back at me. I was sure many of them had no idea what they were getting themselves into.

"Some of you already know Hannah, a registered sex therapist who has been counseling women in her private practice for almost ten years. I think you'll find she has some interesting insights and experiences to share with us. I've also invited my good friend Cheryl Clifton, who is the owner of the Chicago Babeland adult store on Michigan Avenue, to show us some of the fascinating new sex toys that have recently come to market."

I glanced toward Cheryl and she raised her arm to acknowledge her presence. Some of the ladies nodded toward her, recognizing her from their previous trips into her store.

"Hannah," I said, who was sitting beside me. "Did you want to start things off with a few opening comments?"

"Thanks, Jade," Hannah smiled. "Jade and I were talking the other day over lunch about some of the concerns many women still have about their sexual health. She thought it might be fun to share some of our mutual experiences and learnings in a safe and learning environment."

She reached down and opened the case beside her and pulled out an unusually shaped stuffed toy.

"I didn't want to get overly formal about what should be a fun subject, so I thought I'd try to lighten the mood using my favorite puppet."

She placed her right hand in the back of the stuffed toy then held it up for the whole room to see. Many of the women giggled when they recognized the familiar shape and features of a woman's vulva.

"Hi, I'm Valerie, the vagina puppet," Hannah squeaked in a playful voice. "While I may not be proportioned to the correct relative scale, I think you might recognize some of the familiar features on my body."

Hannah caressed the velvety sides of the puppet framing the organ like two puffy parentheses.

"These are the labia majora," she said. "Their job is to cover and protect the more sensitive internal parts of the vagina. Though I must say I rather enjoy having this part of me stroked and caressed as a prelude to deeper exploration of my body."

Many of the women around the circle chuckled as they watched Hannah playing with her puppet. But they shifted uncomfortably in their seats as her fingers moved closer toward the inside of the faux vulva.

"These thinner folds are the labia minora. They're even more sensitive to touch than my larger siblings and can get quite wet when properly stimulated. Their purpose is mostly to provide a slippery surface for easy penetration of a man's penis, but I like to insert *other* phallic-shaped devices inside me when the mood strikes. These lips also connect at their top edge to the clitoris and help provide some very pleasant friction during vaginal thrusting."

Hannah placed the fingers of her left hand over a puffy red ball at the apex of the inner folds. Then she flipped up a flap of silk covering the nub and smiled.

"And this is the hood of the clitoris that helps protect this super-sensitive organ when it is not in use."

She pinched the fingers of her left hand together and inserted them into the opening of the vulva, thrusting her hand gently in and out. The silky hood of the clitoris pulled back and forth over the nub as she stroked her pretend pussy.

"Notice how the hood pulls forward and back over the glans as the labia minora are stretched and contracted with each penetration."

Some of the ladies around the arc crossed their legs and squeezed their thighs excitedly together, becoming aroused by the vivid depiction of their private anatomy.

"Many women think they can't come just from penetrative sex," Hannah continued. "But this design is intended to increase the stimulation on our most sensitive organ even from indirect touching. Did you know that the clitoris is the only organ in either a man's or a woman's body with the sole purpose of providing pleasure? And that the head of the clitoris has over *seven thousand* nerve endings—even more than in the glans of a man's penis? So much for penis envy. If guys had any idea how good it feels to stimulate a woman's clit, they'd gladly switch places with us."

Everyone in the group laughed out loud and nodded in agreement, starting to loosen up.

"But here's the really interesting part," Hannah said as she angled her puppet from side to side for all the women to see. Surrounding the vulva behind each of the labia majora were two puffy 'wings' connected to the outside shaft of the clitoris, making it look like an inverted wishbone.

"The clitoris is actually far larger than many of us believe. The little nub and shaft on the outside is just the tip of the iceberg."

She lifted the two wings framing the internal walls of the vagina to reveal a larger pair of puffy tissues.

"These tissues extend inside and around the walls of the vagina and connect directly to the clitoral shaft and glans. The thinner flaps are called the *crura*, and the puffier tissues underneath them are the *bulbs*, corresponding in many ways to the corpora cavernosa in the shaft of a man's penis. They're all part of the greater clitoral structure, extending more than four inches around each side of the vaginal wall at rest."

Many of the ladies leaned in closer as their eyes widened in surprise, realizing for the first time just how large and all-encompassing this sensitive part of their anatomy was.

"The male and female genitalia both develop from the same embryonic structures," Hannah continued. "They don't actually differentiate until fairly late in fetal development. Just like a man's penis, these structures swell and extend fifty to three hundred percent when stimulated. So the next time someone tells you there's no such thing as a vaginal orgasm, don't believe it. A woman should be able to come just as easily from proper internal stimulation as from external manipulation of the outside glans."

Recognizing that some of the women were eager for the next

phase of the demonstration, I signaled to Hannah that it was time for a shift in the discussion.

"Thank you, Hannah, for that entertaining and enlightening explanation of a woman's sexual anatomy. I don't know about you guys, but I'm feeling a lot more empowered about my sexual health knowing that my lady cock is just as big and powerful as any man's."

The women around the circle cheered and clapped their hands excitedly, equally surprised and impressed with Hannah's presentation.

"What do you say we put Valerie away for a little while and focus on learning some the interesting ways we can stimulate our *real* peachkas now that we understand a little better where all the interesting parts are?" I nodded toward Cheryl and she switched places with Hannah, placing a much larger case on the floor in front of her. "Cheryl is now going to demonstrate the almost infinite varieties of toys we can use to stimulate our wonderful flower in the privacy of our own homes."

"Or with a partner," Cheryl suggested. "I think you'll find these sex aids are equally stimulating used either alone or as part of communal play. There's no reason why you shouldn't be able to introduce some of these toys into your partnered sex life to keep it vibrant and interesting."

I smiled at her and winked, happy that she'd planted the seed for broader group exploration.

She reached down and flipped open her case. Inside, was a treasure trove of multicolored and unusually shaped toys. She picked up two phallic-looking objects of different sizes.

"Following on Hannah's illumination of the shape and structure of the clitoris," she said. "Women's sex toys fall into two general categories: internal and external."

She held up the smaller object and turned it around in her hand for everyone to see.

"This little guy may look familiar to many of you as the trusty 'pocket rocket' vibrator. It's only about two inches long and less than an inch in diameter, but it packs quite a wallop for its small size."

Cheryl ran her fingers teasingly over the nubby end of the finger-sized device.

"You can place these ridges overtop of your clit and twist the tube to select one of three different vibration settings."

She twisted the shaft of the pocket rocket and the device began to hum with a soft whine.

"The good news is that you can carry this guy around in your smallest purse and use it fairly discreetly, since it's no bigger than your index finger."

She pulled two more pocket rockets out of her case and handed them to the women at opposite ends of the semicircle.

"Feel free to pass these around and see what they feel like as you experiment with the different settings. This is what I like to call our 'entry-level' vibrator. It's very basic, but it definitely does the job."

I pulled my own pocket rocket out of the pocket of my jeans and placed it playfully between my crotch.

"If any of you want to see what it actually feels like against your clit," I said, "don't be shy about giving it a try. Clothes on or off, this is a judgement-free zone. We're all liberated ladies here and I don't want anybody to feel self-conscious about enjoying each of these toys to their fullest limits. You'll notice that I've placed some alcohol wipes and clean towels beside every chair, so you can safely and comfortably clean each device after each use."

"And that's another point I want to make about sex toys in general," Cheryl chimed in. "Different toys are made out of different materials. But some are more *hygienic* than others. You should always buy toys made out of medical-grade silicone or hard plastic. Avoid any device made out of a soft jelly or rubber. These materials have thousands of microscopic pores that trap bacteria and can spread disease. The other types are easily cleaned with regular soap and water, or alcohol wipes if you want to be really safe. It goes without saying that all of the toys we'll be demonstrating here tonight use the safe, non-porous materials, so feel free to experiment away!"

As the women passed the little vibrators around the circle, some of them held it in their hands experiencing the different vibrations, while others pressed it gently between their legs as their eyes widened in surprise.

"Pretty powerful for such a little device, isn't it?" Cheryl said, nodding toward the more adventurous ladies. "But this is really just the most basic of sex toys. There's been a surge of innovative new designs to hit the market over the last couple of years."

She reached down into her case and picked up a donut-sized device with two pointy ends that looked like rabbit ears.

"This is the *Form* 2 clitoral vibrator made by JimmyJane. The lovely thing about this sex toy is that you can place these two little fingers on opposite sides of the shaft of your clit to receive a heavenly stimulation, almost as if someone is stroking you with their hand. It's got a quiet but powerful internal motor that you can quickly recharge using the available charging cable. Unlike the pocket rocket, which uses a regular double-A battery. So you'll need to keep plenty of replacement batteries on hand to be sure you don't run out of power at the worst possible time."

Cheryl handed two models of the Form 2 vibe to me and I passed them to the girls in the middle of the circle.

"This one is best appreciated with a minimum of layers between you and the device," I hinted.

I nonchalantly unzipped my jeans and pulled them down to the floor, then slipped my own Form 2 vibe under my panties. A few of the girls raised an eyebrow at my bold gesture, but it didn't take long for them to refocus their gaze at my midsection as they watched me squirm and grunt from the pleasant sensations emanating between my legs.

Most of the other women were also wearing jeans and were reluctant to drop their leggings as they pressed the vibe gently against the seam of their pants. But a few had come prepared with skirts and summer dresses, and I watched excitedly as they slipped the two-pronged device under their hems and began to moan in pleasure. Unfortunately, nobody seemed quite ready to carry their self-stimulation to the ultimate peak and come in full view of the others as they politely passed the two devices around the circle.

Recognizing their hesitation, Cheryl reached into her toy case and pulled out another vibrator. This one looked like a small egg with two grooves on top and a little O-shaped loop connected to the end. She slipped her index and middle fingers through the loop and cradled the egg in the palm of her hand with her two fingers resting inside the grooves.

"This interesting device is called the *Fin*, manufactured by Dame Products, a female-founded and female-run adult toy company. The nice thing about this vibrator is that you can use it almost like an extension of your own hand. It's great to use in couples play to bring an extra level of stimulation to your partner. It's also equipped with a rechargeable battery and provides a quite satisfying sensation to the outer clitoris and overall vulva area. I happen to have four of these on hand, so I'm going to pass these around for more of you to enjoy."

Cheryl handed another one to me and smiled.

"As usual," she said, "Jade will be demonstrating some of the many ways you can use this for maximum enjoyment."

I placed the Form 2 vibrator over my hand then pressed my fingers under the top lip of my panties. As I felt the buzz spread over the head of my clit, I closed my eyes and spread my legs, sinking down in my chair. As I began to feel the rising tide of pleasure spread over my pelvic region, I opened my eyelids a slit and noticed three other women had unzipped the front of their jeans and had the palm of their hands gently rolling over their vulvas. As the rest of the girls squirmed in their seats looking on, the four of us mewed in obvious delight from the sublime tingling between our legs.

Feeling a bit sorry for the other girls being left out of the fun, I pulled the vibe out of my panties and tapped the button to turn it off.

"I'm saving myself for the *next* one," I winked. "I have a feeling Cheryl is getting ready to pull out the heavy guns."

Cheryl smiled at me as she reached into her case and pulled out a much larger device with a plum-sized ball attached to the end of a long handle.

"Right you are, Jade," she said. "This one has the generic name of magic wand and is made by various manufacturers, but my favorite version is this one with the trade name *Le Wand*. This is a major league vibrator, with a deep, penetrating rumble and twenty different vibration settings. It's not to be taken lightly, as it can set you off in a matter of seconds and can be quite addictive. You might want to be careful about pulling it out when your husband or boyfriend is around, since they might be more than a little threatened by both its size and how powerful it is."

Cheryl clutched the head of the device with her hand and twisted the round ball on the top.

"It's got a flexible neck, which makes it feel a bit more natural and it also comes with a bunch of fun attachments."

She reached into her bag and pulled out a variety of odd-shaped covers, placing each one over the end of the wand.

"This nubbly cover," she said, running her fingers over the spiny surface, "feels a bit like a French tickler when pressed against your vulva.

"Whereas *this* attachment," she said, replacing it with a cap having four large protruding nubs, "is billed as a deep tissue massager. But of course, it has much more interesting *sexual* exploration uses."

Then she reached into her case and pulled out a cone with a large curved finger extension.

"But this is my favorite attachment. It's perfectly shaped to stimulate the G-spot on the inside front surface of your vagina, and it will take you to an entirely different level. I'm going to hold off on passing this attachment around because we're going to have a special demonstration of the internal vibrators soon."

Cheryl turned to me with a devious smile.

"Jade, would you like to have first dibs at demonstrating this little gem?"

She passed me one of the wands and handed two others to the women at the edge of the circle.

"I thought you'd never ask," I said with a wicked grin. "But this time I don't want anything getting between me and my vibrating friend. If you girls don't mind, I'm going to get buck-naked to properly enjoy this thing."

As many of the women around the circle widened their eyes in shock, I pulled my panties all the way down to my ankles. Then I flicked the switch on the side the wand and placed it against the front of my vulva, holding it with two hands.

"Fuck, yes!" I purred as the vibrator began to rumble between my legs.

I noticed it was starting to get dark outside and glanced through the crack in my curtains, recognizing some movement on the balcony across from my back yard. Just as I'd suspected, my neighbor Alana couldn't resist spying on me to get a closer look at what was going on inside. I couldn't tell if she was holding her binoculars, but I spread my legs as wide as I could as I rubbed the bat-shaped vibrator between my legs. If she was watching, I planned to give her a show she'd not soon forget.

Suddenly, I heard some moaning coming from the other ends of the circle and I turned my head to see the other women had thrust their magic wands down under their panties and were gripping the handle tightly as they rolled their hips sensuously in their chairs. I locked eyes on one of the girls, a married friend who'd previously been reluctant to share details about her sex life with her husband. As Heather and I began to feel the swell of pleasure sweeping over our bodies, we grunted and groaned in delirious pleasure.

Most of the other women who were without a vibrator had already shoved their hands down their pants or under their skirts as they watched the three of us tremble in our chairs. When Heather gaped her mouth wide open and began to shake uncontrollably in her chair, I couldn't hold back any longer. My orgasm overtook me and I grunted loudly as I hunched over, convulsing in ecstasy. Suddenly, the room was filled with the soft sighs and moans of twenty oversexed women losing themselves in the pleasure of intense self-stimulation as we watched each other rise to the culmination of pleasure.

3
———

Seconds after I came, the doorbell rang. I was tempted to ignore it, but the interruption provided a welcome distraction from the awkwardness of twenty women peering at one another with their hands still down their pants. I threw on a robe and scampered up to the front door and looked through the peephole. It was my neighbor Alana, fidgeting self-consciously on the doorstep. I smiled for a moment, then swung open the door.

"Sorry I'm late," Alana stammered, staring at my curvy body wrapped up in the robe. "I had to finish making dinner and cleaning up after my husband. Have I missed much?"

I looked down at the wet patch in the crotch of her jeans and knew that she'd been touching herself as she watched me through the drapes.

"Not much," I said. "Come on in. We're just getting started."

I led Alana back to my family room and pulled up an extra chair at the edge of the circle.

"This is my neighbor Alana," I said, not wanting to interrupt our flow with a long introduction. "She was held up with a few unavoidable distractions, but better late than never to our party."

I motioned toward Cheryl, who was cleaning the wand I'd just used with an alcohol swab.

"This is my friend Cheryl from the Babeland store in downtown Chicago. She's been demonstrating some of the latest offerings from her establishment. Make yourself comfortable. We were just starting to get to the interesting items."

I looked at Cheryl and smiled.

"What other exciting toys have you got in that magic box of yours?"

"I'm glad you asked, Jade," Cheryl said. "I was just getting ready to demonstrate our line of *internal* vibrators."

She reached down into her case and lifted up two familiar-looking dildos. One had the traditional shape of a pointy pink cucumber and the other looked like an oversize erect penis.

"Until recently, these were the only kinds of internal vibrators that women had to choose from. One's shaped a bit like a pickle and is made out of hard plastic. The other one looks like a super-veiny cock, and is made out of soft silicone. While both come equipped with a handy internal vibrator, their designs are not very inspiring and, just like a man's cock, have limited functionality."

The lesbians around the circle chuckled, but more than a few of my straight friends also nodded, acknowledging their dissatisfaction with their one-dimensional sex lives. I glanced at Alana and she smiled at me nervously as a light blush spread over her cheeks.

Cheryl placed the vibrators back in her case then lifted up another dildo shaped like a banana with a little bump on the end.

"This is called the *Gigi* vibrator, from Lelo," she said. She turned the device slowly in her hand, stroking the tip teasingly. "It has a gentle curve and a specially shaped tip that makes it perfect for stim-ulating the G-spot."

Cheryl looked toward Hannah and smiled.

"Hannah, would you like to demonstrate how to properly position this device using your little puppet?"

Hannah lifted her stuffed toy off the floor then slowly inserted the curved vibrator into the puppet's hole with the little bump facing up.

Then she pressed the shaft downward, angling the tip toward the inside front surface of the vagina.

"As you can see," Cheryl said, "this vibrator is much better suited to stimulating the sensitive G-spot than a straight dildo. And the best part is that it's whisper-quiet, so you can use it discreetly in the privacy of your own bedroom without your husbands being any the wiser. Some women find it's easier to insert with a bit of lube, so we've placed a tube of body-safe cream beside everyone's chair if you want to give it a try."

As before, Cheryl passed one of the vibrators to me and three other girls in the circle. The women turned the wand curiously in their hands as they experimented with the different vibration settings, not quite ready to plunge it into their pussy in full view of the other participants.

Recognizing their apprehension, I flipped open my robe and spread my legs apart. I glanced over at Alana and noticed she had her legs crossed as she squeezed her thighs together while staring at me with wide eyes.

"I don't know about the *rest* of you," I grinned. "But I'm still pretty wet from using the last vibrator. Screw the lube—I'm ready to get *fucked*."

I inserted the dildo deep into my pussy and angled it upward, then turned the vibration setting up all the way.

"Holy shit!" I growled. "This feels absolutely heavenly. You girls have *got* to give this a try. Remember, what happens in Jade's house, stays in Jade's house. We're all big girls and this can stay between us. No one else needs to know how much fun we really had at our little sorority party. Feel free to take off your pants and dresses and get your groove on!"

Two of the women holding the Gigi vibrator looked at one another for a moment, then they pulled their jeans down simultaneously, inserting the wand between their lips. They pressed the shaft in about four inches and angled it downwards as their eyes rolled under their lids and they slithered down in their chairs. I looked at the third woman, who'd slipped the vibrator under her dress, concealing it under her panties. But within seconds, all three of them began moaning and panting as they grasped the handle of the wand and thrust it firmly inside their pussies. I glanced at Alana, who had her hand down the front of her pants as the stain on her jeans spread further down her thighs.

The sight of so many women playing with themselves as they watched our glistening dildos plunging in and out of our pussies raised my excitement to an entirely new level, and I moaned loudly as I began to feel my passion rising. Within minutes, the four of us were trembling in our chairs as we watched each other fuck ourselves with this magnificent tool. As I began to feel the familiar tingling feeling spreading throughout my pelvic region, I spread my legs further apart and began to groan uncontrollably.

"Fuck—that feels so good," I said, shifting my gaze between the three women. "I'm going to cum soon. Are you girls getting close?"

They all nodded as their moans began to rise with a heightened urgency and their eyes glazed over. When one of the girls suddenly slumped over in her chair and pulled her legs together, shaking convulsively, I groaned as I felt the contractions inside my pussy clamping against the shaft of the vibrator.

"I'm cumming!" I hissed, pulling the vibrator hard up inside me, pressing it firmly against the front of my cunny.

"Yes—Yes!" one of the other girls panted as she also began to quake in her chair.

But I was most turned on by the sight of the girl in the summer dress shaking in her chair as her mouth silently spread open and a deep rash washed over the top of her chest. By now, Alana was rubbing her clit furiously under the front of her jeans, and it didn't take long for her to slump forward, trying unsuccessfully to conceal the look of ecstasy on her face. Even Cheryl and Hannah were getting in on the action as they plunged their fingers deep inside their pussies.

After we all came down from our highs, Cheryl composed herself and sat back up in her chair.

"I knew you guys would enjoy that one," she said, trying to collect her breath. She panned around the room and made a mental note of who still hadn't had a chance to use one of the sex toys. "I see there's still a few of you who've been left out of the fun. Let's see if this next one might entice you into the fold, in a manner of speaking."

She reached down into her bag and lifted up another large penis-shaped dildo. But this time, two projections looking like little fingers protruded from the device about halfway up the shaft.

"Some of you ladies might recognize this little baby made famous by Samantha on Sex in the City. It's called the *Rabbit* because of these cute little ears that stick out from the side of the vibrator. But this device can stimulate you in so many other ways."

She flipped on the switch at the base of the unit and little chrome-colored beads began circulating around the middle of the translucent shaft. "These rotating balls provide quite a lovely sensation when you have it inserted inside you." She flicked another switch and the tip of the vibrator began rolling like a bobble head. "This vibrator might not be curved like the *Gigi*, but if you angle it properly inside your vagina, the twisting head does almost as good a job stimulating your G-spot."

Many of the women around the circle nodded, having had first-hand experience with the toy.

"But the best thing about this vibrator are these little rabbit ears," Cheryl said, flicking the two flexible flaps on the side of the device. "If you place them directly over your nub, you can get a full-body orgasm from the simultaneous stimulation of your inner and external clitoris. There's a reason why this is a staple in just about every woman's bedroom—it's the definitive multipurpose dildo for today's liberated woman. I've got two more of these to share with the girls who haven't yet had a turn, and I know Jade also keeps one of her own in her private collection."

I smiled at Cheryl as I pulled my brightly colored rabbit vibrator out of my bag resting on the floor.

"Damn straight, girl," I said. "This is my number one vibrator whenever I go on vacation, and I also keep it handy in the night table right beside my bed. This little guy has given me many an intense orgasm over the years. It's quite a special little toy. Although in this case—" I smirked, stroking the shaft, "it's not so *little*."

The girls laughed as I switched on my Rabbit and it began to whirl and roll like some kind of possessed robot-cock. Cheryl handed the other two vibrators to the women near the middle of the group, and I was disappointed not to see one of them passed to Alana. But I knew we still had a couple more toys to show, and I was confident that by the end of the evening she'd be fully participating like the rest of the girls. I was glad to see another one of my straight girlfriends holding one of the rabbit vibrators in her hand, and she looked at me devilishly as she smiled with a wide grin.

"You might want to use a bit of lube with this one," I said, looking at my gyrating vibrator in mock trepidation. "It's considerably bigger and girthier than the others, and you might find it slides in a little easier with a bit of help."

I picked up my tube of lube on the floor and squirted a healthy dollop up and down the shaft of the device, placing a few extra drops on the wide head. Then I placed the dildo between my legs and ran it up and down the inside of my labia to entice the other women to take off their clothes. Within seconds, the other two women had taken off their jeans and panties and were mimicking the movement of the dildo between their legs. As I watched their chests beginning to rise and fall in pleasure, I inserted my Rabbit into my hole and slowly pressed it further inside until the rabbit ears rested against my clit. When I felt the fingers trilling against my button, I sloped down in my chair, grasping the end of the dildo with two hands.

"This is one hell of a magic cock, don't you think ladies?" I grinned. "Who needs a man when you've got one of these to play with."

By now the other two women had inserted their Rabbits deep into their pussies and were nodding vigorously in agreement. The sight of two big vibrating dildos planted deep inside their snatches was an incredible turn-on, and by now almost all the other women had removed their clothing and were jilling themselves unabashedly as they watched the three of us fucking ourselves with our big vibrating cocks. I glanced over at Alana and saw that her jeans were now resting around the base of her ankles with her fingers rotating under the front of her panties. I smiled at her and nodded, moaning approvingly at her loosening inhibitions.

I was still buzzing from my last orgasm, and it didn't take long for the feeling of impending climax to spread over my body as I watched the rest of the girls grunting in their chairs. But this time I didn't want to come so fast that I couldn't enjoy everybody else's experience to the fullest. I bit my lip and pulled the vibrator slightly away from my clit, concentrating on the feeling of the rotating beads and gyrating head moving inside me.

I wasn't sure if the other two girls had used a Rabbit before, but from the expression on their faces, they looked like they were having a transcendental experience. As their passion began to rise, I watched their bodies progressively tense up as they gripped the shaft of their big dildos with two hands and pulled it harder against their vulvas. I could see the rabbit ears flapping against their clits as they thrust the vibrating cock harder and harder inside their pussies until they both began to whine at the onset of a powerful orgasm.

"That's right," I encouraged, "let it go, girls. Let me watch you cum all over your big dildos. I'm going to cum with you."

Suddenly, the three of us wailed out loud as a powerful orgasm washed over us while we held the big dildos tightly against our vulvas, our legs stretched out in front of us, convulsing in a long simultaneous orgasm. I heard a squeal coming from the other end of the circle and I turned my head just in time to see Alana thrusting her fingers deep inside her cunny as she mimicked our action, lost in her own powerful orgasm. I smiled at her as we both shook deliriously in our chairs.

4
———————

It was hard to imagine getting any higher than this from any other of Cheryl's toys, but she smiled at me with a devious grin as she pulled her dripping fingers out of her panties. I was a little disappointed that she hadn't yet removed all of her clothes like most of the other ladies, but I guessed she wanted to maintain some degree of modesty while she continued her demonstration. After pausing a while for everyone to recover from their last episode, she reached down into her case and lifted up a U-shaped device with two flattened ends.

"I know you're all probably thinking it can't possibly get any more intense than that," she said. "But I've been saving the best for last. This interesting little device was developed by a woman who wanted to feel something different from the typical vibrator. It's called the *Osé*, by Lora DiCarlo. Unlike just about every other sex toy, this one doesn't have a conventional vibrating motor. Instead, it *undulates*, mimicking the feeling of a human touch on your vulva."

She turned on the device and it began to writhe in her hand like an animated snake.

"This end of the device flexes in a *come-hither* motion as if your partner is drawing his or her fingers gently against the inside of your G-spot.

Every woman, including myself, leaned in and squinted their eyes, mesmerized by the unusual movement of the toy.

"At the same time," Cheryl continued, "this end of the device slithers with a *pulsing* motion that mimics the feeling of a tongue licking the glans and shaft of your outer clit."

"Holy shit!" I said, shocked at the innovative design of the toy.

Cheryl turned her head toward me and nodded.

"Even *Jade* hasn't tried this one yet. It's just literally come onto the market and we're one of the few stores to be given exclusive distribution rights. Since none of you have tried it yet, I'm going to take the liberty of showing you how it works *myself* before I hand out a few extra models."

Cheryl lifted her hips off her chair and slipped her panties down to the floor, then raised her feet to shed the lower half of her clothes.

"As you can see," she said, holding the device directly in front of her separated legs. "This toy is shaped in the form of a 'U' and can be used hands-free once properly inserted. The fatter end goes inside and the thinner part rests on top of your outer clit."

She angled the device so the bottom of the U was facing the circle of women, then she inserted one end into her hole. As she gently pressed it upward, the thinner end slid up her vulva until it rested firmly over her clitoral shaft.

"There are two buttons on the bottom edge of the Osé that you can use to easily adjust the pace of the undulations."

She placed two fingers on the bottom of the U and tapped each one in turn.

"The button with the *Plus* symbol on the right-hand side increases the speed and the button with the *Minus* symbol beside it lowers the speed. But you won't notice a buzzing or throbbing sensation like the other vibrators. The buttons simply change the pace and rhythm of the undulations, much like your partner does when he or she adjusts the way they're licking and stroking you."

I could hear a gentle hum emanating from between Cheryl's legs as she spread her thighs apart and closed her eyes, concentrating on the feelings inside her.

"Before I get too lost in the pleasure provided by this incredible toy," she said, briefly opening her eyes, "I'm going to pass out three more models to the group. Please hand them along to those who haven't yet had a chance to test one of our vibrators. If I'm doing my math right, this last toy should cover the remaining girls who haven't yet had a try. But don't worry, ladies—you'll be glad you saved yourself until the end. This is one amazing sex toy that you won't soon forget."

Cheryl handed me three Osé toys, and I passed one to Alana and one to my straight friend Barb, keeping the last one for myself.

"You know what might be kind of fun this time," I smiled, noticing a few of the girls still partially covered up. "Is if we remove *all* of our clothing so we can watch and enjoy each other fully unencumbered with any camouflage. I don't know about the rest of you guys, but I get just as turned on *watching* your bodies as I do by touching myself. If you're all feeling comfortable enough, let's shed the rest of our trappings and revel in the beauty of our feminine bodies!"

It didn't take long for every single woman around the room to take off the last vestiges of their clothing. Even Alana had dispensed with the last of her inhibitions as she pulled off her blouse and unclasped her bra behind her back. I panned around the semicircle, admiring the different shapes and sizes of all the sexy women.

"Let's get started then, shall we?" I said, winking at my friends.

Some of the girls still had a few of the earlier models of the sex toys resting beside their chairs and they picked them up as the three of us began to insert the curved Osé into our pussies. Those who didn't have access to a toy spread their legs wide apart and began to massage their clits with their fingers.

It felt strange slipping the unusual-shaped device inside my pussy, but as I pressed it further and further inside me, I hummed in satisfaction at the way it gripped my crotch. I almost felt like someone was cupping their hand over my vulva with their fingers touching my G-spot on the inside and their thumb resting over my clit on the outside. But when I tapped the On button at the base of the device, my eyes flew open in surprise.

Just as Cheryl had suggested, the sensation was unlike any other vibrator I'd previously used. Instead of a concentrated vibration sensation, the two ends of the device rolled and undulated against my tissues in a most natural way. On the inside, the long end curved and stroked me in a come-hither motion. On the outside, the other end undulated over my bulb, teasing and caressing my clit with its animated tongue-like action. I looked at the other two girls who had the Osé embedded in their pussies, and they had an equally incredulous expression on their faces.

I smiled at Alana, and she responded by spreading her legs further apart. I noticed the juices coating the inside of her thighs as she rolled her hips sensuously on her chair and locked eyes with me. The otherworldly feeling of someone touching me in my most sensitive areas was driving me insane, and for a brief moment, I fantasized about our two bodies pressed together so we could enjoy the feeling in unison. I knew this was likely the first time she'd had sex openly in the presence of other women, and it didn't take long for her to begin thrashing and moaning as she watched me and the other girls enjoying themselves. After only a few minutes of stimulation from her new sex toy, she suddenly threw her head back and screamed as her thighs began flapping together from the intense contractions washing over her. Not long after, Barb groaned equally loud as she shook violently in her chair from the orgasm taking control of her.

Within seconds, virtually everyone around the room including Cheryl and Hannah were squealing and shaking from the most erotic show any of us had ever witnessed. I was the last one to shoot off, and as I grabbed each of my tits in my hands, I gushed all the juices that I'd been building up inside my pussy out the two sides of my ring all over Cheryl and Barb, sitting directly in front of me. I sat convulsing in my chair for almost a full sixty seconds as the rest of the women watched in amazement. When I finally slumped forward in my chair, completely spent and exhausted, everyone stood up and clapped with a standing ovation.

5

---

fter the three of us who'd used the Osé vibrator had come down from our highs, everybody looked at one another wondering what to do next. We were all dripping wet and buck naked, and nobody was in a hurry to end the party. But Cheryl had shared with me how she planned to step up each activity, and I knew she had one last trick up her sleeve that would bring everyone together in the end.

"That was fun, wasn't it?" she said, breaking the awkward silence. "It looked like some of you shared a pretty intense connection during that last demonstration. With that idea in mind, I had a few more toys to show you that were specially designed for multiple partner enjoyment."

She suddenly stood up and walked behind the sofa positioned against the far wall. She lifted an ottoman-sized object draped in a bedsheet off the floor and placed it in the center of the arc between the main group and our two chairs. Then she pulled off the cover with a flourish and threw it behind her. The device looked like a squat pommel horse, but in place of a saddle in the middle of the curved midsection were two diamond-shaped dildos pointing up about one foot apart.

"This strange contraption," Cheryl said, "is the *Sybian Sex Machine*, and it delivers quite a ride. It can be used by one or two people at a time, but as you can see from the double dildos positioned on top, it's best enjoyed as a partnered activity. Each person can face one another and caress the other as they receive powerful internal stimulation from the uniquely shaped dildos. The secure base of the unit allows both participants to ride the machine cow-girl style."

I panned around the circle and noticed the women looking at the device slack-jawed with wide eyes. It was obvious that few of them had seen or tried anything like it, but their erect nipples and swiveling hips suggested they were eager to give it a try.

"Those of you who like to have sex with a man once in a while," Cheryl smiled, "know that the girl-on-top position during intercourse allows for better control and provides a nice firm surface to rub your clits on. You'll notice this device comes with a vibrating pad under each dildo that delivers full-body stimulation to your entire vulva region. You really have to try it to appreciate it. Who'd like to volunteer to be our first test subjects?"

A few girls raised their arms and Cheryl pointed toward two women she recognized from their earlier trips into her store with their husbands. I was unsure if she purposely chose two straight girls to help break down their inhibitions about trying same-sex lovemaking, but I was nevertheless thrilled to see Dawn and Julie approach the device. They both had tight, athletic figures and I'd long fantasized about fucking one or both of them whenever we'd been out on group playdates together. I crossed my arms over my chest and pinched my nipples as I rubbed my legs together in anticipation of watching the two girls try the sexy machine.

"All you have to do is straddle the device," Cheryl instructed, leaning back in her chair holding a control box wired to the base of the unit. "Then sit down gently as you ease the dildos inside of you, facing one another. You might want to place a little lube on them first to make it go in a little easier."

She handed each woman a tube of lube and they generously lathered the dildos underneath them before sitting down over the plugs. The sight of the glistening phalluses disappearing into their neatly shaved snatches made the hairs on the side of my arms stand up on end. Suddenly I became aware of how wet my chair cushion had become as I watched the two women.

"How does that feel?" Cheryl said to the women.

They both made a soft mewing sound as they peered silently at Cheryl, afraid to look at one another and acknowledge that their naked bodies were mere inches apart.

"Can you feel the bulge in the middle of the plugs?" she asked. "They're designed to provide better stimulation of your G-spot once the action gets going."

"Um-hmm," Dawn nodded.

"Yup," Julie replied curtly.

"Let's see if we can make it a little more interesting," Cheryl said as she began to twist one of the dials on the control box.

A soft hum began to emanate from inside the machine, and the two women's eyes widened as they began to roll their hips unconsciously over the seat.

"Better?" Cheryl asked.

"Yes," Dawn panted, closing her eyes to concentrate on the buzzing feeling inside her.

"We've only *begun* to experience what this device can do," Cheryl winked.

She turned another knob on the control box, and the pads under the base of the dildos began to flap against the girls' clits. Julie gasped as she placed her hands behind her on the bench, unsure where to put her arms. Dawn crossed her arms nervously over her chest as she grunted and flitted her eyelids in pleasure.

"Feel free to touch one another," Cheryl said, trying to get the girls to loosen up and become more engaged with one another. "The whole point of this device is to revel in each other's pleasure and make it an interactive experience."

Dawn reached out tentatively and cupped each of Julie's trembling tits in her palms. Julie leaned forward and placed her arms around Dawn's back then the two women pressed their bodies together.

"There we go," Cheryl nodded. "Feel the pleasure coursing through each other's bodies as you caress one another. Lose yourself in the experience as you become one. We're going to begin ramping up the intensity level now."

She twisted both knobs further to the right then flicked a switch on the side. Each of the dildos suddenly began gyrating inside the women's pussies, pressing more firmly against the front of their tunnels. Both women groaned and locked lips, probing their tongues inside each other's mouths. As they began to mash their breasts together and moan in unison from the incredible sensation enveloping their pussies, I glanced around the room.

All the other women were playing with themselves in one form or another as they watched the sexy show in front of them. For my part, the sight of two straight girls rubbing their bodies together as they were being remotely stimulated by an innocent bystander was too much to resist. I picked up my rabbit vibrator off the floor and flicked the speed to max as I jammed it inside my pussy, pulling it hard against my tingling button.

"That's what I'm talking about," Cheryl purred, watching the two women beginning to lose themselves in each other's passion. "Are you ready to take it to the penultimate level?"

"Mmm-hmm," the two women nodded as they ran their hands over each other's bodies while they continued to kiss passionately.

Cheryl twisted the two dials to their maximum setting, and the hum inside the machine deepened as the flaps under their pussies began to flap wildly. Dawn and Julie pressed their hips forward, gyrating their hips together as they got closer and closer toward climax. Within seconds, they began wailing in tandem as their bodies shook violently with their arms clasped tightly around each other. Seeing the two women coming together soon put me over the edge also as my pussy clamped tightly over the vibrating shaft of my

Rabbit toy. I glanced over at Alana and noticed that she was holding a Form 2 vibrator over her clit while she quaked in her chair watching the other women in the room jilling themselves as they took in the action.

6

———

After everyone had finished coming once again, Cheryl looked at the two girls still sitting on the now-silent Sybian machine.

"What do you think, ladies?" she said. "Does that feel anything like riding your husbands on top?"

"Fuck no!" Dawn said. "This is way better!"

Julie nodded enthusiastically in agreement, and everybody around the room laughed out loud.

"Well at least now you know how much fun it can be to play with some of your own kind," Cheryl said. "And while we're on that subject, I'd like to demonstrate a couple of toys that will allow you to be even *more* actively engaged with your same-sex partners." She peered at Dawn and Julie and smiled. "You guys are welcome to stay there if you wish or return to your seats for this next demonstration."

The two women kissed each other one last time then eased themselves off the bench, revealing two glistening, pearly-white dildos. When they returned to their seats, I noticed they were holding hands beside one another. I smiled at their new special friendship and nodded at them approvingly.

Cheryl moved the Sybian machine off to the side of the circle then reached back down into her display case. When she sat up, she revealed a giant flexible dildo with a raised ring running around the middle of the shaft.

"This is a two-sided or double dildo," she said, running her fingers over the two ends of the object shaped in the form of the head of a man's penis. "As you can see, it's a little longer than a regular man's cock and it has two heads for double the pleasure. Perhaps *most* interesting though, is this raised band in the middle."

She squeezed the shaft near the center and the band began flapping like the pads on the Sybian machine.

"When two women press this dildo inside them from opposite ends, the vibrating ring in the middle provides some very pleasant supplemental stimulation as they grind their pussies together. Unlike the Sybian machine, which you experience in more of a passive role, with this device you can actively fuck each other in a multitude of positions."

Cheryl looked around the room and smiled mischievously.

"Who'd like to give this one a try?"

Two of my lesbian friends raised their hands but I quickly pre-empted them. Watching Cheryl demonstrate her toys all this time had gotten me seriously worked up and I jumped at this opportunity to have some fun with her.

"I notice that *you* haven't yet had a chance to use any of your toys today, Cheryl," I said. "If you're game, I'd be happy to demonstrate this one for the rest of the group with your participation."

"I thought you'd never ask," Cheryl said, winking at me. "Let's get down on the floor and show these ladies how two lesbian women can get it on."

I lay down on the carpet in front of the chairs with my hips facing up and spread my knees apart. Cheryl lay down in a similar position facing me, with our vulvas about a foot apart. Then she squirted a drop of lube on each end of the dildo and pressed one end against her opening. As she shimmied her hips toward me, half of the dildo slowly disappeared inside her pussy. When the other end pressed against my hole, I mimicked her movement until the plug was fully inserted inside our bodies with our vulvas mashed together.

"Are you *in* yet?" Cheryl joked, lifting her head off the floor and peering toward me.

"Judging by the feel of your wet pussy pressing against mine, I'd say so," I meowed.

"Shall we get started then?" she said.

"By all means," I purred.

As we both began rolling our hips together, I felt the dildo thrusting in and out of me as it plunged deeper and deeper inside my cunt. Although it wasn't vibrating yet and it didn't have the beneficial shape of some of the other curved vibrators, the feeling of Cheryl actively fucking me with the unicock and the sensation of her wet lips grinding against mine more than made up for the lack of other features.

Suddenly, she rolled over onto her side and straddled me with one leg under my ass and the other one over my tummy. As she humped me more aggressively, she began to grunt like a wild animal. I was enjoying the experience of being on the bottom for a change, but just as I began to feel the familiar feeling of another orgasm rising up within me, she turned over another ninety degrees until she was facing face-down on the carpet.

"Fuck me from behind, Jade," she groaned. "I want to feel your ass slapping against mine."

"Fuck yes!" I said, quickly rolling over so we were both facing down.

We pulled our knees forward and lifted ourselves up until we were resting on all-fours with our butt cheeks pressing against one another. Cheryl reached between her legs and pinched the middle of the dildo, and the snake suddenly began writhing inside our pussies as the ring between our legs flapped against our two clits.

"Oh God," I moaned as Cheryl began rocking her hips against me, slapping her ass against mine.

The simultaneous feeling of the gyrating dildo in my pussy with

Cheryl's ass grinding against mine and the vibrating ring trembling against my burning clit felt incredible.

"*Fuck*, Cheryl," I hissed. "I'm gonna cum. I'm gonna cum so hard all over your pretty ass. Come with me baby."

"I'm close," Cheryl growled. "Spray all over my wet hole. Let me feel you cum all over my burning cunt."

Whether it was Cheryl's sexy dirty talk or the sensation of being watched by all the other women around the room, I felt my orgasm suddenly wash over me as I began to shake uncontrollably against Cheryl's ass. My pussy clamped down hard on the flexible dildo as I felt the juices squirting out of my hole all over her opening.

"Yes, Jade!" she wailed. "Spray me with your cum. I'm coming baby! Fill up my hole as you cum inside me!"

As we both pawed the carpet like two cats in heat, I heard the sighs of other women around me and turned my head to see every one of them fucking themselves with one device or another as they watched us, their breasts trembling as they came in simultaneous union with Cheryl and me.

7

___

A s the two of us lay spent and exhausted on the floor, I looked up at the other women peering at one another expectantly. It was obvious that they were ready to engage more actively with some of the others, and this seemed like the ideal time to open things up for broader participation. Cheryl and I looked at each other, thinking the same thing, and nodded.

"This seems like a good time for the rest of you to find a partner and try some interactive play," I said. "Feel free to grab whatever toy you can find and experiment away. It's always a lot more fun when you bring someone else into the mix, and there's a limitless degree of combinations you can create when you bring other partners into the equation. Grab a spot on the sofa, or use one of my private rooms, or join the rest of us on the floor. This party is a long way from being over!"

Almost immediately, all the other girls joined us on the floor, pairing up with new and old acquaintances, as they picked up various loose toys and rubbing them against each other's bodies. I peered over in Alana's direction and noticed that she was sitting by herself, looking at my naked body longingly. I turned to Cheryl, still joined at the hips with me on the floor, and she motioned for me to go to her. I pulled myself off my half of the dildo and Hannah quickly took my place, smiling at Cheryl as they pressed their hips together.

I was happy to see my friends hooking up and enjoying themselves so openly, but as I walked toward Alana crossing her legs shyly, I felt sorry for the one person in the group who still seemed hesitant to participate in the group fun.

"Haven't you been enjoying the party?" I said, taking a seat on the chair beside her.

"Yes, of course," Alana said, placing her arms shyly over her chest.

"I've noticed you participating at various times," I smiled. "But you seem reluctant to engage with the others. Are you feeling uncomfortable?"

"No—not really," she said. "It's just that no one else here...*interests* me."

I sensed what Alana was getting at, but I wanted to be sure before taking the next step.

"No one else meaning..."

"*You*, Jade," she said, peering into my eyes. "I've been watching you for so long, wanting to make love to you."

I slipped off my chair and kneeled in front of her, kissing her softly on her lips.

"I've been watching you from afar also, Alana," I said. "I've had many a sleepless night fantasizing about your beautiful figure, imagining myself touching and licking your naked body."

I lowered myself down the front of her body, nibbling the side of her neck and kissing the top of her chest. When I reached her firm breasts, I cupped each one in my hands and ran my tongue over her nipples in gentle circles. I could feel her nubs hardening in my mouth as I sucked on them gently. Alana tilted her head back and moaned, pressing her body toward me. As I moved in closer, she spread her legs further apart, and I could feel the heat emanating from her pussy.

Eager to feel her in my mouth, I continued lower until my face was level with her mound. I was a little surprised to find her so smooth and bare down there, and I looked up at her with a quizzical look.

"I shaved myself just for you," she said. "I didn't want anything coming between the two of us tonight."

I smiled up at her then rolled my cheeks against her soft pubis, flapping my eyelids with butterfly kisses against her skin as her thighs trembled in anticipation of my touch further below.

"Suck me, Jade," Alana whinnied, pressing her hips harder toward me. "I want to feel your lips on my most private parts. I've been dreaming about this for so long—"

Before she could finish her sentence, I lowered my face and encircled her flaming clit in my mouth, rolling my tongue over her pearl. Alana gasped and grabbed the back of my head, pulling me harder against her soaking vulva. I hummed in approval, alternating between flicking my tongue over her erect shaft and sucking her button deeply into my mouth. Her clit was larger than most, and I could feel her sex extend a full inch into my mouth as I sucked on her little cocklet.

Alana began rocking her hips wildly on her chair as she fucked my mouth shamelessly. Her groans grew progressively louder but just as I was sure she was about to come in my mouth, she suddenly pulled away and peered down at me with a possessed look on her face.

"I want to feel you inside me when I cum," she said. "Fuck me, Jade. Fuck me with one of Cheryl's sexy toys. I want to be your bitch."

I shook my head in shock, momentarily taken aback by Alana's newfound boldness. Whether this was simply her straight side wanting to get fucked in the manner she was accustomed to, or she was demonstrating her desire to adopt the femme persona in our new lesbian tryst, I didn't care. I just wanted to take her and consummate our long, lingering relationship as quickly as I could. My eyes darted along the floor to find something I could fuck her with, but seeing that all the other toys were in use by the other women engaged in heated affairs, I peered into Cheryl's case and noticed a strap-on dildo.

"Wait here, babe," I said. "I think I have just the thing."

I walked gingerly around all the writhing bodies on the floor and reached slowly into her case. Hannah and Cheryl were nearing the point of no return as they fucked each other wildly with the two-ended dildo, and they smiled at me devilishly as my breasts wobbled above their faces.

"Go fuck that girl," Hannah said. "Show her what it's like to experience a real orgasm."

I nodded at her then scampered back to Alana's chair where I found her already kneeling on the floor with her glistening ass pointed up toward me.

"Yes, Jade," she purred. "Fuck me with that big dildo. Let me feel your big cock deep inside me."

It didn't take more than a few seconds to wrap the belt around my waist and legs to secure the big phallus over my mound. It had a gentle downward curve and a thick head specifically intended for G-spot stimulation when used from behind. I noticed a couple of buttons on the front of the harness, but I was in too much of a hurry to feel Alana's pussy wrapped around my cock to figure out what they did. I reached between her legs to see if she needed any lubrication and she was slippery as a runny faucet. I pointed the tip of the dildo against her hole and wasted no time slamming it inside her cavern. If she wanted it rough, I thought, I was only too happy to oblige.

"Oh *fuck*!" Alana groaned. "That feels so good. Can you feel me squeezing you?"

I couldn't of course, because it was an artificial dildo. But I could feel the resistance of her tight pussy clamping against my faux cock as I pulled it out and slammed it back into her. The feeling of her ass cheeks slapping against my mound and my throbbing clit just amplified the feeling of fucking her like a man. I wondered what her husband would think if he knew what I was doing to his wife behind my closed curtains.

From her escalating moans and movements, I could tell that she was close to popping off, and I selfishly wanted to come with her. Maybe it was from me channeling the replacement of her husband or maybe it was just me desperately wanting to get off again. But either way, as sexy as it was to screw this little vixen with my artificial cock, I wasn't getting quite enough direct stimulation to get there with her.

I pulled out of her halfway for a moment and tapped a few of the buttons on the front of my harness. Suddenly, the dildo began throbbing with a deep rumble and another motor began vibrating against my nub under the harness.

"Holy shit," Alana hissed. "This thing is *way* better than my husband's cock. Whatever you're doing, it's driving me crazy. Fuck me harder, Jade. I'm getting close."

"So am I," I grunted, overwhelmed by the multiple sensations of fucking my neighbor from behind while simultaneously getting jilled on my clit. "Come with me baby. Let me feel you gushing all over my dick."

"Yes, Jade!" Alana cried. "Here it comes—I'm cumming!!"

Suddenly, I lost all sense of control as every ounce of my pent-up passion poured out of my body. As I began shuddering with intense contractions, I gushed my wetness out the sides of my harness down both sides of Alana's inner thighs. Feeling me cumming all over her, she wailed at the top of her lungs as her hips began shaking in spastic convulsions. I leaned over and squeezed her tits firmly with my hands as we both grunted in ecstatic union. When the two of us finished our long and intense climax and finally collapsed together on the floor, I noticed the rest of the girls lying beside us with silly grins on their faces.

This was one party none of us would soon forget.

VOLUME THREE

NAKED TWISTER

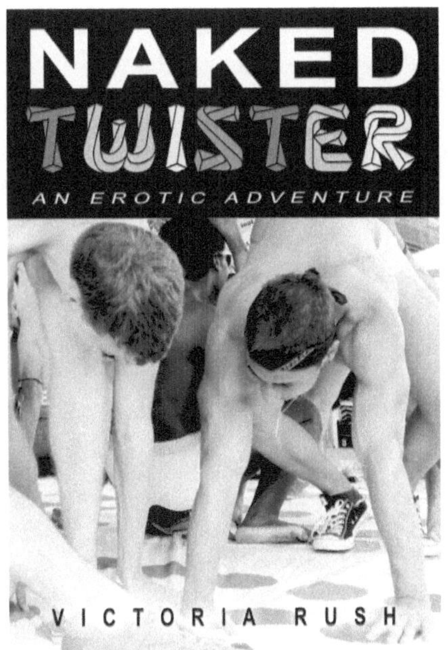

1

When I saw the new email message from my friend Madison with the cryptic heading *Don't get your knickers in a knot,* I had to open it right away. Madison was famous for hosting the most interesting and sexy parties, and as I began to read the message, I could already feel my heart racing in excitement.

Dear Jade,

You are cordially invited to a party at Madison's place this Saturday at 9 p.m.

As with my other events, there will be a special activity that will be sure to keep everyone engaged and spread the love around. I don't want to spoil the surprise by giving away too much, other than asking you to wear loose fitting or stretchy clothing.

And you might also want to work on strengthening your abs at the gym or the yoga studio. Because you're going to need a fair amount of 'stamina' to play the game I have in mind.

I think you'll find this variation on a classic game will be sure to please! Be there or be square,

Maddy

P.S.: Make sure you're freshly polished and scrubbed, and I do mean everywhere, because you know, one thing often leads to another at my parties. ;-)

What the–? I thought, as my mind raced trying to decipher what she was cooking up this time. *It's going to be some kind of 'physical' game requiring strength and stamina, and it sounds like there's going to be a fair amount of body contact, with or without clothes. It could be anything from flag football to dodgeball to nerf tag.*

After stewing over what she had planned for most of the day, I finally succumbed later that evening and gave her a ring.

"Hey, sexy!" she answered, after seeing my caller ID on her phone.

"You know I can't sit on that mysterious invitation without wanting to pry for more details."

"Pry away," she teased. "But you're not going to get much more out of me. Finding out what the surprise is when you get here is half the fun. Plus, I want everybody to be charged up and ready to jump in the moment they arrive."

"Jump in?" I said. "Does it involve your swimming pool?"

"At some point it's pretty likely," she said. "If only to cool off after all the strenuous exercise. And I'm pretty sure most of the attendees will have their clothes stripped off within an hour or so, so it seems like a logical place to finish off."

"You are *such* a tease!" I huffed, more confused than ever about what she had planned. "Who's invited?"

"It's a pretty mixed bag," she said, knowing my preference for sex with women. "Some people you know, plus a few new faces. But I can guarantee they're all hot! You might even be tempted to switch sides once or twice during all the merrymaking."

"Jesus, Mad!" I squealed into the phone. "You're killing me!"

"That's the whole idea," she said. "I want you to be on pins and needles by the time you arrive at the party. And to keep your options open. Because there's going to be a fair amount of random touching and interaction. Who *knows* what body parts might get intermingled others during all the hijinks?"

"Where do you come up with these crazy ideas, anyway?" I said, marveling at her ingenuity in finding ever more creative and exciting games.

"What can I say?" she said. "I guess I'm just a kinky kind of girl."

"You got *that* right," I smiled, reflecting back on our last erotic encounter at her previous game night involving blindfolds. "But I can't guarantee I'm going to be all polished and pristine by the time I get there. I'm *already* getting wet imagining what you've got in store this time."

"Don't you worry your pretty little pussy over it," she said. "A little extra lubrication might come in handy in more ways than one for what I have in mind. And I use the word 'come' very loosely in this context."

"Fuck you," I said, playfully.

"Mmm, I hope so," she purred. "But it will depend which way the bottle spins..."

"Bottle?!" I said, shaking my head. "What does a bottle have to do–"

"See you Saturday at nine," she said. "And don't be late. This will be an all-hands-on-deck kind of activity. You don't want to miss your chance to get in on the action early."

When Madison hung up on me, I was tempted to call her back, but I knew from previous experience that she wouldn't reveal any more details. Even though I was one of her closest confidants, she knew how quickly gossip traveled around our close-knit group of friends. And she also knew me well enough to know that the less knowledge I had about the details of her sexy party event, the more turned on and eager I'd be to play her game.

You got that right, girl, I smiled as I pulled my panties down and began to finger my soaking slit.

2

———————

On the night of Madison's party, I drove to her place with a certain degree of trepidation. The only loose clothing I could find in my closet were an old pair of flannel pajamas. I'd considered wearing my stretchy yoga tights, but with my tendency to soak my crotch when I got worked up, I figured the pajamas would help protect my modesty–at least until things heated up later in the evening. Besides, I still wasn't sold on the idea of touching my intimate body parts with a bunch of unknown men, and the thick material would provide an extra degree of insulation.

When I arrived at her house and she opened the door, she eyed my ensemble up and down, then smiled and nodded.

"A bit unconventional, but that'll do," she said. "Come on, we're just about ready to get started."

I could hear the buzz of male and female voices coming from her living room, and when she escorted me to the group, I was surprised to see a dozen or so people sitting barefoot around a plastic Twister mat on the floor.

Of course, I thought, shaking my head at my stupidity. *Stretching, exercise, random touching of body parts. How could I not have figured this one out?*

I peered around the group, recognizing a few of my friends. There was my BFF, Hannah, of course, plus a couple of girls from the office where Madison and I used to work. But there was also a fair number of unfamiliar faces of both genders. My pussy twitched as I scanned the group, noticing quite a few hot and sexy bodies bedecked in tight yoga outfits and skimpy gym clothes. And I smiled when I recognized my transgender friend Shae, who worked as a dancer at the local cabaret club. We'd shared an impassioned weekend together a few months ago, and I was suddenly glad I'd chosen the loose-fitting pajamas to wear as a dribble of lubrication trickled down the inside of my thigh.

"Now that we've got the last member of our group here," Madison said. "Let's finish up with the introductions. Most of you know Jade of course, but we also have a few new faces in the crowd.

"This is my friend Natalie from work," Maddy said, motioning to a cute blond girl in her twenties.

"And my college roommate, Taylor," who's in town for a few days visiting family.

"And my sexy neighbor Laura, who I'm totally envious of stealing all the attention on our block while she suntans all day long in her skimpy bikini around her pool."

I could see a number of both men and women around the circle nodding as they eyed her sylphlike body wrapped up in a tight two-piece yoga uniform.

"And on the other side of the mat," Maddy said, motioning to an equal number of men seated opposite the women. "Besides Dylan, Jake, and Marco, who you already know, we have my ex-boyfriend Brett, my current partner-in-crime Tyler, and Laura's husband Brad."

I glanced at each of the men and nodded, lingering for a little longer at Laura's husband, with his smoldering eyes and chiseled jaw. He was wearing a tight-fitting pair of sweat pants and a tank-top that showed off his perfectly sculpted athletic figure. Apparently I wasn't the only one distracted by his good looks and hot body, noticing some of the men frowning that his pretty wife Laura was already taken, while the women simply gawked at him with wide eyes.

"Okay," Madison said, taking a seat at one end of the rectangular-shaped mat with its four rows of green, yellow, blue, and red polka dots. "Let's go over the rules of this fun little game. As you can see from this plastic mat in front of us, it has a bunch of different colored circles. In a few moments, we're going to divide up into teams. Two partners will stand side-by-side on the four dots on one end of the mat and another team of two will stand opposite them on the other end of the mat."

She motioned to a compass-shaped device nestled between her legs with a needle pointing to the four alternating colors arranged in a circle.

"Then I'm going to spin this little needle and call out which body part each person must use to touch which colored circle. Only one body part and one person can occupy any one circle at any given time. But as you'll soon discover, the availability of circles quickly diminishes as the game advances, so you'll have to move fast to capture the circle closest to you."

"How do you decide who wins?" my friend Lily from our last camping trip asked.

"It gets harder and harder to keep yourself balanced over the mat as the players get into increasingly twisted positions," Madison said. "Whichever player or team falls first onto the mat or touches any body part other than their hand or foot loses."

"What if two people reach out and touch one of the circles at the same time?" Dylan asked.

"As the referee, I reserve the right to decide who got there first." Maddy clamped her hands together in excitement. "Are you guys ready to start?"

"How do we decide on the teams?" I asked, peering at the sexy group of men sitting opposite me. "And why are the men and women sitting on opposite sides of the mat?"

"At first, *I'll* decide who will pair up with whom. But as people get winnowed out, the winner of each round will move on until there's literally only one last man or woman standing. As for the separation of the boys and girls, the reason for that will be revealed soon enough. Shall we proceed?"

Everybody glanced around the circle excitedly at one another, then they peered toward Maddy and nodded.

"Alright then," Madison said. "Who shall we get started with?"

She panned around the group slowly, then nodded while rubbing her hands together with a mischievous grin.

"Let's mix it up a little to get started. We'll have Lily and Dylan form one group and Hannah and Brad form the other group. If you haven't yet removed your footwear, please do so now since you'll definitely want bare feet to maximize your traction on the slippery mat."

The four players stood up and took positions on opposite ends of the mat as Madison had instructed. Then she spun the needle on the game card and called out the first move.

"Okay, the first move is: left leg on a yellow circle."

The four players hesitated for a moment trying to figure out the easiest and quickest route to the designated circle, then each of them awkwardly extended their legs forward, bumping their knees and ankles against their partners' bodies. The ones who already were standing on a yellow circle only had to take one simple step forward, but their partners who were a little further away from that side of the game mat had to stretch and bend over them to reach the next available circle.

"*Oooo,*" some of the people sitting around the circle chortled, realizing how soon the game would have the participants tied up in knots.

"So far so good," Maddy said, smiling at the two teams leaned over one another. "How are you guys doing so far?"

"Piece of cake," Dylan said with his left leg hovering a few inches overtop his partner Lily's bent knee.

"I can see how there's a certain *first-mover* advantage here," Hannah nodded, watching her partner Brad grunting to hold his position stretched further out toward the center of the mat, with his head now lowered to the same level as her loose-fitting T-shirt showing her braless breasts bouncing inches away from his face.

"True," he said, smiling up at Hannah. "But the view isn't all bad."

Everybody in the group chuckled, while his wife Laura looked at him playfully with dagger eyes.

"Okay," Maddy said, returning her attention to the spinner. "Let's ramp up the degree of difficulty a little bit."

She spun the needle once again, and it stopped on a new color.

"This time," she said. "You need to touch a green circle with your right hand."

The players quickly scanned the game mat to decipher the easiest way of getting to the nearest dot, then they lurched forward, bending and bumping against their partners to reach the designated target. Once again, it was a fairly simple move for Hannah to reach only one circle forward and to her right, while her partner Brad had to reach all the way to the opposite side of the mat overtop of both his knee and Hannah's to reach diagonally across the game board.

By the time all four players had twisted their bodies to successfully reach the intended target, both teams had become further entangled, with their crotches rubbing up against their partners legs and hips, and their heads pressed up tightly against their torsos. I noticed a fair-sized bulge in the crotch of Brad's tight sweat pants, but I wasn't sure if he was becoming aroused from all the suggestive moves and rubbing of body parts, or if he was just a little better hung than most of the other guys. I peered over at his wife Laura and noticed her giving him a devilish smile while staring at his tumescent package. Either she was giving him tacit encouragement to rub whatever body parts came in contact, or they had already discussed the possibility of the game taking a 'swinger' turn.

"Ohh!" the group murmured in appreciation as they watched the players move into tighter and more stretched positions. Both Dylan and Brad were puffing more heavily now as they struggled to hold their newly strained positions, having deferred to their female partners to give them the easier first-mover advantage.

"*That* looks a little more interesting," Madison nodded approvingly while peering at each of the players. "I hope you guys have been working out at the gym, because it's only going to get more difficult from here on."

"No sweat," Dylan said, grunting to hold his position.

"That's not what the beads of perspiration on your forehead are telling me," Maddy smiled. "I hope you're all wearing sturdy clothing, because we're about to test the strength of your seams with this next move."

She spun the needle again and this time it landed on the red color.

"Now you have to touch a red circle with your–"

She paused, giving everyone a moment to prepare for their next move.

"*Left* hand!"

This time, Hannah had to reach overtop of Brad's bent leg to reach the circle closest to her, while he had to twist his body facing up to reach his left hand all the way to the other side of the mat. By the time they both had rested their limbs on the designated markers, Hannah was leaning overtop of his crab-shaped body, with her dangling tits rubbing against the rapidly bulging bump in his sweatpants.

For his part, since he was already positioned on the red side of the mat, Dylan only had to reach one circle forward to place his hand on the board. But this time, his partner Lily had the tougher stretch, having to lean over his back to reach the last red dot between the two men's hands. With her body hunched forward into a doggy-style position, it looked like she was humping Dylan's butt with her crotch.

"Woo-hoo!" the group cheered at the erotic ways the two couples had chosen to position themselves.

"Well that certainly looks like fun," Maddy said, raising a playful eyebrow. "Are you guys starting to enjoy yourselves yet?"

"That's one way of putting it," Brad huffed while struggling to hold his upturned position with Hannah resting her body on his hips to support herself.

"I could hold this position for *hours*," Dylan kidded as Lily rubbed her crotch against his ass in their bent-over positions.

The group chuckled, but I noticed Laura shifting her position awkwardly as she watched her husband get increasingly turned on rubbing his thickening rod against Hannah's swinging tits.

"We'll have to see about that," Madison snickered as she spun the game needle one more time a little more forcefully.

After spinning around four or five times, it finally landed on a green circle again.

"Your next move," Madison announced with a glimmer in her eye, is to move your right leg to a green circle," she announced.

The four players peered down at the mat then back up at Maddy with a puzzled expression.

"But all the green circles are already occupied," Hannah said. "What do we do now?"

"In this instance," Maddy said. "Two people may occupy the same circle, but only with their own partner, not someone from the opposing team."

The players paused for a moment trying to determine how they could reach around everyone's twisted body parts, then Brad stepped his foot forward two circles, resting it beside Hannah's downturned hand. The action pressed his crotch even tighter against Hannah's compressed tits, and she caressed his little toe playfully with her index finger while he struggled to hold his position.

But this time it was Dylan's turn to be put into an increasingly difficult position. He had to move his right foot in front of his left leg on the same plane, while Lily had to simultaneous reach forward with her own right foot, trying to place it beside his. With her full weight already boring down on top of Dylan's back, and with his legs no longer in a spread position to balance himself, the two players quickly toppled onto the mat in a jumble of limbs.

"Nooo!" the crowded roared in laughter while Dylan and Lily embraced each other, completely exhausted.

"We appear to have a winner," Madison nodded, motioning for Hannah and Brad to extricate themselves from their twisted position. "You two can relieve yourselves now if you'd like. Although it looks like you're kind of enjoying yourselves in that position, so if you need to take a moment to compose yourselves, don't let me rush you."

"Mmm," Hannah purred, smiling at Brad prostrated beneath her with an arched back. "I wouldn't mind taking advantage of my partner in his currently vulnerable position, but something tells me his wife would prefer we separate before one of us gets some other ideas."

"Don't let me get in the way of your fun," she said, winking at Brad with a sly smile. "It's all part of the game. Whatever happens at Madison's place *stays* at Madison's place. Isn't that right, honey?"

"I suppose so," Brad grunted. "But I'm not sure I can hold this position much longer. Perhaps I should save my strength for the next round if this means the two of us will be moving on."

"Actually," Madison smiled with a devilish grin. "Only *one* of you will be moving on to the next round. I have a slightly *different* idea for how to make the next step it a little more interesting."

As Hannah and Brad untangled themselves and lifted themselves off the mat, they looked at Maddy with a suspicious expression. They undoubtedly were thinking the same thing the rest of us were regarding Madison's email instruction to wash our bodies thoroughly in preparation for the event, intimating that we would soon be intermingling our bodies without clothes in subsequent rounds.

The only question now was who would be volunteered to join with whom, and would it be with the men or the women? As I contemplated all the combinations and permutations, I watched Brad resume his position at the other side of the mat while crossing his legs and folding his hands over his crotch to conceal the swelling in his sweat pants. Meanwhile, the growing wetness between my *own* legs suggested I wasn't quite done with the idea of playing a slightly different version of this 'twist and groan' game with the opposite sex after all.

3

After the two teams sat back down and everybody had their wine glasses topped up, Maddy continued with her instructions for the next round.

"So, as you can see," she smiled. "This game has a tendency to get you tied up into some pretty imaginative, close-contact positions. I thought to make it even more interesting in the next round we might try it without clothes..."

Some people from both sides of the mat began darting their eyes around the circle, already thinking about who they hoped to get hooked up with.

"I know most of you pretty well," Madison continued. "And I chose you specifically because you're pretty open-minded about these things. Some of you have already participated in a similar type of group interaction at my last nude blindfolded party game. But if any of you are hesitant to expose yourself in front of the group, you're welcome to remain clothed and sit out the action while you enjoy the rest of the show."

Most of the guys simply nodded their heads with a sly smile while I listened to the escalated breathing from the girls around me indicating their willingness to get involved.

"Is this going to be a *unisex* sort of thing or..." Marco asked, eager to mix it up with some of the girls he was eying up on the other side of the mat.

"It's funny you should mention that, Marco," Maddy grinned. "I thought to make it even more interesting, we'd do it a little differently each round. I'm thinking first we do just the girls, then just the guys, then we finish up with a mixed group. I know some of you like to swing one way or the other, so this way everybody will have a chance to mingle with their preferred partners."

"How do we decide who'll participate in each round?" Marco continued, shifting uncomfortably at the idea of getting naked and rubbing his body together with a bunch of other straight guys.

"The winners of each round will move forward of course," she said. "So Hannah moves into the next round and Brad the one after that. Plus, two more guys will move forward to the last round after it's their turn. So that'll be a little extra incentive for you to try to win your round. As for the remaining participants, that will be my choice."

Marco nodded his head and pursed his lips as he ran through the possibilities in his head.

"So for this next round, it's going to be all girls. Hannah is on deck by virtue of her team's win in the last round. And to join her, how about we have Jade and Laura..."

Maddy paused as she glanced tentatively at Shae sitting on the girls' side of the mat.

"I don't want to make any presumptions about *you*, Shae," she said. "Do you have a preference for which group you'd like to join?"

"Actually," she said with a sly grin, glancing across the mat toward the guys eyeing her curvy body greedily. "I think I'd rather join the guys if that's okay with you."

"Absolutely," Maddy said. "So then to finish up the girls' group, let's go with...*Natalie*. Are you guys all good to go?"

The four of us peered at one another with raised eyebrows, then slowly nodded in agreement.

"Okay," Madison smiled. "You know the next step then."

"Um, okay," I said, standing up to slowly unbutton my pajama top. But who will team up with who this time?"

"Good question, Jade," Maddy said, pausing to consider the most appropriate mix. "How about you and Laura form one team and Natalie and Hannah form the other?"

The four of us stood up and slowly removed our clothes, then walked tentatively toward the opposite ends of the game mat. Every single set of eyes in the room including our own, ran wildly over the sea of naked flesh, and I could feel tummy fluttering in knots knowing that soon we'd be rubbing our naked bodies together in front of the rest of the group. As I stood at one end of the game mat and placed my feet on two of the adjacent dots, Laura reached her hand out to my side and squeezed it gently. I could feel a charge of electricity shooting through me, realizing that soon I'd have a chance to molest her body with near impunity right in front of her husband, whose growing bulge in his pants was now impossible to hide.

"Alright then," Maddy said when she saw all of us standing in the starting position. "Are you guys ready?"

"Ready as we'll ever be," I said, feeling the goose bumps spreading over my entire body.

Maddy spun the game needle and it landed on a blue color.

"Your first move is: right leg to a blue circle."

Since my right leg was already resting on the first blue dot on the board, I simply had to step forward one circle. But with Laura's right foot resting two rows over on the other side of the mat, she had to reach three rows over toward me, stretching her leg over top of my thigh to reach the next blue circle. As her naked vulva grazed the top of my leg, I gasped at the sensation of her touching me with her private parts. With her legs now spread almost three feet apart, everybody who was seated at floor level could see her gaping slit exposed inches above my flesh.

On the other side of the mat, I watched Hannah step one circle forward and one to her left, while Natalie had to similarly stretch overtop of her knee to position her foot on the last blue dot next to Laura's foot. With the four of us now pressed forward against one another and our feet positioned only inches apart, we stared at each other's faces, trying not to let our eyes dart below our direct line of sight.

"Looking good, ladies!" Madison, nodded approvingly at our tight bodies flexing and straining to hold our partial squats. "Are you ready for the next move?"

"*Bring* it," Hannah joked, elbowing Natalie good-naturedly in her abdomen while pressing the side of her stomach against her firm breasts.

Madison spun the needle again and this time it landed on the red color.

"Your next move is, left hand to a red circle."

Everybody paused momentarily, trying to figure out the easiest path to the designated target. Realizing that my partner would have to reach all the way across the game board to reach a red circle, I moved one dot forward so she'd have a little more room to maneuver over my hunched body to reach the next circle. She had to squat her body quite a bit lower to reach the distance, and as she leaned her torso over my bent right leg, I felt my tits sliding across the top of her back and the wetness of her slit pressing against my upper thigh.

By the time she placed her left hand in front of mine, we were both groaning softly, partly from the strain of holding the more crunched position of our bodies, but also from the erotic sensation of feeling our intimate parts touching one another. I wasn't sure if she'd ever had sex with another woman, but I was pretty sure the slick mark she was leaving on the top of my thigh wasn't just sweat from overexertion. For his part, I noticed Brad darting his eyes over the two of us as he watched Laura's breasts dangling down in front of her with her pointed, hard nipples. The bulge in his pants was now pointing unabashedly straight up, tenting almost an entire foot, and he was no longer making much of an effort to conceal it.

At the same time, Hannah and Natalie were struggling to fill the remaining two red dots on the other end of the game board. Once again, Hannah had to move her hand only slightly forward, but with her legs already crossed from the first maneuver, by the time she placed her left hand forward of her right hand, she looked like one of those twisted donut sticks or a piece of braided rope. But Natalie had a much more difficult task trying to reach the last red circle, since it was almost five feet away from her position on the other side of the mat. She tried repeatedly to stretch to reach it, bumping her hips and breasts all over Hannah's body in the process, but it was simply too far away for her to reach.

"What do we do now?" Hannah said, peering toward Maddy in frustration. "Natalie isn't tall enough to reach the last available circle."

"Remember," Maddy smiled, obviously enjoying the four of us stretching and rubbing our slippery bodies together trying to follow her instructions. "Two people from the same team can occupy the same circle, you don't always have to find an unoccupied one. Also, you're allowed to lift one limb temporarily to permit your partner to reach a circle, if that's the only way to achieve it."

"*Now* you tell me," Natalie joked, looking at Maddy with a mock frown. The rest of the group laughed, but I noticed the guys closer to her end of the mat were more interested in staring at her upturned ass and her glistening pussy, which was spread wide open for their viewing pleasure.

After taking a moment to discuss amongst themselves the best strategy for reaching the new target, Hannah finally lifted her right foot a few inches off the mat while Natalie hunched underneath her outstretched leg and positioned her hand on the same red dot that Hannah was occupying. By the time they were finished, Natalie was precariously balanced in a low squat position with her pussy mere inches off the mat and Hannah's bare mound pressing against the side of her torso with her tits pressed firmly against the small of her back.

I noticed the plastic mat underneath Natalie's pussy was glistening with a shiny film, and I wasn't sure if it was from the sweat dripping off her body or from her slit dripping in excitement from all the interbody rubbing and the lascivious stares of both the men and women sitting around the board looking on in fascination. One thing was for certain though. Judging by the universal tenting of the guys' loose-fitting sweatpants and the squishing sound of the women shifting their weight on the floor next to me, everybody was enjoying the show tremendously.

"Wow," Maddy said, shaking her head in surprise. "You guys are really showing great teamwork. Do you think you've got enough energy left for another tough move?"

"The *stretchier* the better," Laura purred, rocking her wet pussy against my tensing thigh as she pretended to adjust her position to support herself. Between the sensation of her humping my leg and the feeling of my erect nipples caressing the soft skin on her over-turned back, I was getting just as turned on as she was, and I wondered if the spectators on my end of the mat had noticed the trickle of lubrication running down the insides of my thighs.

"Alright then," Maddy nodded. "Here goes..."

She spun the needle once again with a hard flick, and it turned around the card a few times, finally landing on a yellow circle.

"Your next move is–left hand, yellow."

The four of us looked at the board then peered up at Maddy with a confused look.

"But our left hands are already on the *red* circles," I said. "Are we allowed to move them?"

"Of course," Madison said. "You only have to stay on a designated circle until the spinner shows a new position."

Natalie was the first person to move, relieved to have a chance to reposition her left hand closer to her side of the mat and reduce the tension on her straining quads and shoulder muscles from having to crunch down so low and spread her entire weight over the board. This time, it was Hannah's turn to twist further toward her partner as she moved her left hand from the right side of the mat toward the side closer to Natalie. In the process, the two girls ended up mashing their tits together with their faces right next to one another. Not missing an opportunity to give the rest of the group a little show, they locked lips and groaned loudly while rolling their erect nipples together.

Whether they were doing it out of fun or because they were

genuinely turned on by the tight connection of their intimate parts, it certainly emboldened Laura and me to ramp up the action on our end of the mat to try to match their performance. Fortunately, the new hand placement afforded both of us a chance to relieve some of the tension in our bodies, with Laura moving her hand closer to her side of the board. But with my legs already crossed over one another, I had reach over the side of her overturned back to position my left hand diagonally across her body. By the time I was finished, I could feel the muscles of her buttocks pressing hard against my mound, and I reached my free hand around the side of her back to squeeze her perky breasts and pinch her nipples.

"Mmm," she purred as she humped my pussy with her ass while I felt her up. "Are you sure we have to move one more time?" she asked Madison. "Because I'm kind of digging this position."

"Well I'll be happy to give you guys a little longer if you need a moment to pause," Maddy smiled. "But something tells me that the boys are getting a bit restless over there on the other side of the mat. We better keep the action moving before they blow a gasket or something. You girls are certainly giving everybody plenty of food for thought in terms of experimenting with new positions, wouldn't you agree, guys?"

"Absolutely," Taylor gushed, as she watched me trib the side of Laura's ass with my wet pussy.

"Mmm-hmm," Shae nodded, revealing a sizeable stiffy of her own bulging to the side of her brightly colored leotard.

"Okay, let's see what *other* creative positions you can invent," Maddy said, spinning the game needle one more time. When it finished turning, this time it pointed toward a green circle.

"Your next move is with your left leg onto a green dot."

The four of us looked at one another, then shook our heads trying to figure out how we were going to make this one work. For Laura, it was a fairly simple maneuver. She could have easily crossed her left leg over her right leg and squatted a little lower to reach the nearest circle. But for me, it was going to be considerably more difficult reaching all the way over to the opposite side of the board, especially with my right knee already pressing up tightly against my stomach. We glanced at one another, then Laura winked at me with a sly smile.

"You said we can lift one or more limbs to permit the movement of another partner, right?" she called out to Madison.

"Well *technically*," Maddy said. "I said you could lift one limb, but under the circumstances, I suppose we can give you a little more latitude..."

Laura smiled at me, then lifted her left hand and right leg one at a time until she flipped her body all the way around with her breasts now pointing up and her two knees spread apart in an arched position directly underneath me. I took one look at her splayed legs and dripping pussy, then studied the board to determine how I could best adjust my position to achieve maximum contact with her while still placing my limbs on the required spots.

After a few moments of contemplation, I decided to turn my body around a hundred and eighty degrees, so that I was now facing away from her with my ass pointed directly toward her pussy. Then I threaded one foot over her right thigh to place it back on my previously occupied blue dot, and snaked my other foot under her other leg to place my left foot on the green dot next to hers. As I leaned over to place my left hand back on the last red circle, I lowered my pelvis toward her until our pussies melded together in a slippery scissors position.

"*Ohhh!*" I could hear some of the women sitting beside us gasp as they watched us grind our vulvas together while we pretended to exert ourselves holding the strange reverse squat position. Meanwhile, the men simply groaned as they stared at our wet pussies while they rubbed their legs together, desperate to give their aching hard-ons some much needed direct stimulation.

Hannah and Natalie regarded us with amusement for a few seconds, then not to be outdone, they tried to simulate a similar maneuver on their end of mat. But with both of them already in a more precarious position to begin with, first Hannah, then Natalie, attempted to stretch their elongated bodies across the board to reach the last available green circles, but they bumped into each other and fell over.

"*Wooo!*" the crowd cheered boisterously, impressed at Laura's and my inventiveness pulling off the tricky maneuver.

But with the round technically over, neither one of us was in a hurry to stop the sexy grinding of our pussies in full view of the rest of the group. And with Brad nodding enthusiastically at us while stroking his dick under his sweats, Laura lifted her head towards mine and we kissed passionately while grunting and moaning from the mutual pleasure building between our connected thighs.

Within seconds, both of us had a powerful climax connected together in our erotic position as we hummed loudly into each other's mouths while jerking our hips together in a mutual spasm. As usual, I made a bigger mess than usual, squirting all over the mat when I came, causing the guys' eyeballs to almost pop out of their heads. After we both finished coming, we plopped back down onto the sticky mat, pressing our nipples and breasts together while we embraced each other in a soft hug.

"Wow," Maddy said after a long pause. "That was certainly an *exciting* finish to this round. I don't know about *you* guys, but I'm already chomping at the bit to see some more action in the next round."

She peered over at the lineup of guys sitting at the side of the mat with sheepish looks on their faces and raging hard-ons poking up out of their pants.

"How about it, boys–are you up for a little grinding and drooling of your own?"

"Oh, we're *up* for it all right," Shae said, standing up as she pulled down her leotard to reveal an eight-inch throbbing erection pointing straight up toward the ceiling.

$$4$$

After Laura and I took a moment to compose ourselves, we all distracted ourselves cleaning off the slippery mat, then Maddy refreshed our glasses of wine for the third time. By now, all of us were feeling tipsy enough to lose whatever inhibitions we might have previously had about getting naked in front of the group. When we all sat back down around the game board in preparation for round three, I noticed the boys were still sporting partial woodies in their loose-fitting sweats.

Whether it was because they were still turned on from watching Laura and me rubbing our pussies together or because they were looking forward to getting up close and personal with Shae in the next round was unclear. Although she definitely had a man's equipment down below, as a female-identifying transgender person, she otherwise had a beautiful feminine figure, with firm natural-looking breasts, a narrow waist, and long, slender legs. Plus, she was absolutely gorgeous to boot, with full lips, high cheekbones, and large, brown doe-eyes. On top of all that, she was an absolute *minx* in the sack, as my fluttering pussy reminded me from our last time together.

Whoever Maddy chose to join her with in the next round was in for a pleasant surprise.

"Alright, then," she said, resuming her position at the end of the game mat with the spinner card nestled between her crossed legs. "We're going to move on to the boys' round now, or should I more correctly say–" smiling in Shae's direction, "the *open* round.

"Brad's up first, by virtue of his win in the first round. And Shae has also generously volunteered to join the group. And since Marco's already expressed his eagerness to get in on the action, why don't you join this group too?"

Then she paused as she scanned the remaining three men.

"And to round out the group of four, let's have...Dylan."

I smiled when I heard Maddy's choice of players for the next round. Although Marco and Brad appeared to be straight-as-an-arrow heterosexuals, I knew from previous experience that Dylan was unabashedly bisexual, and that Shae would swing whichever way the wind was blowing.

And something told me there'd be a little more than *wind* blowing in this next round.

"So, if you guys are ready," Madison smiled. "Assume the positions."

"*Naked?*" Marco said, still not entirely comfortable with the idea of rubbing his body against a bunch of other nude guys.

"Of course," Maddy said. "That's more than half the fun. Of course, if you'd rather *sit out* this round, I can't guarantee you'll be chosen in the last round..."

Marco peered across the game board at Shae who had already fully disrobed, staring at her gorgeous figure and her swelling, half-erect dick.

"Um, no, it's fine," he said, beginning to pull off his t-shirt. "I mean it's not going to be *all* boys this time around..."

Madison simply smiled and nodded while the rest of the men removed their gym togs then paused at the side of the mat with their pendulous dicks throbbing in anticipation of the next move.

"Who'll be joining with *who* this time?" Brad asked, his body language also revealing a certain degree of unease standing next to three bouncing cocks on his side of the mat.

"I suppose it doesn't really matter, does it?" Maddy smirked, knowing full well the men would soon lose their inhibitions once the round got underway. "Let's have you and Shae on one team, and Marco and Dylan on the other."

Brad nodded his head and smiled, relieved to be paired with the sexy transgender girl rather than one of the guys at the opposite end of the game board. For his part, Marco simply frowned, refusing to look at his partner, who had a curious grin on his face.

This should be interesting, I thought, noticing everyone's peckers slowly inflating and lengthening over their tight balls. All four of the players had well-toned bodies and beautiful penises with trimmed bushes and shaved balls. *Straight, my ass,* I thought, noticing Marco's dick slowly rising in spite of his best attempt to hold it down with his covered hands.

Brad and Shae stepped up to one end of the game mat, while Marco and Dylan stood side-by-side on the opposite end. While the three men stared stoically straight ahead at each other's faces, Shae shamelessly darted her eyes up and down each of their figures with a big Cheshire Cat grin on her face.

"Are you guys ready?" Maddy asked.

"Oh, I think we're *ready*, alright," Shae smiled.

Madison spun the game card and the needle landed on a yellow color.

"Okay," she said. "Your first move is with your left hand to a yellow circle."

With all the dots open beyond the four at each end of the game mat, the first move was always the easiest. Since Dylan was already standing on a yellow circle, he only had to twist his torso forty-five degrees to place his hand on the nearest dot. But because Marco was standing slightly further away and had to reach forward to the next unoccupied circle, he had to extend his arm over top of Dylan's, lowering his head to the same level as his midsection. With their bare skin touching for the first time, I noticed Dylan's member twitching between his legs. As the only uncircumcised member of the group,

Marco couldn't help staring at it hanging only a few inches away from his face.

On the other side of the game board, Brad and Shae peered at one another before they took their first move, discussing who would go where. It was nice to see them collaborating right out of the gate, and I wasn't sure if it was because Brad was just trying to be polite with his ladylike partner, or because he was hoping she'd take the initiative in bringing them into closer contact. After a few seconds, Shae motioned for him to bend over and move one circle forward, then she twisted her body and leaned over his back, placing her hand on the last available yellow circle in the middle of the board.

The move forced her pelvis onto the side of Brad's angled knee, with her plump tits rubbing against the top of his back. It hadn't taken long for her to regain her full erection, and at eight-inches-plus in length, it flapped up against the underside of his thigh as he tried to maintain his composure staring towards the other players, similarly bent over. But I noticed Laura, who'd chosen to sit next to me to watch the rest of the proceedings, was watching her husband's physical reaction carefully as she resting her palms between her crossed legs. When he glanced briefly over at her, she spread her legs further apart for him to see her glistening pussy while she rubbed the fingers of her right hand softly over her clit. Within seconds, Brad's big pole lengthened until it was almost touching the floor.

"You *did* say that any body part other than our hands or feet touching the mat would disqualify us, right?" he said to Madison, somewhat chagrined at his inability to hold his libido in check under the full gaze of the other participants in the group.

"Well, *yes*," Maddy smiled, noticing his huge, stiffening erection. "But under the circumstances, I think I'll make an exception for certain—er—*autonomous* appendages. I'm just happy you guys seem to be enjoying yourselves so early in the round. Shall we ramp up the action with the next move?"

"By all means," Brad said, staring at his wife's pussy while she played with her clit watching Shae rub her stiffy along the soft hairs on the underside of his thigh.

Madison spun the needle again, and this time it landed on a green dot.

"Your next turn," she said, "is with your left leg to a green circle."

With Dylan already standing on a green dot, it would have been a fairly simple maneuver for him to step one circle forward. But knowing that it would be a far more difficult for his partner to reach all the way across the board with his left leg, he chose instead to move two circles forward, which necessitated Marco reaching underneath his bent-over torso and upturned ass, directly under his swinging balls and rapidly growing dick. Marco tried his best to achieve the maneuver without touching his partner's skin, but with their hands already planted directly on the floor in front of one another and their bodies hunched over close to the surface of the mat, it was impossible for him to snake his leg under Dylan without grazing his balls and flapping dick.

I smiled at Dylan's ingenuity in forcing the direct body contact with his partner, recognizing that he was determined to force Marco to touch their body parts at one point or another. As Marco struggled to hold his awkward three-point position with his upper thigh quivering against his partner's bouncing pole, I noticed the pink head of Dylan's cock begin to emerge from the end of his foreskin, revealing his growing excitement from the touch of his reluctant partner.

On the other end of the board, Brad and Shae took another moment to plan their strategy then they nodded at one another and Brad stepped two circles forward and one diagonal, exposing his shaved balls and anus to the rest of the group and his partner, with his now fully erect penis flapping up against his belly. Just like Marco, Shae had to make an equally strenuous stretch to move her left leg all the way to the other side of the mat. In the process, she had to twist her hips and torso almost one-hundred-and-eighty degrees, placing her penis and balls directly in contact with Brad's. By this point, they were staring directly into each other's faces and for a moment, there was an awkward silence as everybody wondered how the two of them would react from their intimate contact.

"How are you guys doing over there?" Madison said, trying to break the awkward tension in the room. "Cause, uh, from this angle at least, it looks like your arms and legs aren't the *only* body parts getting a little workout there."

"Well, I've never been in this kind of situation before," Brad said with an embarrassed flush on his face. "You know what they say about the little head having a mind of its own. I don't exactly have full control over these things."

"So I *see*," Maddy nodded. "But I'm not quite sure I'd call that your *little* head."

Then she turned her attention to Marco, who was trying to hold his position while maintaining minimum intimate contact between his and Dylan's equally tumescent body parts.

"How about you, Marco and Dylan? Are you guys managing to navigate your way around each other's dangling participles in that convoluted position?"

"This is harder than it looks," Marco panted.

"So I can *see*," Maddy smiled, staring at his hard poker, now pointing straight up between Dylan's splayed legs, only inches away from his face. Don't let us interfere with your fun if you want to take a few moments to enjoy yourselves in your currently advantageous positions. We're all big boys and girls here. None of us are going to judge if you want to grab the bull by the horns, in a manner of speaking. Am I right, gang?"

"Damn *straight*," Laura said, beginning to jill her clit more vigorously as she watched her husband's and Shae's big cocks bobbing against one another.

"Fuck, yeah," Jake nodded, stroking his dick under his sweats as he stared at the four twitching hard-ons mere inches away from his face. "This is *way* hotter than I ever imagined when I played this game as a kid."

"Speaking of," Maddy said, trying to encourage the two teams to abandon their final reservations. "Haven't we *all* experimented a little bit with our same sex when we were younger? The only difference now is that it's no longer taboo, and we're surrounded by like-minded friends."

Dylan took one look at Marco's twitching hard-on poking up between his open legs, then peered over at his partner to gauge his readiness to proceed to the next level. Marco was too shy to give direct verbal assent, but the look of lust on his face was more than enough for Dylan to take the next step. Without hesitating any further, he lowered his head and began sucking on Marco's flaring bulb with a loud slopping sound. Marco threw his head back and pressed his hips upward, forcing his dick further into her partner's mouth.

When you're horny and someone's sucking on your dick, I smiled, *everyone's gay at one point or another.* I uncrossed my legs in sympathy with Laura and thrust two fingers into my sopping slit, egging them on even further.

With Marco giving his unconscious approval to engage more intimately with his partner, Brad and Shae seemed to take this as a sign that all bets were off and that anything was fair game at this point. Without missing a beat, Shae tilted her head up towards Brad and he bent down and kissed her passionately on the lips. As they grunted into each other's mouths, Shae reached between their stomachs with her free hand and wrapped it around their connected poles as they both began humping her hand vigorously.

"Oh my *God*," Laura moaned watching her husband frotting his big dick with Shae while she rubbed her tits against his chiseled pecs. "Yes baby," she purred. "Fuck her gorgeous cock. I want to watch you cream all over her tits."

By now, virtually everybody around the game mat either had their hands stuffed down their pants or had pulled off their clothing and were madly jerking and jilling themselves taking in the erotic action at both ends of the mat. With Dylan using his well-practiced technique to expertly suck off his partner, it didn't take long for Marco's breathing and groaning to reach a crescendo as Dylan deep-throated him down to his balls while caressing his perineum with the fingers of his free hand.

"*Oh fuck, oh fuck...*" Marco panted. "I'm going to come! Fuck, I'm going to *come!*"

With one last powerful thrust of his hips into Dylan's mouth and a loud grunt, his hips suddenly began shaking as his buttocks trembled while he emptied his seed into Dylan's mouth. It seemed to take almost a full minute for him to stop grunting and shaking as Dylan calmly swallowed his load.

I smiled realizing he'd probably never experienced a blow-job like that ever before.

Meanwhile, watching the erotic scene play out between their opposing partners seemed to embolden Brad and Shae to ramp up the action at their own end of the mat. Listening to his wife egging him on and seeing her fingering her pussy while she watched them rub their big dicks together had a similar effect on Brad. A long string of pre-cum dangled down from the tip of his hard-on, and the extra lubrication made a sexy slurping sound as Shae squeezed their two dicks harder together.

"Mmmft!" the two of them groaned with their faces joined together in a vice-grip as they thrust their tongues into each other's mouths. By now, they were humping each other wildly, and I could see their purple heads popping in and out of Shae's fist as the fingers in her hand got redder and redder while she gripped their poles more tightly. With both of their dicks considerably larger than most men's, she could barely get her hand half way around their joined organs, and this simply added to the excitement of the moment.

With both of them nearing the height of their pleasure, Laura and I both pounded our pussies with our fingers, spreading our legs ever wider as we neared our own orgasms. When Shae and Brad suddenly began jetting long streams of cum all over the mat in front of them between her clenched hand, the two of us squealed in delight as we both gushed our juices in front of us onto the mat, jerking in unison with the couple directly in front of us.

While all this was going on, I was so lost in my *own* pleasure and those of the players on the mat, I hardly even noticed everybody else around the board jerking and moaning in mutual ecstasy while they took in the incredible view of everybody climaxing simultaneously. Glancing briefly over in Madison's direction, I noticed that even *she* had her hand down the front of her pants while jilling her clit, mesmerized by the orgy of activity all around her.

It only took two spins, I smiled to myself as my contractions slowly began to subside. *Two spins, for the self-styled straight boys to lose their inhibitions and get their freak on. What can possibly happen in the in the final round?*

5

———

After everybody climaxed around the game board, there was some awkward silence in the room while the four players lay in a heap on the game board. After a few minutes, Maddy stood up and brushed herself off for dramatic effect.

"Well, *that* was certainly a little more stimulating than I imagined," she smiled. "I don't know about *you* guys, but I'm kind of hungry after all that exercise. Who wants to join me in the kitchen to help put together some snacks before our final round?"

A few of the girls raised their hands while the boys shifted their equipment awkwardly, looking at their stained sweatpants.

"If the rest of you need to clean up, there's one washroom on the main floor and two upstairs. Maybe you can bring down some extra towels to clean up the game board."

Madison peered at the slick plastic mat and grimaced.

"Cause, um, I'm pretty sure there's nowhere safe to step on it right now."

Everybody chuckled, then the group separated to prepare for the next round. When we all reassembled around the mat a half hour later, everyone seemed to have regained their composure, munching noisily on nachos and popcorn. After drinking a couple more glasses of wine, we had a pretty good buzz on again, and Maddy reached over to place the Twister spinner card back between her legs.

"Are you guys ready for the big finale?" she grinned.

"Absolutely," Jake chimed in, eager to get in on the action. "But if I'm doing the math right, I've counted a total of five winners from the three previous rounds, but only four available spots on the board?"

"Good catch," Maddy nodded. "Hannah and Brad won the first round, Jade and Laura won the second, then Brad and Shae somehow managed to stay on their feet in the last one. And we can't have an uneven number of participants if everyone's going to team up again. So, to make this last round a little more entertaining, I thought we'd add one more player and have *three* teams instead of two. It will be a little more challenging to twist around the extra bodies, but it'll also provide even more opportunities for group interaction. Are you guys up for changing it up a little in the final round?"

"Okay..." Jake continued, looking around the circle at the people who still hadn't participated in the game. "That definitely sounds more interesting, but that still leaves six of us on the sidelines. When will the *rest* of us have a turn?"

"That's a good point, Jake," Madison nodded. "But as you may have noticed from the last round, being on the sidelines doesn't mean you have to miss out on all the action. I would encourage the *rest* of you to join up in whatever way strikes your imagination so you can have just as much fun as the players on the board."

Jake darted his eyes around the circle, noticing the rest of the attendees glancing at one another as they nodded in agreement. With four boys and two girls still unaccounted for, there'd still be plenty of opportunities to mix it up amongst the group.

"So that just leaves the matter of who'll join the other five players who've earned the right to move on," Madison said. "Since we already have four girls in the group, I think we should have one more guy to balance it out a little bit. That will also help balance out the rest of the group looking on from the sidelines. Since I'm pretty sure just about everybody else got off one way or the other in that last round, I think it's only fair that we invite Dylan back up on the board for this final round. What do you say, Dylan–are you up for another turn?"

"I never really went *down* after that last encounter," he said, pointing to his still swollen member leaning against the side of his upper thigh.

The rest of the group chuckled, admiring his impressive package.

"Okay," Madison said. "We're going to line everybody up a little differently this time with the two extra players. I was thinking about the best way to do this while we were working in the kitchen. If you guys can take your position one at a time on the board as I call your name, it'll minimize the confusion."

Everybody looked at Maddy with a puzzled expression, curious to see what she had in mind.

"First up," she said, "I'd like Brad to stand on one end of the mat with his feet on the two middle circles."

Brad dutifully walked over to his designated position, then peered at Madison with a wrinkled forehead.

Don't worry, beautiful, I smiled, peering at his retracted penis. *I'm pretty sure we'll be ironing out those wrinkles pretty soon.*

"Next up," Madison smiled, "I'd like Jade to stand on the next set of circles directly in front of Brad, facing away from him."

I jumped off the mat and took my position, playfully wagging my butt over Brad's flagging dick.

"Now let's have Shae stand in front of Jade in the same manner."

As Shae took her position on the board, I began to nod at Maddy's devious plan. With each of us lined up boy-girl in a daisy chain pattern, there would be an almost infinite number of ways for each of us to connect once we began to stretch into position.

"Now on the *other* end of the board," Madison continued. "I'd like first Hannah, then Dylan, then Laura to take similar positions facing the other three."

After everybody had taken their place on the game mat, we all peered at one another and smiled. I could feel Brad's dick already beginning to press against my ass as he got excited pondering the possibilities, especially with his wife directly facing him and Shae. I wasn't sure if this was their first swinging affair, but *one* thing was for certain. They probably didn't imagine in a million years that both of them would end up hooking up with a sexy transgender girl in the space of a single night.

"Okay," Madison said, nodding approvingly at the lineup of contestants on the board. "Do you guys think you can make this work?"

"It's going to be a little tougher to find an open spot to place all our hands and legs," Dylan said.

"True," Madison smiled. "But look at it this way. There's also going to be a lot more open 'spots' to place a few *other* things, if you catch my drift. Plus, this time, I'm going to allow multiple people to place their limbs on any one circle."

"Oh, I'm pretty sure the mood's gonna strike," Laura smirked, ogling Shae's elevating dick, only a few inches in front of her belly.

"I hope so," Maddy said. "Let's see if we can set a new record for group interaction in this final round. Here we go..."

She flicked the needle with her middle finger, and after a few spins it landed on a red dot.

"Your first move," she announced, "is to a red circle with your right hand. But since one team is pointed in the opposite direction on the board, I'm going to allow Hannah's team to move their hands to the other side of mat onto a green circle."

Everybody paused for a moment, realizing they had a little more latitude as to who could go where. I saw the wheels turning in the other team's heads as they tried to plan how best to configure their bodies to take maximum advantage of everybody's rapidly swelling body parts.

Shae was the first person to move as she reached one circle forward and one to her right, bringing her face down to the same level as Laura's pussy directly in front of her. Seeing Shae's sexy ass pointing up in the air in front of me, I moved next, placing my hand directly on top of hers, causing my breasts to press atop her back. With two sexy girls bent over in front of him, Brad decided the best way for him to gain maximum contact would be to reach one circle forward, causing him to bend forward just enough to angle his now fully erect spear atop the small of my back. Shae and I hummed in approval at the feeling of our partners' intimate parts touching our tingling skin.

With Laura watching how the three of us had chosen to arrange ourselves, she placed her hand on her chin and massaged it slowly, crafting her plan. While the two others behind her waited for her to make the next move, she surprised all of us when she arched her body backwards, placing her palm on the green dot opposite Hannah's foot at her end of the board. It was definitely a more challenging position to put herself in than she might have otherwise performed, but it forced her knees further forward to balance herself, pressing her dripping pussy even closer to Shae's downturned face.

Seeing Laura prostrated beneath him in her inverted crab position made it easy for Dylan to choose the next move, and he smiled as he reached for the green circle opposite her midsection, causing his erect organ to point directly down over her upturned face. With Hannah having the last move, she glanced at Dylan's tight balls hanging between his legs, then reached two circles forward to rest her hand beside his as she proceeded to dry-hump him from behind.

"Looks like things are unfolding very nicely," Madison purred, nodding her head at the ingenious way each of us had chosen to arrange ourselves to maximize contact with our preferred partners. "I don't know how long some of you are going to be able to hold those positions, but it's certainly going to be interesting to see where the game play takes us next."

Without any further hesitation, she spun the needle again, and it landed on a green circle. I could see from my bent-over vantage point that the needle pointed toward our right hand again, but after noticing how carefully we'd all arranged our bodies to bring our private parts closer together, she decided to create a new instruction.

"This time," she said, "Brad's team will move their left leg to a green circle and Hannah's team will likewise move their left leg to the opposite side to a red circle."

This time it was Laura who made the first move, as she quickly repositioned her left foot one dot sideways to rebalance her weight and relieve the strain on her arm extended behind her. As she watched Laura's pretty pussy opening up in front of her face, Shae moved next, moving her left leg forward to the opposite side of Laura's hips, placing the tip of her bobbing cock directly in contact with her glistening slit.

"Mmm," Laura groaned, trying to push her hips further forward to take Shae's wand in her hole. But with her body already in a fully stretched position, she had limited freedom of movement. If anything more exciting were to happen between the two of them, it would have to be *Shae* taking the initiative. Instead, she simply peered at Laura with a sexy grin, and rocked her hips from side to side, dripping precum over the insides of Laura's thighs.

As he watched his wife moaning in delirious frustration, Brad's hard-on pressed harder into the small of my back, and he stepped forward two steps to place his left foot on the green circle next to my shoulder. With his hot balls pressing up against the back of my ass, I paused trying to decipher the best way to bring us closer together. It would have been easier for me to stretch my left leg forward only one dot, but that would have angled my ass further down toward the mat and out of reach of his throbbing organ. Instead, I threaded my leg under his bent knee and placed my foot directly behind me, next to his on the green circle. By so doing, I tilted my ass further up in the air, and he pulled his hips back a few inches, letting his organ flap down under my quivering slit.

Meanwhile, with Dylan staring at the tempting combination of Shae's hard-on probing Laura's upturned pussy and her tits staring him in the face, he stretched his leg one dot sideways to the nearest red circle. In so doing, he lowered his balls onto Laura's face, where-upon she began licking the sensitive area between his testicles and his anus.

"Uhnn," he groaned, enjoying the combination of the erotic show on display in front of him and Laura's teasing of his perineum.

Once again, Hannah had the final-move advantage, having seen how everybody else had arranged themselves. Realizing her only chance to gain any direct stimulation on her throbbing clit would be to grind her pussy against his tailbone, she leaned forward two circles, placing her left foot beside Dylan's as she began to make a wet slick mark rubbing herself against his ass.

"*That's* what I'm talking about," Maddy panted, getting just as worked up as the rest of the group watching the players on the mat move into a tighter formation and beginning to rub their bodies together. I noticed some of the other viewers had already begun to reach over and start caressing one another. I smiled, knowing that it wouldn't just be the players mixing it up on the game board who'd have a chance to hookup and get off.

"I'm not even sure you guys are going to be able to *make* another move stretched out the way you are overtop of one another," Madison smiled. "This is beginning to look a little more like a game of *K'Nex* than Twister, with everybody looking ready to plug each other's holes. But let's give it one more try to see where the spinner will take us next..."

Madison spun the needle again and glanced down at it only briefly before turning her attention back to the game board to decipher the best way to consummate our tentative connections. After a few moments, and without even bothering to consult the position of the needle, she called out the last instruction.

"Your next move, if you can pull it off, is with your right leg to a red circle for Brad's team and right leg to a *green* circle for Hannah's team."

I looked down at the board and smiled, realizing that Maddy was instructing us to spread our legs even wider apart, giving our partners easier access to our waiting holes. By now, Brad's huge prick had extended all the way up the underside of my stomach to my belly button, and eager to feel his full manhood buried inside me, I shifted my right leg directly to the side, placing it next to his hand on the mat. By so doing, I tilted my pussy further upward in the direction of his tight balls. Fortunately, he only had to shift his foot over one circle so that he was now perfectly balanced over my quivering ass. I reached between both of our legs and pointed his throbbing pole into my dripping slit, and he slowly began to slide it inside me. I groaned as it began to fill me up while Laura tilted her head up and moaned along with me seeing her husband fuck me from behind.

"Yeah, baby," she purred. "Fuck Jade's sweet pussy. Make her squirt all over Shae's beautiful ass while I suck on her tits."

"*Fuck* yes," Brad groaned as he watched Shae shift her right leg one row sideways and behind her so she'd have better leverage to plow his wife's pussy. Eager to facilitate the connection, Laura also shifted her leg over one row so that she was now perfectly balanced in an upside-down position with her pussy spread far apart directly in front of Shae's flapping cock. She wasted no time inserting her throbbing prick into Laura's hole, burying it up to her balls. As she began to hump Laura in her bent over position, Laura sucked loudly on her hard nipples, groaning in pleasure along with the rest of the bystanders who were getting increasingly bold touching one another at the edge of the mat.

By this point, Dylan was just about ready to burst a gasket having observed the erotic act unfolding before him twice now with no direct stimulation on his part. As he watched Shae's tongue dancing over Laura's tits directly below his cock, he pressed his right leg forward and one row sideways, shifting his weight forward just enough for poke Shae in the forehead with his raging hard-on. Not skipping a beat, Shae immediately engulfed his organ in her mouth while she continued fucking Laura, prostrated beneath her.

Seeing everybody else now connected together, and with no way to fill her own streaming pussy with any warm object, Hannah shifted her right leg one circle over to her side so that she was now riding Dylan's ass like she was on a horse. With her right hand resting on the mat beside Dylan's lurching body, she reached around with her other free hand and grasped his cock hard in her fist, stroking his shaft forward and back while Shae sucked on his head and swirled her tongue around the crown. Watching the whole scene inches away from her upturned face, Laura lifted her head a few more inches and engulfed Dylan's balls in her mouth, sucking them hard.

At this point, with virtually everybody in the room groaning and panting in pleasure from their combined connections with one person or another, Brad finally sunk his enormous pole all the way into my snatch, while his tight balls rubbed up against my dripping labia. Watching Shae bent over directly in front of me fucking Laura, I reached between her legs with my free hand and squeezed her balls as she began to pant more heavily. With the sweet smell of sex permeating the room, one person after another began to howl as they reached the height of their pleasure humping and sucking whatever hard or wet body part happened to be closest nearby.

By the time the six of us on the game board fell exhausted and spent onto the slippery plastic mat, I noticed that even *Maddy* had removed her clothes, impaled on her previous boyfriend's hard cock while her current beau straddled his face, pulling his head onto his own spurting cock as emptied his seed into his mouth.

Wow, I thought shaking my head in amazement. *This game really does have a way of creating some unexpected twists and turns.*

VOLUME FOUR

THE COSTUME PARTY

1

———————

I woke up to the sound of my best friend Hannah calling me from the other end of my house. She'd let herself in early on a Saturday morning and for some reason was yelling at me as she ran up the stairs.

"Jade!" she hollered. "Where are you? I've got some exciting news!"

I rolled over and squinted at my clock on the nightstand. It was a little past eight. Saturdays were the only day of the week I allowed myself to sleep in, and I was more than a little ticked at her rude intrusion.

"Aren't you up yet?" she called. "Get up—you're not going to believe what I just heard."

I rolled over and wrapped my pillow around my ears as she dashed into my bedroom. She paused for a minute smiling at my feeble attempt to block her out of my morning daze, then she pounced on the bed below my curled-up knees.

"Wake up, sleepyhead!" she squealed, pushing my shoulders to rouse me from my slumber.

"This better be good," I said, raising my pillow a few inches and peering at her through thin eyes. "You know how much I worship my weekend sleep-ins."

"You'll be glad I woke you when you hear what I have to tell you," she said. "Besides, you're gonna want to get up and begin planning your day right away. We're going to need a few extra hours to go shopping."

I pulled my duvet cover over my shoulders and huffed.

"What could possibly be so important to drag me out of my soft and cozy bed this early in the morning?"

I peered outside, looking at the gray clouds hanging low in the late October skies. I was in no hurry to venture out into the chilly autumn air.

"Only the biggest private shindig of the year. Steve Bannon is hosting his annual Halloween party at his mansion on the lake, and we're invited!"

"Isn't that the party with all the A-list celebrities? How did you score an invitation?"

Hannah peered at me with a wicked look in her eyes.

"Let's just say I know somebody who knows somebody. Someone with whom I may have pulled a few strings to earn some special favors."

"I bet that's not the *only* thing you were pulling to earn those favors," I said, raising an eyebrow.

"Possibly," she smirked. "But I apparently impressed him enough with my naked gymnastics to land an invitation to this special event. Except this year, it's got an extra twist. This time it's going to be a *nude* costume party."

I lifted my head and propped the side of my face on a crooked elbow, suddenly intrigued.

"Isn't that an oxymoron? How can you be in costume and naked at the same time?"

Hannah smiled and handed me a gold-embossed card inscribed with fancy calligraphy writing. I felt the raised surface of the script on the tips of fingers, rubbing it gently trying to divine its meaning through my still bleary eyes. Somebody had gone to a great deal of effort to create an invitation card on par with the most extravagant wedding.

I pulled myself up and leaned against my headboard, slowly reading the message.

You are cordially invited to attend my annual Halloween costume ball at my estate overlooking Lake Michigan.

This year I've added a special twist to make it even more interesting. You're encouraged to wear as little or as much trappings as you feel comfortable—including nothing at all beyond a simple mask. With everyone baring a little more than usual, who knows what kind of shenanigans might break out, and we're always mindful of protecting the anonymity of our special guests.

Of course, I encourage everyone to be playful and creative with their choice of costumes, as this is always the highlight of the event. As in previous years, there will be a special prize for the best costume of the evening and we hope you'll be suitably daring and inventive.

Feel free to bring a partner and let down your britches! As always, what happens at the Bannon residence stays at the Bannon residence. I look forward to seeing you this Saturday, starting at midnight. We'll all have a ghoulish good time!

I peered up at Hannah and grinned.

"No RSVP?"

"There's no need with a Steve Bannon invitation," she said. Everyone who's invited always goes. It's the go-to event of the year in the Chicago area. Models, actresses, rock stars, billionaires—everybody who's anybody in this town will be there. There's even a rumor that the Governor and his wife will attend this year's event."

I looked down at the card, rubbing my fingers over the embossed script.

"The invitation says you're allowed to bring a partner. Was that a condition of your little tryst with your friend—that you accompany him as his plus-one?"

Hannah peered at me devilishly as a tiny curl formed on the sides of her mouth.

"When I told him I had a friend who was even prettier than me and had a body to die for, he didn't hesitate to hand me an extra invitation. *You're* my plus-one, girl." She pulled another card out of her purse and handed it to me. "You know I'd never pass up an opportunity like this without bringing my bestie along to share in the fun."

I looked at Hannah with a quizzical look and shook my head in confusion.

"How are we ever going to find a decent Halloween costume on the Saturday before the end of the month? All the costume stores will be sold out of the best stuff."

Hannah kicked off her shoes and lifted the covers, then scooched in excitedly next to me against the headboard.

"I've been searching online for some ideas. We don't have to wear anything too elaborate, and there's no reason why we have to stick to a Halloween theme. Remember, this is a *nude* costume party. We already look pretty hot for a couple of girls nearing middle age. The less we wear, the better. Let's flaunt it while we've still got it!"

She pulled an iPad out of her purse and tapped the screen. A website opened showing a collection of sexy models wearing risqué costumes. She scrolled through the images, commenting on the various themes.

"Just look at some of these possibilities. We can play any role we like, wearing as much or as little as we please. Most of these costumes can be put together with a simple trip to Walmart and maybe a bit of needle and thread. Plus, we can easily remove one of two pieces from each outfit to reveal a bit more skin. The most important element is the headpiece. We just need something to conceal our identity and highlight our girly figures with a bit of flair."

Hannah paused at a picture of a sexy blonde wearing a Playboy bunny costume. She wore a tight corset and a rubber mask that covered the top half of her face with tall ears pointing up in the air.

"What about this one? You have to admit, it's pretty hot. You'd could even dispense with the bodice altogether and just keep the bunny tail on your naked ass. Imagine the looks you'd get prancing around his mansion in that costume!"

The images of sexy half-nude models wearing unusual masks

reminded me of my encounter at the Fantasy Feast naked dinner party. Suddenly, I became mindful of the wetness that had begun building between my legs.

"Not bad," I said, shifting my weight uncomfortably off the wet spot on my sheets. "Show me some more."

Hannah flipped through a few more images and stopped at a picture of a sexy maid wearing a lacy dress, holding a feather duster in her hand. Her firm tits pressed against the flimsy fabric, creating an irresistible focal point from the sensuous shadows on her bosom.

"How about this?" she said. "You'd look stunning in this outfit. You'd be covering up just enough to drive every man and woman at that party absolutely crazy. And imagine all the fun you could have teasing the naked guests with your little duster!"

"*Intriguing...*" I said as I squeezed my thighs together, trying to quiet my burning clit.

The more images Hannah showed me, the more turned on I got. Whether it was from me imagining myself in the costumes or imagining myself playing with the guests dressed up in the provocative outfits, was unclear. Either way, the more my mind began to ponder the possibilities, the more excited I became about going to this event.

"The only problem is, it will be difficult to cover my face without looking unnatural in that outfit," I frowned. "Show me more costumes with masks."

Hannah refined her search by typing in the words *sexy mask costumes* and the screen refreshed showing a new set of models in racy outfits. Many of the themes revolved around superheroes, with the male models sporting Batman and Superman motifs and the female models wearing Wonder Woman and Batgirl-type costumes.

"Not very original," I frowned. "I bet there'll be a ton of superhero costumes among all those egotistical celebrities. I'm looking for something a little different."

Hannah paused for a moment, then tapped on her photo library pulling up an image of me wearing a business suit painted on my naked body.

"Remember that time you went to the nude bodypainting workshop? You're a graphic artist. You can be virtually anything you want and show off all you wish with a little bit of well-disguised paint. Whether it's Catwoman, Black Widow, or Wonder Woman–all these characters wear is a mask and tight outfits to show off their beautiful physiques. You could even dress up like Mystique in the X-Men movie and wear absolutely nothing other than a full coat of body paint."

"Been there, done that," I said. "If I'm going to really enjoy myself, I want to wear something I've never worn before that will absolutely blow everyone away."

"You sure are a tough customer," Hannah said, shaking her head. "Let's try something a little different..."

She reopened her browser and typed in the words *naked masquerade costumes*. A gallery of Google images popped up with a collection of half-naked men and women.

"*Now* we're talking," I said, squirming on the bed as I scanned the toned bodies of the sexy models.

"Look at that one," Hannah said, pointing at the screen. "It's a picture of Rihanna at last year's Met Gala dressed as Nefertiti. With her sheer lace dress and silver headdress, it doesn't leave much to the imagination. A bit more makeup around the eyes, and you'd be able to mask your identity quite easily."

"That's pretty hot," I said, beginning to feel the sheets getting wetter and wetter between my legs. "She definitely looks fuckable. But it's been done before. I don't want to wear something half of these people will have already seen."

"Damn, girl, you're *impossible!* Remember, less is more. The idea is to show as much of our bodies as possible to attract the attention of all these beautiful people. You could get away with a simple mask, a painted emblem on your chest, and a shiny belt. Who really cares what you're wearing as long as you get the attention of the guests?"

"Humor me for a little longer," I said, squeezing Hannah's leg. "I'm starting to get a few ideas. I just need a bit more inspiration."

Hannah began flipping through the images more quickly until one picture suddenly caught my attention.

"Wait!" I said. "Go back a few frames. I saw something

interesting..."

She scrolled back until an image of six men dressed in contrasting costumes popped up.

"That's the one," I said, scanning the image slowly.

"*The Village People*?" Hannah said. "That might be okay for a gay guy, but how could you possibly look sexy wearing any one of those cheesy costumes?"

My eyes darted back and forth between the sexy cowboy wearing chaps and the indian warrior wearing a feathered headdress and a skimpy loincloth. Suddenly I nodded as a mischievous smile formed on my face.

"What?" Hannah said. "What could you possibly be thinking?"

She glanced down at my breasts peeking above the covers, noticing my hardening nipples.

"Because I know gay dudes—even ones with hard bodies like these guys—don't do it for you. Where is your mind going with this idea?"

"I've decided what I'm going to wear," I said, crossing my arms over my chest. "But I'm going to keep it a secret until we get to the party. It'll be all the more fun and surprising if I reveal it at the last second. But I promise you, it'll be one-of-a-kind and extremely provocative."

Hannah's eyes darted across my face, trying to imagine what I had in mind.

"Now you've got *me* all excited thinking what you're going to do. Judging by your obvious state of arousal, your head is already at the party. Can I crawl under the covers with you and have some fun fantasizing which one of those costumes you're going to wear?"

"By all means," I said, disappearing under the covers with her. "Just imagine me as one of those hot dudes with his clothes off."

"Mmm," Hannah purred, slithering between my slippery thighs. "I'd rather imagine you as a hot *chick* with her clothes off."

"In a couple of days," I said, spreading my legs further apart and pulling her face into my steaming crotch. "You might be able to have it both ways."

2

———

Just after midnight on the day of the party, I pulled my car up beside a call box in front of a large wrought-iron gate protecting the entrance to Steve Bannon's estate. After providing our names and the identification numbers on the front of our invitation cards, the gates opened and we followed the curved driveway up to the front of a giant French-styled chateau. As a parking attendant approached our car, I turned to Hannah seated next to me and smiled.

"It's show time," I said.

"Not a moment too soon," she huffed. "I've been dying to see what you're wearing under that coat ever since you picked me up."

I'd intentionally worn a long western duster to cover my body all the way from my shoulders to my ankles. Part of it was meant to surprise Hannah when I finally reached the event, but it had much more to do with my desire to shock everyone else once I got in the front door. I reached behind my seat and pulled a thin black mask out of a bag on the floor and wrapped it around the top of my face.

Hannah's forehead wrinkled as she looked at me, still confused.

"Let me guess: Kato, Zorro, Nightshade?"

"You're moving in the right direction with the first two," I smiled, reaching back into the bag and pulling out a pair of western boots.

"Cowboy boots?" Hannah squinted. "I don't know my cowboy characters quite as well—"

"Maybe this will help," I said, donning a white Stetson.

Hannah looked at me blankly for a moment, then her eyes lit up, recognizing the familiar image of the famous cowboy with the white hat and black mask.

"The Lone Ranger?"

"Yes, but with a little twist. You'll have to wait for the full reveal until we get inside."

"You're such a tease," she said as I handed the attendant my keys and we stepped out of the car.

We paused for a moment, taking in the full scale of the Bannon estate close-up. The four-story mansion extended almost a hundred feet in either direction, with tall arched windows and ornate brickwork. The bright spotlights illuminating the front of the house lit up the entire courtyard, reflecting off Hannah's shiny Batgirl outfit.

"Holy shit!" she exclaimed. "This place is gigantic. We're going to have to drop *breadcrumbs* to not get lost in there."

"More like *caviar* or *foie gras*," I chuckled. "Something tells me everything about this affair is going to be top shelf."

"What are we waiting for?" Hannah giggled, rushing ahead of me toward the front door.

My gaze drifted down while I soaked up her tight ass in her black latex outfit. She had a beautiful hourglass figure, and the tight Batgirl costume highlighted every curve of her sexy body. I smiled as I imagined the two of us mingling among the high rollers. But I had a feeling they'd be focused on someone *else's* ass tonight.

With the large double entrance doors pulled back, we peered into the bright marble-floored foyer as we approached the front steps. A large crowd of costumed guests had already begun to gather in the main ballroom, and we could hear soft jazz music wafting out into the courtyard.

"Good evening ladies," a man wearing a crisply tailored tailcoat and black tie said as we stepped into the entrance hall.

He looked at my long shawl and smiled.

"May I check your coat, Madam?"

"Yes, thank you," I said, turning my back to assist him in its removal.

When he pulled the cape off my back and viewed my naked backside, I heard him gasp. To complement my Lone Ranger disguise, I'd chosen to wear a tight-fitting black leather vest and long black chaps with nothing underneath. My tight ass poked out the back of the open leggings, and I could feel him running his eyes up and down my body as he hesitated hanging my coat in the closet.

But when I turned around, both Hannah and the doorman took a step back in shock. On the front of my open pants, I wore a large dildo fashioned in the shape of a man's cock and balls, framed by two silver pistols on either side of my hips. The long phallus slapped against the sides of my naked thighs as it swung from side to side.

"Holy *fuck*, Jade!" Hannah squealed. "That's *outrageous*! Where did you ever come up with that idea?"

"Remember the Village People picture you showed me a few days ago? I decided to borrow elements of both the cowboy and the indian characters to create my own design." I shook my hips to juggle my equipment and smiled. "I thought it would be kind of fun playing *both* sides of coin, so to speak."

"Uh—*yeah*," she said, flicking her eyes between my tight bosom spilling over the top of my vest and my faux genitals. "I'd have to say you pulled it off. With that getup, I expect you'll be the center of attention all night long."

"Um," the doorman said, shyly interrupting. "May I have your tickets, please?"

"Of course," I said, rustling my rubber balls as I fished in the pocket of my chaps for my ticket. When the butler turned to collect Hannah's ticket, I could see the front of his pants tenting in obvious arousal.

"Enjoy your evening," he said, motioning for us to enter the ballroom.

"Oh, I have a feeling we will," Hannah winked, as she nodded toward the lengthening pole pushing down his pant leg.

A waiter approached us with tall glasses of champagne on a silver tray and did a double-take when he noticed the swinging package between my legs.

"Whoa boy," Hannah said to the server, taking two glasses off his unsteady tray. "We wouldn't want you to spill your load before we've sampled the goods."

As we moved into the main entrance hall, the patrons milling in small groups began to turn around to view the newly arriving guests. Suddenly, the gentle buzz of group conversation receded until the only sound we could hear was the hum of the background music. Everyone was so stunned taking in my outfit, they were literally dumbstruck with their mouths agape.

Many of the guests had chosen to wear predictable Halloween costumes with little bits of flesh showing here and there, but nobody was letting it all hang out quite as brazenly as I had. Amid the predictable sprinkling of ghosts and goblins, there was a profusion of superhero figures and Disney characters bedecked in various stages of undress. I shook my head at the lack of imagination of the high-powered group and began to wonder if the event was going to live up to Hannah's hyperbole.

"Damn, girl," she said. "It looks like you're going to be this evening's scene-stealer. You've already stopped the show. I don't know what everybody's thinking right now, but that thing looks so realistic, they must be wondering if you're a legit tranny wearing that impressive package."

I smiled a crooked grin, suddenly feeling self-conscious with all of the eyes in the room surveying my exposed body. Fortunately, a handsome couple dressed as Anthony and Cleopatra began to approach us, providing some distraction.

"Welcome to our little costume party," the man said, extending his hand to Hannah and me. "I'm Steve Bannon and this is my wife

Genevieve. You'll have to excuse me, but I don't recognize either of you under your—*interesting* disguises."

I was taken aback by how handsome the eccentric billionaire looked close up. With his square jaw, dimpled cheeks and thick head of salt-and-pepper hair swept back in a dense poof, he looked like a slightly older version of the famous actor Patrick Dempsey. He wore a loose toga draped over his well-muscled chest, and I could see his pecs flexing as he shook my hand.

But I found his wife even more beguiling. Wearing a tight-fitting gold-lamé dress slitted at one side of her hips and a pretty beaded headdress, she looked like a dead-ringer for a young Elizabeth Taylor. As I ran my eyes shamelessly over her luscious figure, I felt a sudden dampness building under the weight of my latex balls pressing against my flaring clit.

"Jade," I introduced myself, not yet wanting to reveal my full identity.

"Hannah," my partner responded, politely shaking their hands.

"It appears that you two have already captured the attention of my guests," Bannon said, turning to appraise the congregation still gazing awkwardly in our direction. He extended his arm in the direction of the main hall and nodded. "Please, come in and mingle. There are so many fascinating people to meet. I'm sure we'll catch up with the two of you a little later this evening."

"I'll look forward to that," I said, smiling at Genevieve, lingering for a moment longer at her dazzling figure. She returned the gesture, widening her eyes as my member twitched while I held my palm over the handle of one of my six-shooters.

"Holy shit," Hannah said, as Bannon and his wife melted back into the crowd. "Did you see the way he was looking at you? He was practically *raping* you with his eyes. Something tells me this is going to be a very interesting night. It seems the men are even more enamored with your disguise than the women. Either there's a lot of bi-curious guys in here, or they're attracted to that whole futa thing."

"I dunno," I said. "I'm showing off a lot of *girl* parts too. Who's to say what they're more attracted to? But did you notice his wife? I'd far rather get into *her* pants."

"It's too bad that thing isn't animated," Hannah chuckled, glancing at my pendulous dick. "If you could actually get it up, you could probably have your way with just about everybody in this place."

"Who knows?" I said, winking at Hannah. "In my current state of arousal, I wouldn't be surprised if this thing had a life of its own."

Little did she know how much truth in this statement I was about to reveal before the evening was over.

3

A fter Bannon and his wife resumed mingling with the rest of the crowd, Hannah and I wandered into the main ball-room. At first, most of the assembled groups gave us a wide berth, unsure what to make of the two girls dressed in such revealing costumes. Hannah's latex Batgirl outfit clung to her naked body like a second skin, the shiny fabric accentuating every crease and curve like it was painted on her. And the cutouts on both sides of my leather chaps left little to the imagination, even with the modicum of cover provided by my fake genitals covering my bare mound.

I was glad to have the freedom to mill about the room for a while, surveying the faces and costumes of the high-powered gathering. I recognized a fair number of public figures from the senior ranks of the local political, business, and media fields. The mayor was there with his wife, dressed as Little Red Riding Hood and the Big Bad Wolf, which seemed fitting given the ongoing level of corruption at City Hall. Bannon's business partner and fellow billionaire Kent Schiffer circled the room with a familiar supermodel, outfitted in matching red tights as Mr. Incredible and Elastagirl. And our local news anchorman was paired with his pretty sidekick, dressed as Woody and Bo Peep from the movie Toy Story.

Many of the guests were dressed as famous characters from superhero movies or nursery rhyme stories, with most of the men playing the more dominant role. *Typical display of macho-entitled privilege*, I thought. *Why does it seem every man who achieves a certain degree of power have to lord it over everyone else, thinking they're better than the rest of us?* My cheeky cowboy costume seemed a perfect counterpoint to the heavy dose of testosterone permeating the room, mocking their oversize male egos as I swung my big dick around like I owned it.

As Hannah and I began mingling with the small cliques scattered around the room, I found it amusing that while most of the women praised my cocky outfit, their male partners seemed threatened by it, silently stealing glances at my huge dong while their wives and girlfriends chatted with me comfortably. I wasn't sure if it was because they felt intimidated by my outsize genitals, or because they were secretly fantasizing about fucking me.

As more and more people began gravitating toward us, intrigued by my outrageous costume, Hannah slowly drifted off to the other side of the room. I couldn't blame her, with everyone asking me silly questions like what it felt like to be a woman carrying a man's dick. For a while I amused them, swinging my hips from side to side and playfully grabbing my balls, flaunting my male persona.

But I soon tired of the incessant stares and never-ending quips about my tranny disguise, and began looking for an excuse to break away. Just as I was about to excuse myself to go to the ladies' room, the governor and his wife approached our group and introduced themselves. They were dressed in matching his and hers chef outfits, the only difference being that his wife wore a less poofy hat and a backless apron that showed off her sexy ass and legs.

"That's quite a provocative costume," the governor said, extending his hand to me. "I'm Jack Scanlon and this is my wife, Alicia."

"Pleased to meet you, Mr. Governor," I said, quickly seeing through his thin disguise. "But no less daring than your wife's, which I dare say is even *more* revealing."

"In some respects, possibly," he said. "Except you're revealing both sides of the coin."

"Heads *and* tails, you mean?" I smiled.

"In a manner of speaking," he said, temporarily at a loss for words by my sassy attitude. "Are you here alone tonight?"

I scanned the room and noticed Hannah chatting it up with a hunky guest dressed in a Tarzan outfit.

"It seems my partner is out looking for greener pastures. I guess she felt this one had been fully tilled."

"Oh?" the governor said, glancing at my pendulous prick. "Who's been doing most of the figurative plowing—you, or all these other farm animals?"

"At this point, I'd say everybody's just getting the lay of the land," I said, dragging out the metaphor. "Surveying the landscape, deciding the best place to position their hoes."

"I see what you mean," the governor said, his eyes widening from my double entendre. "You seem to be particularly–*ambidextrous* in that respect."

"I'm just having fun pretending what it might be like to cultivate both sides of the field," I said, running my eyes up and down his wife's sexy body before locking eyes with her. "You never know when a particularly fertile plot might need tending."

"Well put, my lady."

"Please—call me Jade," I said, turning my attention to his wife, who'd been staring at my outfit the entire time. "What about you, Alicia? Have you been enjoying the evening so far?"

"Yes," she said, happy to deflect attention away from her over-bearing husband for a moment. "So many interesting people and costumes."

"I find yours very alluring also," I said, staring at her plump breasts pressing against the front of her skimpy apron. "But it seems that all your fun parts are hidden from view, at least while we're talking face-to-face. It's only when you turn around that you reveal your adventurous side."

"I guess you'll just have to catch me when my back is turned then," she said, winking at me sexily.

"I'll definitely be keeping a lookout. Hopefully we can catch up later."

As much as I wanted to continue our playful flirtation, I knew I'd never have a chance for some alone time with her as long as I continued to engage them as a couple. Besides, I was getting tired of her husband's thinly veiled sexist comments.

"Will you excuse me for a moment while I use the restroom?"

"Of course," she said. "But be careful in there. It's not as simple for us ladies to pee standing up as it is for the men."

"Not to worry," I smiled. "Fortunately, this thing is easily removed. Though it might be kind of fun to try it just once."

"Will you be using the men's or the ladies' room?" the governor smirked.

"I'm pretty sure the toilets are unisex in this place," I said, gently admonishing him for another chauvinist remark. "Which will be a refreshing change from the usually cramped ladies' rooms we have to endure in other public places. Enjoy your evening. Perhaps we'll see each other a little later."

"We'll look forward to that," the governor smiled.

As I pulled away from the crowd, I shook my head at the impudent tone of the governor, ignoring his beautiful wife while he shamelessly flirted with me. Little did he know that I was far more impressed with Alicia than by the trappings of his high political office. I felt like I needed to wash myself off after dealing with his sexist attitude and while looking for a place to freshen up, I recognized the familiar red and white uniform of the mayor's wife as she waited outside the closed door of an adjacent anteroom. As I approached her from the side, I admired her shapely legs and full bosom pressing against her tight bodice. Her Little Red Riding Hood costume seemed the perfect outfit to highlight her youthful face and figure.

"You'd think we wouldn't have to wait to use a toilet in this place," I said, sauntering up next to her. "There must be at least twenty washrooms in this mansion."

"No doubt," she laughed. "But even in a place like this, with this many guests, unfortunately we ladies still have to wait to use the lavatory." She glanced down at my faux genitalia and smiled. "It's too bad they don't have his and hers toilets like in most public settings. With that getup, you'd probably get away with slipping into the men's room."

"Maybe," I said. "But I'd still have to pee sitting down. I'm just looking to freshen up anyway. I was hoping for a respite from all the overcharged testosterone out there."

"Tell me about it," she nodded. "I've been dealing with city politics from the other side for almost twenty years now. It's still very much an old-boys network in this business. Women are just treated as chattel, to be trotted out as eye candy whenever there's a public relations opportunity like this."

"That's partly why I wore this outfit," I admitted. "I thought it would be kind of fun to swing my own dick around all these heavy hitters at this posh event."

The washroom door suddenly swung open and a woman wearing a Victorian costume brushed past us, sneering at our haughty outfits.

"Judging by the heft of that thing," she said, "I'd say yours is the biggest one here by a large margin. Do you want to join me while I freshen up inside? It looks like the last thing you need right now is to stand outside alone while everybody wags their tongues at you."

"Thanks," I said. scurrying in behind her as we locked the door, giggling like two schoolgirls. "I'm Jade, by the way," I said stretching out my hand.

"Haley," she said, grasping my hand firmly as she smiled into my eyes.

As we leaned in to the doublewide mirror over the marble vanity to check our lipstick and mascara, I noticed Haley's gaze drifting lower to check out my package.

"You know, if it weren't for the straps holding that apparatus onto your hips, I'd swear that thing was real," she said. "It's so life-like. Even your *testicles* look authentic."

"The whole thing is made out of a special latex engineered to mimic real skin. With all the advances in artificial dolls these days, it's amazing what they can do with sex toys."

"Do you mind if I—*touch* it?" she asked.

"I thought you'd never ask."

As I stepped back from the vanity, Haley turned to face me, reaching her hand down to touch my artificial cock.

"My God," she said, squeezing it firmly. "It even *feels* like a real dick. If only it could get hard, I shudder to think how big it would be angry."

As she reached further down to cup my balls, her face came closer to mine, and we kissed. I pressed my tongue into her mouth and she reached lower still, running her fingers over my moist labia. I purred in pleasure, pressing my crotch harder into her hips. She hiked up her skirt, and I was pleasantly surprised to see that she was completely naked underneath. Recognizing my opportunity to have a little fun, I positioned my hand over my right pistol, gently pumping the trigger. Slowly, my synthetic cock began to fill with air and inflate between her legs.

"What the—" Haley gasped, pulling back to see what was happening. "You've got to be kidding me. You can *animate* that thing?"

"In a manner of speaking," I said. "You want to give it a try?"

"*Hell* yes!" she said. "I'm so horny right now, I could fuck just about anything. But first, let me take a closer look at what I'm working with."

As I smiled at her wickedly, I pumped my trigger harder until my organ rose to a full ten inches of erect flesh. Haley couldn't help herself as she fell to the floor and took my member into her mouth while she proceeded to give me a pretend blowjob. As I watched her stretch her lips around my thick pole, I placed my hands behind her head and imagined fucking her face like a man. Although I was being far gentler than most, it was fun fantasizing being in the man's role for a change, having my way with my muse.

"That's it," I purred. "Suck my big cock, baby. Squeeze my balls while I fuck your pretty face."

Without hesitating, Haley reached underneath me and began

rubbing my balls against my raging clit. The sensation was not unlike what I imagined a real man would be feeling as she stimulated my sex organ.

"Fuck, yes," I panted. "That feels good, Haley. I want to fuck you so bad."

Suddenly, she stood up and smiled at me.

"That makes *two* of us. I'm so turned-on, I could pop off any second."

She reached behind her, placing her hands on top of the vanity and lifted herself up onto the counter, hiking her skirt all the way up. I took one look at her glistening pussy and leaned in to kiss her passionately. She reached down and pointed my hard pecker toward her opening and when I pressed it into her, she gasped.

"Oh God, Jade," she groaned. "Your cock feels so good. Fill me up with your big dick. I want to feel your balls slapping against my pussy."

Her dirty talk got me even more worked up, and as I pressed my hips forward, she moaned loudly. As we began to grind our hips together, our tongues danced in each other's mouths. Haley flapped her thighs against me as I plowed in and out of her, grinding my clit against the underside of my rubbery balls. While we grunted and moaned with abandon, anybody who might have been waiting to use the restroom must have surely known what was going on inside. But neither one of us cared, lost in the moment by the rising feeling of ecstasy engulfing our joined bodies.

Suddenly, Haley wrapped her legs around my ass and pulled me even deeper inside her pussy.

"*Damn*, girl," she panted. "You're going to make me come with that big thumper of yours. Fill me up while I come all over your pretty pussy."

"Yes," I groaned. "I'm close too. I'm going to cum with you. God damn, I like fucking you."

"Here it comes," Haley moaned. "Take me over the edge."

I grabbed Haley's hips by both sides and pulled her strongly toward me, grinding my cock and balls as hard as I could against her while ramming my cock in and out of her sloshing pussy. Suddenly, a wave of passion rolled over me as my clit began pulsating against the underside of my faux balls.

"Oh God, Haley," I groaned. "Cum with me baby. Come all over my big dick."

"Yes!" Haley howled. "I can feel you pounding my G-spot. It feels soooo good!"

Suddenly, I felt Haley spraying all over my balls and mound as her pussy clenched down over my phallus while we ground our hips against one another. We moaned inside each other's mouths as we locked lips in a tight and passionate kiss. After what seemed like a full minute of shaking and convulsing in each other's arms, our breathing finally returned to normal, while we kissed with me still inside her.

"*Ahem*," a woman's voice called impatiently from outside the door, from someone waiting to use the facilities.

"I guess we'll have to vacate the premises," Haley smiled. "Though I could make love to you all night long."

"Same here," I said. "Let's clean up and get out of here. Maybe we can find a more private place to continue our fun."

While Haley pulled down her skirt and reapplied her smudged lipstick, I unfastened my appendage and washed it under the tap before reattaching it to my mound. When we finally got ourselves put back together, we opened the door and walked past a long line of stunned onlookers as their eyes widened in shock ogling my still-dripping, semi-hard cock.

4

—————

It didn't take long after Haley and I returned to the main ballroom for her husband to spot us. While we giggled amongst ourselves about the pretentious costumes of all the men in the room masking their tiny peckers, the mayor approached us with an angry scowl on his face.

"Where've you been?" he barked at Haley, his ruddy, pockmarked face making his wolf costume look all the more ridiculous. "I've been looking all over for you. There are a lot of prominent people I wanted to introduce you to."

"Jade and I were just freshening up. No need to get your knickers in a twist, dear."

"*Freshening up*?" he said, darting his eyes back and forth between Haley's face and my tumescent cock. "How long does that take? You must have been gone for at least a half hour!"

"Well, you know how we women are when we hang out in the ladies' room," she replied with a straight face. "There's no telling how long it might take to get ourselves put together in front of the mirror. You *do* want me to look pretty and proper for all your important friends, don't you?"

"I—suppose so," he stammered, distracted by my glistening

joystick. He grabbed Haley's hand, trying to drag her away from me. "Come, I want you to meet one of my biggest fundraisers, Kent Schiffer."

As he steered Haley toward a gathering in the center of the room, she looked back at me with an apologetic expression, mouthing the words *later*. Soon after, Hannah came up behind me and cupped one of my bare cheeks with her hand.

"What was *that* all about?" she said. "It looked like the Big Bad Wolf was about to bite off his wife's head."

"He might as well have," I huffed. "The way he was acting as if he owned her. All these upper-class snobs seem interested in is congratulating themselves around their buddies while showing off their arm candy."

"He did seem a little distracted by you," Hannah said, noticing Haley peering in my direction with a flushed face. "And he wasn't the *only* one. What kind of trouble did you get into with his wife? You've got a strange glow about you."

"Nothing much," I lied. "We were just freshening up in the ladies' room, looking for an escape from all the overbearing egos in this place."

Hannah looked at me suspiciously, pinching her eyebrows as she peered at my puffy appendage.

"Well, judging by the flush on your chest and the sweat dripping down your ass, I'd say you were up to a little more than just fixing your makeup. If I didn't know better, I'd swear even your *dick* looks more excited than usual."

"We may have been touching up a bit more than just our *faces*," I admitted. "We started admiring each other's costumes and one thing led to another..."

Hannah reached down and squeezed my tumescent dildo, then her eyes widened as her lips curled up into a knowing smile.

"Is it just my imagination, or does it seem a little *bigger* than when we first came in? You better be careful—you could poke somebody's eye out with that thing."

"That's not the only thing it's good for poking," I grinned.

"No way!" she said, stepping back in mock indignation. "You were *fucking* the mayor's wife in the washroom? Did he have any inkling?"

"I don't think so. But judging by how much noise we were making in there, I imagine it won't take long for word to spread around the room."

"Not to worry–just stick with me, girl," Hannah said, moving closer to protect me from everyone's disapproving glares. "If any of these jokers cause you any trouble, I'll give them a batkick to the groin."

"I doubt that'll be necessary," I sighed, catching Hannah's Tarzan friend stealing glances at me from the open bar on the other side of the room. "Most of the men in here seem reluctant to engage me in any kind of conversation, let alone actually approach me in this getup. I don't know if they're more threatened by my provocative outfit or they're just afraid to admit they're attracted to a pretty girl with a big cock."

I noticed Tarzan moving to the other side of the bar to get a clearer look at me. I found it strange that he seemed so focused on me after Hannah had spent so much time with him earlier. Unlike me, I knew she had a preference for men, and I suspected she was hoping to land a wealthy boyfriend at this event.

"What about you?" I said, shifting my position to deflect Tarzan's gaze. "What kind of trouble have you been getting up to around all these society types?"

"Not as much as I'd like," Hannah frowned. "I've found a few interesting candidates, but so far everybody's been politely keeping their dicks in their pants."

"Well, you know how it is. With all their extra ornamentation, it might be kind of hard to just whip it out. Most of these guys seem to have gone to great lengths to gussy themselves up with all this embellishment."

"I know what you mean," Hannah said, pulling her tight latex skin down uncomfortably under her crotch. "I guess I didn't give this costume as much forethought as I should have. I'm sweating like a pig under here. I have to dismantle the whole thing just to go pee."

"Not exactly conducive to pulling off a quickie in this place," I chuckled.

"Not as easily as you," she grumbled. "You don't have to remove a single stitch of clothing to get your freak on. All you have to do is find a willing accomplice and insert your magic wand."

With Hannah's back turned away from the bar, I saw Tarzan adjusting his equipment under the counter. His loincloth had begun pouching in front of his penis, and he seemed to be getting more and more aroused watching me.

"What about that hunky Tarzan character I saw you flirting with earlier?" I said, hoping to redirect his attention. "He seems worthy of a little deconstruction."

"It crossed my mind, believe me," Hannah said. "But he seemed more interested in talking about everyone else in the room. Either he's just here for the people watching, or he's gay. I mean, I'm still a *catch*, right? Who can resist a sexy chick in this tight outfit? I was practically throwing myself at him."

Tarzan turned away from me holding his hands in front of his crotch, trying to keep his rising member from making too obvious an appearance. Then he suddenly stood up and exited through a door next to the bar.

"He's probably just trying to keep up appearances," I said. "It's a pretty snooty affair, you have to admit. People would likely get their nose out of joint if they caught a couple getting too carried away in public."

"That's what *powder rooms* are for, right?" Hannah grinned.

"Speaking of, I gotta go pee for real this time. Catch up with you in a bit?"

"Sure," Hannah said. "Just try not to dip your dick anywhere it doesn't belong this time. There's no telling what kind of hullabaloo it might generate if one of these heavy hitters caught you getting it on again with another one of their wives."

"Don't worry," I smiled. "I'll be staying far away from the ladies this time."

As soon as I left Hannah, a flock of men suddenly converged on her, no longer threatened by the presence of her sexy androgynous partner. But I was happy for the distraction, because there was something about this Tarzan hunk I needed to check out. He was the first man I'd met at the ball who'd demonstrated any genuine interest in me, and I wanted to see which persona he was more attracted to.

I meandered through the crowd making small talk with some of the guests then I ordered a cocktail at the bar and slipped quietly out the same door I'd seen Tarzan use. It led to a large wine cellar, darkened and chilled to a frigid fifty degrees. I looked around the room, catching sight of Tarzan huddled between two kegs with his hand moving suspiciously between his legs.

I strolled over in his direction and smiled when I noticed his predicament. His cock was at full mast, flapping up over his flimsy loincloth, high up against his belly. I nodded when I saw how well hung he was, his organ standing a good eight inches in length and at least two inches thick.

"Aren't you a bit underdressed for this place?" I asked.

"I suppose so," he said in a shaky voice. "But I didn't know where else to go." He looked down at his crotch with a sheepish expression, vainly trying to cover up his erection. "It seems I'm having a bit of a wardrobe malfunction."

"Is *that* what you call it?" I said. "Can I offer some help? Provide a little body heat at least? You're shivering in that skimpy outfit."

"Maybe," he hesitated, peering down at my even bigger cock hanging down over my naked belly. "At least you can provide some cover if anyone else comes in here."

As if on cue, the door on the other side of the wine cellar opened, and a uniformed waiter entered the room, walking in our direction. He appeared to be looking for a particular bottle, but when he caught sight of the two of us, he stopped and did a double-take. Without pausing, I stepped closer to Tarzan and flung my arms around him, pretending to make out. It was just the cover he needed, and this was the perfect excuse to get a little closer. The waiter smiled as he nodded toward us, then collected his items and exited the room.

"Thanks," Tarzan said, pulling away awkwardly. "This is beyond embarrassing. I can't seem to make this thing go down and I have nothing to cover up with."

"I can't imagine why you'd *want* to," I said, running my fingers over his hard chest muscles. "With a body like this, you should be showing off as much of it as you can."

He glanced down at my full breasts pressing up against him in my tight leather vest.

"I hadn't counted on getting quite so—*aroused* at this event," he stuttered. "I thought I'd be able to keep it together around all these stiff necks. This has never happened to me before in a public place..."

"Not to worry," I said. "This little accident will stay between us. But if you don't mind my asking, may I ask what's gotten you so worked up? I saw you looking in my direction, and all of a sudden you wanted to hide."

"I'm sorry," he said, his face flushing like a teenager. "I just couldn't help staring at you. I find you incredibly sexy, and with so much of you hanging out for everyone to see, I guess I just had a visceral reaction."

"I understand," I said, darting my eyes over his handsome face, finding myself getting surprisingly turned by his shy demeanor. "But which *part* of me were you most attracted to? I'm hanging out on both sides."

"Both," he said, without hesitation. "You have a sexy body and you're absolutely stunning. But there's something especially alluring about a woman flaunting a man's genitals overtop their naked body. It's very—*ballsy* of you."

"You like *cocky* women, do you?" I said, leaning in towards him as I brushed my thick cock against his tight balls.

"In a manner of speaking," he huffed.

"Did you want to play with it?"

"May I?" he said. "I've never really touched another penis before..."

"You mean besides your *own*?" I kidded. "Is that what you were doing in here? Stroking it trying to make it go down before you went back into the ballroom?"

"I was so turned on, I didn't think there was any other way to get myself back together."

"Maybe I can help you with that," I smiled, reaching down and grasping his throbbing cock with my left hand. "Is this warming you up a little bit?"

"Yes," he panted, clutching my ass while he rocked his hips toward me, trying to create some much-needed friction against his throbbing hard-on. "But you've got goosebumps too. How can I help warm you up?"

I wasn't sure what he had in mind, but I wasn't interested in him fucking me in the usual manner. I'd long been fascinated seeing gay men play with themselves. I found one of the most erotic things was when they rubbed their erect cocks together. Something about the playful jousting of their erogenous parts always got me turned on.

"Well, we're both equipped with similar equipment," I said, raising an eyebrow. "I've always wondered what it would feel like to rub two cocks together..."

"Oh my God," Tarzan said. "I've fantasized about that too. But you're not exactly *functional* in the way most men are—"

"You might be surprised what this ladyboy is capable of," I grinned. "This little package comes equipped with a few extra features."

As I began stroking his hard-on, I squeezed the trigger of the pistol on my right hip, slowly inflating my rising pecker. Tarzan looked down and widened his eyes, seeing my love muscle inflating to its full ten inches. When it reached its maximum length, I placed it against the underside of his prick and began rocking my hips in tandem with his. Even though he was better endowed than most men, my giant phallus looked like an anaconda slithering up next to his garden snake. As the rubbery veins of my dildo rolled over the sensitive flesh on the tip of his rod, he shuddered and emitted a drop of dew out of his hole.

"Uhnnn," he groaned. "This is incredibly hot. I've always wondered what this would feel like, but to do it with such a sexy woman is a dream come true."

"You've always wanted to get it on with a *tranny*?" I smirked. "Well now you've got your wish."

I reached down and cupped my hands around both of our cocks and began humping him more vigorously. Tarzan groaned as he placed his hands against my chest, squeezing my breasts over my cowboy vest.

"Open it up," I nodded. "See what it's like to fuck a real ladyboy. I want to feel your hard pecs rubbing against my tits."

He didn't need any more encouragement as he fumbled with my buttons until he freed my boobs from their tight enclosure. When he saw my firm breasts bouncing on my chest, he circled them with his hands and pinched my nipples gently while I continued frotting our cocks together in my hands.

"Fucking hell," he said. "You are so hot. You are truly the woman of my dreams."

"And *man* also?" I smiled.

"Yes," he admitted. "I've long fantasized what it would be like to hold another man's penis in my hands."

"Why don't you take the driver's seat then?" I said, acknowledging his bisexual nature. "Let me admire the scenery for a while."

When I removed my hands, he placed his palms around our joined cocks and squeezed them together firmly. More precum oozed out of the head of his pole, and he moaned as he began to pick up the pace of his rocking motion. Neither one of us seemed interested in kissing, fixated on the appearance of our two big cocks frotting in and out of his hands. As he began to moan more loudly, I slapped my sweaty breasts against his hard chest. I could tell he was getting close to the point of no return, and I was eager to watch him cum with our cocks joined together.

"Yes, baby," I purred. "Let it come. Cum all over my big tits. Let me hear Tarzan's call of the wild."

Suddenly, he arched his back and thrust his dick as hard as he could against my organ, pressing his balls tightly against mine. My clit throbbed as he shot one giant geyser after another between my boobs, cumming all over the underside of his chin and face.

"Fuckkkk!" he growled with each spurt. "I'm cumming all over your cock. *Uhn, uhn, uhn!*"

With each throb and spasm, he grunted like a wild animal until he was fully spent. When he finally recovered his strength, he looked up at me with gratitude.

"Thank you," he said. "I needed that. You were even more magnificent than I imagined."

"Glad I could be of service," I said. "Now you should get yourself back in there. Somewhere out there is your *real* Jane, waiting for you to scoop her up and take her away to your jungle."

"What about you?" he said, looking at me confused.

"I'm still looking for my Jane, too," I smiled.

The whole time neither one of us had so much as touched lips. All either one of us wanted was a quickie in the wine cellar, where we could live out one of our mutual boy-on-boy fantasies. As Tarzan tucked his pecker back under his loincloth and staggered out of the cellar, I smiled.

That's one way to get it on with a man, I thought. I wondered what other fantasies awaited me before the night would be over.

5

———

After Tarzan left the wine cellar, I found a sink nearby and cleaned myself up, removing all the cum that he'd splattered over my dildo and chest. Feeling flushed and sweaty, I decided to catch some fresh air before going back into the main room. A side door from the cellar led onto an expansive terrace overlooking the lake. Standing alone in a corner of the balcony stood the governor's wife Alicia with her back toward me. Her arms rested on the stone railing as she puffed a cigarette, leaning over with her naked ass jutting out behind her backless apron. My pussy fluttered as I admired her shapely figure, feeling the moisture accumulating on my lips tingling in the cool autumn air.

Alicia had one of the most magnificent backsides I'd ever beheld. Her long, slender legs were taut and shapely like a professional dancer's and her ass was as tight and firm as a teenager. The rising moonlight reflecting off Lake Michigan shimmered between the space in her thighs, illuminating the dark pit under her mound. It was almost as if she were daring me to approach her and fuck her from behind.

I surveyed the rest of balcony and seeing that we were alone, I began tiptoeing toward her. It was a calm and cloudless night and the light of the full moon shone brightly over the Bannon estate, revealing the splendor of its manicured gardens. Amidst autumn-speckled trees and perfectly manicured flower beds, lay a geometric hedge maze accented with stone sculptures and a flowing water fountain.

I paused for a moment to breathe in the floral scent of the breeze wafting in from the shore. I couldn't imagine a more romantic setting for a private encounter with my pretty temptress. As I edged closer toward her, I stepped on a small pebble and it went skittering over the stone tiles in Alicia's direction. She cocked her head and turned slightly in my direction, then bent lower on the handrail, taking another puff of her cigarette. Whoever she imagined approaching her from behind only increased the boldness of her seductive pose.

Maybe being the wife of the most powerful figure in the state gave her the confidence to blow off any would-be interlopers. Or maybe she was just bored and looking for an anonymous fling to mix up her dull political life. Whatever the reason, her self-assured nature turned me on even more and as the glistening slit of her pussy came into focus, I felt the wetness from my own sex beginning to run down the insides of my thighs. When I came within a few feet of her, she stood up with her arms extended on the balustrade and blew a stream of smoke high in the air.

"Beautiful night, isn't it?" she said to no one in particular.

"Spectacular," I said. "The view is truly magnificent in this light."

"Mmm," she replied, oblivious to the identity of her midnight paramour. "Were you admiring the landscaping?"

"Among other things," I said, staring at her bald snatch. "Everything is so perfectly balanced and neatly trimmed. It really makes you want to pause and appreciate Mother Nature."

Alicia took a step back with one of her legs, arching her ass higher.

"It would be a shame just to *look* at it," she said, "Nature is meant to be immersed in, don't you think?"

"Absolutely," I said, taking a step closer, brushing my bare breasts against her chilly back. "You never know what you might find until you make contact."

"Like the way a woman's nipples pucker when it's cold?"

"Or when they brush against a soft surface," I replied.

"Or her lover's skin," she said

She pressed her ass further toward me and touched my protruding organ, then gasped and turned her head in my direction, checking it before we made eye contact.

"And sometimes—" she mused, recognizing the familiar shape of my leather chaps. "Nature has a way of *surprising* us with her wonderful diversity."

"Do like surprises?" I teased.

"In the right circumstances."

I reached under the front of her apron and squeezed her breasts, pressing my cock harder between her legs. She reached underneath and began stroking my dildo against her wet cleft.

"I particularly like the way nature has a way of adapting to its surroundings—" I said, beginning to inflate my rubber penis with my pistol trigger. "Like the way it expands and contracts to fill the void in any particular situation."

"Yes," Alicia panted, running her hand up and down my giant shaft. "I'd like you to fill *my* void."

By now, my inflatable penis had reached its maximum length and Alicia was busy rubbing the bulbous head against her inflamed clit.

"Fuck me, Jade," she said, dispensing with any further pretense. "I've been fantasizing about you banging me with your beautiful dick all night long."

"As have I," I panted, angling the tip into her dripping opening. I've dreamt of pounding your beautiful ass from the moment we met."

"*Fuck* yes," she grunted, as I pressed myself inside her. "Pound me with your big cowboy dick. Let me feel your balls slapping up against me while you ride me."

As I began to hump her, I marveled at how enthralled all the guests seemed to be with my transgender persona—both male and female. Everyone seemed to want a piece of my girl-cock, no matter how they could get it. While I watched my drumstick pounding in and out of her hole, I had to admit it was kind of fun assuming the male role for a change. There was something strangely empowering about being connected to a man's cock, watching all these strangers bow to my made-up masculinity. As I grasped the sides of her hips and pulled her toward me, she moaned and gyrated her hips, holding on to the rail for support.

"God damn, girl," she hissed. "You feel so good inside me. I've never had a man fill me up quite this way before. I only wish you could cum inside me. I want to hear you get off with me."

There was something about the sight of my big phallus plowing into her tight little ass that was getting me especially worked up. Even though she wasn't providing direct stimulation to my lady parts, I could have come just watching the incredibly sexy scene that was unfolding before my eyes. But I'd been saving up one more special secret. I pressed a button on the inside of my handle and suddenly my balls began vibrating from a battery-operated motor embedded inside. As I pressed my scrotum against her underside, I was instantly taken to a whole new level of excitement.

"Holy shit!" she squealed. "That's *definitely* something no man has ever done to me. Grind your nuts against me, Jade. Trib me with your big fat balls."

"Fuck, yes," I growled, feeling the rising tide of ecstasy building within me.

I couldn't help smiling, acknowledging the multipurpose capability of my male equipment. Not too long ago I was frotting a man with my big firehose, and now I was tribbing a sexy woman with my vibrating balls. For a brief moment, I felt envious of a man's equipment, but as my pussy began throbbing and dripping over my strap-on apparatus, I became acutely aware of my true gender. I leaned forward and rubbed my tits against Alicia's back, pinching and rolling her nipples between my fingers.

"Can you feel my wetness, Alicia?" I panted. "Can you feel how much you're turning me on?"

She reached under my vibrating balls and inserted two fingers inside me, stroking the front of my G-spot.

"Yes," she grunted. "You feel exquisite. You're going to make me come soon. I want to feel you come with me."

"With every part of my body actively engaged in fucking her, I didn't need any further encouragement. Within seconds, a surge of energy coursed through me, as my pussy began clamping down over Alicia's fingers. At the same time, she hunched over and began shaking wildly as she gripped the railing with all her strength.

"Fuck, Jade!" she hissed. "I'm cumming! Pound my ass with your big dick. God, I'm cumming so hard!"

As the two of us grunted and shook in simultaneous orgasm with my buttocks clenching as I pressed my cock deep into her, I suddenly became conscious of the extra light that was being cast onto the terrace from the open windows of the ballroom. When we finally came down from our powerful climax, she turned around and gently kissed me.

"It seems we have an audience," she smiled, directing her eyes toward the adjacent wall.

I peered in the direction of the ballroom and noticed a giant crowd of onlookers staring out the windows with their eyes and mouths agape.

"Good," I said. "It's about time some of these snobs got a taste of the real world outside their sheltered cocoons. "Maybe this will open their minds about the natural order of things."

With that, I lifted Alicia up onto the stone abutment and spread her legs far apart, pressing my still buzzing cock back inside her.

"If they want a show, let's really give them a show."

6

———————

After Alicia and I came a second time in full view of the crowd, we took a moment to compose ourselves then walked back into the main ballroom as if nothing had happened. Neither one of us seemed to care that virtually everyone was staring at us as they continued gossiping in their little cliques. I didn't even bother to refasten my leather vest or deflate my dildo as my breasts bounced freely on my bare chest in tandem with my turgid hard-on.

The two of us approached the bar and ordered matching margaritas then giggled amongst ourselves about the way everyone was trying not to stare as they talked amongst themselves. In spite of the fact that they pretended to carry on normal conversations, it was obvious that they were still highly aroused by our little tête-a-tête.

"I think Mr. Incredible is regretting his wardrobe choice right about now," Alicia chuckled, motioning toward the billionaire and his supermodel girlfriend.

I stole a glance in their direction and noticed Schiffer had a pronounced erection tenting the front of his tights.

"He's looking more like *Mr. Fantastic* with that cucumber wedged between his legs," I joked.

"And check out our favorite newscaster," she said. "It looks like Woody's popping a little Pinocchio of his own."

I peered at the anchorman and noticed him rearranging the front of his denims as a prominent bulge ran down one side of his pant legs.

"Ha," I chuckled. "I bet he's wishing he wore chaps like me."

I had to admit that I was enjoying the attention of all the powerful people in the room, particularly amongst the men who seemed especially attracted by my naked ladyboy costume.

"I don't know about *Jack* though," she said, furrowing her brow as her husband marched toward us with an angry expression on his face. "I have a feeling that his little willie will be even more shriveled than usual after watching you pound me with your big tool."

The governor stormed up to the bar and grabbed Alicia's hand, trying to ignore the pink pole jutting up from my lap.

"What is it, dear?" Alicia said, feigning surprise at her husband's indignation. "I was just enjoying a quiet drink with my new friend."

"That was hardly *quiet!*" he huffed, dragging her off her barstool. "Come on, it's time for us to go."

"But the party was just getting started," Alicia protested. "I was just starting to get warmed up."

The governor glanced down at my flaring joystick then glared at me.

"It looks like the two of you were getting more than just *warmed up.*"

"Oh, come on, Jack," Alicia said, trying to resist his advance. "We were just having a little fun. You said that you wanted me to get more comfortable around your political friends."

"Not *that* way!" he fumed. "You've made a fool out of me and embarrassed me in front of all my colleagues!"

Alicia tried to protest, but the governor pulled her away from the bar and stormed toward the entrance. After collecting their coats from the butler, they soon disappeared out the front door. Alarmed by the commotion, Hannah joined me at the bar and sat on Alicia's stool, taking a sip of her cocktail.

"Jesus, Jade," she said, slapping my dripping dildo. "You sure know how to rock the boat in these genteel affairs."

"That's not the *only* boat I was rocking around here," I said. "Were you watching the show like everybody else?"

"How could I miss it?" Hannah chuckled. "It only took one person to catch you fucking the governor's wife before the entire room joined in the spectacle. Not like they could have *ignored* it, with all the grunting and groaning the two of you were doing."

"I wasn't paying much attention. I was kind of lost in the moment."

"You sure looked like it," Hannah said. "I have to say, It was an incredible turn-on watching you fuck her from behind. I could actually see your buttocks shaking when you came." She glanced down at my swollen cock and shook her head. "How does that work, exactly? I thought you were kind of detached from that thing."

"Not as much as you might imagine," I smiled. "Touch my balls to see for yourself."

Hannah placed her hand over my rubber scrotum and I switched on the vibrator, then her eyes suddenly flung open.

"Holy shit!" she said. "That thing really *is* fully animated. What else can it do? Spurt out fake cum?"

"As much as I wish it could, no. But these two extra tricks seem to be providing all the entertainment I need."

"I'd say so, judging by how loud the two of you were howling out there on the balcony. I fact, I've got a little girly hard-on of my own thinking what that would feel like inside me. I don't suppose we could find our own private alcove for a little fun, could we? I'm so horny right now, this costume is practically glued onto my body."

I glanced around the room and noticed that everybody was staring at us with disapproving expressions.

"Why not?" I said. "After that last escapade, it looks like all bets are off. There's not much to hide any more at this point."

I took Hannah's hand and began heading in the direction of the wine cellar, but Steve Bannon and his wife stepped in front of us, smiling like Cheshire Cats.

"It appears you've been enjoying my party even more than I could have imagined," he smirked, peering at my dripping dildo. "You seem to have gotten a rise out of more than a few of our guests this evening. I'd have to say you win the prize for the most inventive costume."

"I have to admit, it's been far less of a stuffy affair than I imagined." I glanced at Genevieve, noticing the slit in the side of her dress looking even more pronounced than before, revealing her hip bone above her barely concealed pussy. "I've found the conversation very stimulating."

"So it would seem," he said, staring at my tumescent totem. "Would you like to join my wife and me for a little nightcap in our private lounge? We've been admiring you all night long and would love to continue the conversation."

"Hmm," I said, raising an eyebrow toward Hannah. "Do you mind if I bring my friend along? We were just about to explore some private time of our own."

Bannon leered at Hannah's costume then smiled at her.

"I don't see why not," he said. "What do you think dear? Would you like to bring another partner into our little meeting?"

"The more the merrier," she smiled, jumping at the chance to have some more alone time with me. "Besides, now it'll be more evenly balanced. I'm not sure I could manage the two of you all by myself."

"Come then," Bannon said, leading us to a private elevator at the base of his stairs.

As we crossed the ballroom floor, the entire room followed our movement while my protruding penis waggled playfully between my legs. When we got in the elevator and the doors closed behind us, Bannon pressed button number four and smiled at Hannah and me.

"You've already explored many of the rooms in my house," he said. "But I think you'll find the view particularly appealing from the top floor."

I glanced toward Hannah and saw that her pupils were already dilated in excitement. I didn't know if she was more impressed by the fact that Bannon's mansion had four floors and a personal elevator or that she was about to participate in a private orgy with the richest man in the Midwest.

When the lift stopped and the doors opened, we both gasped at the view. The elevator opened to an enormous bedroom with floor-to-ceiling windows providing a panoramic view of Lake Michigan. As impressed as I'd been with the view from his main floor balcony, from this elevation the lake seemed to stretch out in every direction forever. But the view on the *inside* was even more spectacular. Bannon's bedroom was almost as large as most people's houses, with giant expressionist paintings hanging on the walls, a huge wood-burning fireplace next to the bed, and a separate bar beside the sliding glass windows.

"Would you like something to drink?" he said, lifting a crystal decanter off the table. "Perhaps a glass of brandy? I've got a thirty-year-old bottle of Hennessey that I've been meaning to open for a special event."

As much as I admired his impressive collection of personal effects, I was far more attracted to the elaborate trimmings of his beautiful wife.

"That would be lovely," I said, smiling at Genevieve.

Bannon handed each of us a large goblet filled with cognac, then he pressed a remote control device and the large window panes began to separate, bringing in a gust of cool air.

"Would you like to move to the balcony? The view is even more magical at this time of the night."

"Sure," I said, checking with Hannah to make sure she was still feeling comfortable. She simply peered back at me with wide eyes and nodded silently. We stepped out onto the deck and Bannon motioned to a wicker settee encircling a bubbling Jacuzzi.

"It might be a bit warmer next to the hot tub," he said, extending his hand toward the tub. "Please—make yourselves comfortable."

Hannan and I took a spot next to one another, while Bannon and his wife sat kitty-corner to us, a few feet to our left. The view of the lake was magnificent with the light of the full moon reflecting off the ripples like an evening sunset on a secluded beach. A cool breeze wafted in from the shore, and I pulled my vest over my exposed abdomen.

"Feel free to dip your toes in the water," he said. "Or climb right in if you prefer. It's chillier outside than usual tonight."

"I wouldn't mind getting out of these boots," I said, kicking off my footwear and placing my feet in the churning water.

Then I turned to Hannah and smiled.

"This feels heavenly, Han. Why don't you join me?"

She motioned to her all-in-one ensemble and frowned.

"It's not quite as simple for me as it is for you."

"Don't be concerned about *us*," Bannon grinned. "We're all adults here. Besides, I think we've seen just about everything already tonight. No one's watching this time besides Genevieve and me."

Hannah peered at me for a moment and I nodded. I'd never known her to be shy in these kinds of circumstances and it didn't take long for her to shed her clothes and slide under the bubbling water.

"Mmm," she purred, glancing up at me. "It's lovely. You should come in. These jets are good for massaging more than just your feet."

I looked toward Bannon and his wife and they smiled with a knowing grin.

"You said you wanted to find a private spot to continue your engagement," he said. "Don't let us stop you. We'll just finish our brandies while you two make yourselves comfortable."

He glanced down at my bobbing tool then peered back up at me.

"Is your equipment waterproof?"

"It should be," I said, winking toward Hannah. "Would you like me to keep it on?"

"I think we would," Bannon grinned. "I'd love to see how you use that thing close-up. How about you, dear? Are you interested in watching Jade play with her magic wand again?"

"Absolutely," Genevieve said, staring me directly in the eye. "I'd love to see her make another pretty girl come with her big man-cock."

I pulled off my chaps and vest and squeezed the trigger on my pistol to re-inflate my shaft to its full length then pressed the button on the handle to turn on the vibrator. Bannon and Genevieve squinted at the humming device, and I smiled at them as I slipped under the surface next to Hannah.

She scooted up next to me and lowered her hand under the water, stroking my phallus as she caressed the inside of my thighs. I turned toward her and we embraced in a passionate kiss. I could feel the jets of the Jacuzzi shooting between our breasts as we rubbed our tits together while she lifted her leg, straddling my hips. Within seconds, she lowered herself onto my pole and wrapped her arms around my back. As she began to rock her hips together with mine, I glanced up and made eye contact with Bannon and his wife. I noticed the front of his toga was tenting between his legs and Genevieve's hand was moving up and down as he smiled lasciviously toward us.

"Damn, Jade," Hannah groaned as I embedded my rod deep inside her. "That thing feels amazing. Fuck me with your big cock. Rub your balls on my cunt. I can feel it vibrating."

"Mmm," I sighed, as her tits mashed up against mine in the swirling water. "Squeeze my dick, Hannah. Let's put on a nice show for our hosts."

By now, Bannon had dispensed with any form of modesty, flinging his toga to the side where I could see his throbbing erection standing up between his spread legs. Judging by the size of his wife's hand, he appeared to have a decent-sized hard-on, but nowhere near as large as my own. Genevieve had apparently gotten just worked up watching Hannah and me fucking under the swirling water, and before long she kicked off her heels and hiked up her dress, sitting down over her husband's cock while she faced us. As I darted my eyes between her husband's prick thrusting in and out of her pussy and her dark eyes, our mouths began to open in mutual pleasure.

It was an incredible turn-on watching Genevieve's sexy body squirming over her husband's cock as she watched the two of us writhing in the churning water. Whether she was more excited getting fucked by her husband while two pretty girls watched them get it on or by the sight of Hannan and me enjoying ourselves underneath the surface, it didn't matter. Before long, all four of us were moaning loudly as we watched each other fuck our partners with abandon.

Hannah was the first to go off, as she started shaking wildly on my hips.

"Oh God, Jade," she groaned. "I'm cumming! Ram it inside me. Let me feel your balls slap up against me. Uhnnnnnn!"

Seeing Hannah having a powerful orgasm on top of me soon put Bannon over the edge as he grunted with his shaft pulsing inside his wife's pussy. Although he was staring at me, I was more interested in watching the expression on Genevieve's face as she returned my gaze with glassy eyes. I could tell that she was close, but needed a little extra stimulation to reach her goal.

As she locked eyes on me, she placed her hand over the front of her mound and began jerking her protruding nub. As her eyes opened progressively wider, I leaned forward and lifted my ass over one of the jets behind me. While the water gushed against my quivering opening, the vibrating balls pressed against my clit, and I felt a surge of pleasure engulfing my body.

"I'm close," I panted, locking eyes with Bannon's wife. "Come for me, Genevieve. Let me watch you come all over my big dick."

Even though she was planted on her husband's cock, we were both thinking the same thing. In that moment of mutual ecstasy, we were both imagining that it was *my* cock embedded in her pussy instead of her husband's.

"Yes, Jade!" she howled. "I'm cumming! I feel you inside me. I want you so bad. Oh *Gawd...*"

While the four of us panted and groaned in simultaneous climax, I glanced at Bannon, noticing him watching me with a wild look in his eye. Locked on me with laser focus, he had a strange, almost animalistic expression. I wasn't sure what he was channeling at that moment, but I could tell it wasn't his wife he was thinking about.

After we all settled down, Genevieve lifted herself off her husband's cock and slid in the water next to Hannah and me. She cuddled up beside me and her hand disappeared under the water, and soon after I felt her caressing my vibrating dildo. As Hannah leaned over to kiss her, Bannon stood up with his penis dripping a string of cum, motioning with his head inside his bed chamber.

"Why don't we all go back inside?" he said. "There'll be more room for us to play and we can watch each other better on the bed. Something tells me there's still a lot of pent-up energy between you girls."

Genevieve stepped up out of the tub first and led me by the hand into the bedroom as Hannah scampered in behind us, shivering. Bannon returned from his washroom and threw each of us a towel. Then he walked over to the bed and sat on the edge, beckoning for the rest of us to join him.

"Come," he said. "Let's share the wealth. There's plenty to go around."

"What did you have in mind?" I said, raising my eyebrows. After the Tarzan episode, I wasn't sure what part of me he was more interested in.

"There's enough parts between us for us to create an interesting *foursome*, don't you think?" he smirked.

As we all lay down on the bed and began exploring each other's bodies, Bannon seemed immediately drawn to my cock. As he sucked on my nipples, he reached down and began stroking my phallus while he masturbated himself with his other hand. While Hannah and Jenny intertwined their legs and began rubbing their pussies together, Bannon lowered himself down my abdomen until his face was directly in front of my giant pole. Suddenly, he stretched his lips around the head and began sucking it while he jerked his hand over his own dripping dick. Within seconds, he began moaning loudly, as he jetted squirts of cum all over his stomach.

Seeing her husband getting off so quickly again, Genevieve sat up and peered at the two of us with a sly smile.

"You seem quite enamored with Jade's cock, dear. I have an idea, if you're game for a little four-way fun. How would you like a *real* cock inside you this time, Hannah?"

Hannah looked at Genevieve then back at her husband, and smiled. There was little doubt that she'd fantasized about being fucked by the hot billionaire for a long time.

"*Definitely,*" she said.

"Lie down face up on the bed," Genevieve instructed. "That way we can *both* have access to you. And *Jade,*" she purred, with a gleam in her eye. "Why don't you choose whatever outlet looks most enticing to you among the three of us?"

As Genevieve spread her thighs over Hannah's face and lowered her pussy onto her lips, Bannon pulled Hannah's legs apart and straddled her opening with his dripping dick. As I watched them begin to fuck my best friend like she was a piece of meat, something inside me snapped. There was something about the way Bannon thought he could use her any way he wanted that pissed me off.

Just another self-righteous rich asshole, I thought. *This guy needs to be put in his place.*

As I kneeled behind him watching the two of them grinding their bodies against Hannah, Genevieve looked up at me and smiled. She glanced down toward her husband's ass and nodded. It was almost like she was *begging* me to fuck him from behind.

As the sides of my lips slowly curled up in acknowledgement, I brushed my erect dildo over Bannon's cheeks. Instead of flinching, he leaned further forward until I could see his balls waggling above Hannah's pussy. His asshole puckered as he thrust in and out of her, and for the first time in my life, I sensed the attraction of anal sex. There was something incredibly sexy and empowering about fucking a man up the ass. Now I knew why gay men separated into tops and bottoms. Just as with lesbian couples, one had to be the dominant one and one was meant to be the submissive one.

And *this* time, it was *my* turn to be the dominant one. Only in a way I'd never envisioned.

I lifted the tip of my pole, still glistening with Hannah's juices, and pointed it toward Bannon's opening. As I pressed it against his pucker, he grunted and pushed back gently.

So he likes being fucked by a woman? I thought. *It's time to show him who's really in charge here.*

I grabbed the sides of his hips and slowly pressed my cock deeper inside him. It felt strange and titillating at the same time to be fucking a man with my faux hard-on. As my balls pressed back against my clit, I imagined what it would feel like for a man to fuck another man this way. Suddenly, all the times I'd felt used by men who fucked from behind came flooding back. I thrust my dick as far into Bannon's ass as I could and began pounding my hips against his butt cheeks.

As his hole stretched as far as it could go by my coke-can-width hard-on, I found myself enjoying the feeling of thrusting in and out of him. Strangely, Genevieve seemed to be enjoying the show almost as much as me, as she writhed and moaned on Hannah's face while watching the two of us.

"Yes, Jade," she grunted. "Fuck Jack's ass. Make him your bitch. I want to watch him get off while you have your way with him."

Whether it was the sight of her pretty body twisting over Hannah's face or the sense of power I felt fucking her husband, I soon felt the familiar wall of pleasure beginning to overtake me. As I pressed my balls tight against his ass, creating more friction against my clit, I began to moan approaching my peak.

"Damn this is hot," I grunted. "I'm going to come soon. Watch me cum inside your husband's ass, Genevieve."

"Yes," she groaned, suddenly shifting her gaze to her husband's eyes.

I wasn't sure if she was communing with him at that moment or she just enjoyed seeing him at his most vulnerable moment. Either way, the sight of her convulsing over Hannah's mouth as she reached her own orgasm soon opened my floodgates. I pulled Bannon's ass hard toward me as I thrust my cock one last time deep into him, squirting all over my vibrating balls and Hannah's pussy. Within seconds, all four of us were howling in mutual ecstasy as we pounded and quivered atop one another in a mass of sweaty flesh. When we finally collapsed onto the bed in exhaustion, Genevieve leaned over and kissed me, whispering in my ear.

"Thanks for putting my husband in his rightful place," she mewed. "You have no idea how much both of us needed that."

VOLUME FIVE

SPIN THE BOTTLE

VICTORIA RUSH

1

———————

When I saw a new email message with the subject *Fun and Games* from my friend Madison, I had to open it right away. She was famous for hosting the wildest sex parties, and it had been a long time since I'd participated in a group event, so I was eager to see what she was planning this time. As I began to read her message, I could already feel my heart pounding in my chest.

Dear Jade,

You are cordially invited to a party at my place this Saturday evening, starting at 9 p.m.

As with my previous events, there will be an exciting game designed to loosen everyone's inhibitions and get our juices flowing. I don't want to give too much away other than to say you'll definitely walk away with some interesting new techniques to add to your bedroom repertoire.

Get ready to mix it up with friends and foes alike, because in this game, there's no telling who or how you'll be paired up. All I can guarantee is that you'll be stimulated in ways you never dreamed imaginable!

Be there or be square,

Maddy

P.S.: Make sure you're all scrubbed clean, and I do mean everywhere, because we'll be exploring some erogenous zones you probably didn't even know existed!

By the time I finished reading her message, my panties were already soaked trying to imagine what kind of crazy new angle she'd dreamed up. After participating in her blindfold game and naked Twister, it was hard to imagine how she could ratchet the excitement up any further. But the idea of learning some exciting new sex techniques and discovering new erogenous zones had me intrigued. After stewing over what she had planned for the better part of an hour, I finally picked up the phone to give her a call.

"Hey beautiful!" she answered after seeing my caller ID on her phone display.

"*Fucking eh*, girl," I huffed. "You can't leave me hanging like that! What strange and wicked games have you cooked up this time?"

"Keeping it a secret is half the fun," Madison teased. "Besides, with your big mouth, if I told you, half the planet would know before anyone set foot on my doorstep."

"Hmmph!" I grunted. "I didn't hear you complaining about my big mouth the last time I was sucking your sweet pussy."

"Yeah well, you'll want to save that, because I have a feeling you'll be putting it to good use in some *other* ways pretty soon."

"At least tell me who's *going*," I said. "Will it be people I know or a bunch of strangers?"

"A bit of both," Maddy said. "You know how I like to mix it up every time. I plan to stretch your repertoire in more ways than one."

"You're such a dirty girl," I groaned. "Where do you dream up these wild ideas?"

"I guess I have a pretty fertile imagination. I'm always looking for new ways to keep my friends' sex lives fresh and exciting."

"Don't you mean your *own*?" I smiled. "I know you set up these sex parties for your own amusement as much as anyone else's."

"Maybe," Madison purred. "But if I can derive a little pleasure from everyone else's entertainment, can you begrudge me?"

"I suppose not," I said. "I'm just jealous you're the one always coming up with all these crazy scenarios. I feel like such a lightweight around you."

"No one's stopping you from creating your *own* party idea and inviting the next group over to your place."

"I might just do that," I said. "You're not the *only* one with a kinky imagination."

"That's good, because you're going to need every bit of it to participate in this new game."

"In what way exactly?" I probed, pressing for more details. "Give me at least a hint of what I can expect to get my creative juices flowing."

"All I can say is that everything will be completely random. Both in terms of who you'll engage with and in what way. Just be prepared for something entirely new and unexpected."

"You're *killing* me here!" I said, squirming in my chair as I felt my pussy throbbing in excitement.

"That's the idea," Maddy mewed. "By the time this game is over, I intend to have you tingling all over."

"Just *tingling*?"

"Oh, I'm pretty sure there's going to be a lot more than tingling going on."

"Well, there's a lot more than tingling going on right *now*," I panted while I rolled my fingers over my burning nub as I listened to Madison.

"Good," Maddy said. "But don't forget to save some for the party. I'd hate for you to lose your edge before we get started. Unlike my earlier events, this one's going to be *timed*. The more worked up you are coming into it, the more likely you'll be to walk away fully satisfied."

"*What?*" I said. "You're going to put us on the *clock* while we're having sex?"

"Don't worry, sweetheart," Madison purred. "Something tells me that with some of the new techniques likely to be unleashed, it won't take long to get your rocks off."

"You are such a *tease!*" I moaned, feeling my pleasure rapidly rising within me.

"That's the plan," Maddy said. "See you Saturday, sexy. Enjoy!"

After Madison hung up, I came hard within a matter of seconds imagining myself being stimulated by a group of strangers while everyone sat around watching. Part of the fun of her parties was the voyeur aspect, with those doing the watching enjoying the festivities almost as much as those being watched. The more I fantasized about it, the more excited I became, and it took every ounce of my willpower not to jill myself to orgasm ten more times before Saturday night rolled around.

2

When I arrived at Madison's house on the night of the party, she escorted me to her living room where a crowd of people sat around a large mattress covered with a rubber sheet and a single, triangular-shaped pillow. I recognized many of the faces in the crowd, but there were also quite a few new people I hadn't met before. There was an even sprinkling of men and women, and as the last few guests arrived at the house, we made small talk introducing ourselves. After everybody was seated, Madison sat cross-legged at one end of the mattress with a gameboard spinner and a large hourglass positioned between her legs.

"I'm glad everyone could make it this evening," she smiled. "I see many of you have already introduced yourselves, but just to make sure nobody's left out, why don't we go around the circle and have each of you tell us who you are and what your connection to the group is."

She peered at the sexy girl next door that I remembered from her last party and nodded.

"Hi," the woman said. "My name's Laura and I'm Madison's next-door neighbor."

"My very *hot* next-door neighbor," Madison added. "Who likes to skinny-dip in her pool late at night while driving the rest of us crazy with her perfect figure."

There was an awkward pause, then the hunky man sitting next to Laura peered over at Maddy.

"Um, I'm Laura's husband Brad," he said. "Who occasionally can be found guilty of joining my wife naked in the pool."

"And from what I can tell under the rippling water," Madison smirked. "Skinny-dipping isn't the *only* thing you two like to do nude in the pool late at night."

Brad smiled with a lopsided grin then turned to the man sitting next to him, trying to deflect the attention.

"My name's Lucas," the man said, making eye contact with some of the girls around the circle. His smoldering eyes and chiseled jaw had everyone drooling while they stared at him with their mouths agape. "Maddy and I work together, but she twisted my arm asking me to come to the party tonight."

"I didn't have to twist *too* hard as I recall," Madison smiled, peering at Lucas through hooded lids. "After I told you it would involve touching a bunch of *sexy women* in ways you never imagined."

Lucas chuckled, then turned to the pretty girl sitting beside him.

"My name's Amy, and I'm Lucas's girlfriend," she said, blushing slightly.

"Are you going to be okay if your boyfriend has to touch someone *else's* body tonight?" Madison asked.

"Possibly," the girl said. "I suppose it depends on which parts are touching whom."

"What if it ends up being another *man*?" Madison teased.

"*That* could make it a little more interesting," Amy said, grinning at Lucas.

As everybody continued introducing themselves around the circle, we all joked and prodded each other good-naturedly. In addition to Emma, Bonnie, and Lily from last summer's all-girl camping trip, there were two new women—a pretty twenty-something brunette named Amy and a hot African-Asian girl named Mia. On the boys' side, I recognized Ryan and Neil from Madison's previous blindfold game and Dylan from the Naked Twister night. Rounding out the group were two other guys, a young Robert Redford lookalike named Noah, and a barely-legal-looking stud named Alex, who said he was Madison's pizza delivery boy. The last person to introduce herself was Shae, the exotic transgender dancer I knew from the local cabaret club.

"Okay," Madison smiled after everyone finished introducing themselves. "As you can see, we have a pretty eclectic mix of people with different backgrounds and interests, which I think will make this evening's activities all the more interesting. I see many of you have been looking with interest at the vinyl-covered mattress lying in the middle of the floor and these strange objects sitting between my legs."

"Not to mention that weird triangle-shaped pillow on the bed," Lucas said.

"Yes," Madison smiled. "There's a *reason* why it's shaped that way. Allow me to explain the rules of the game."

She held up the game spinner card, pointing to various body part symbols scattered around the perimeter.

"As you can see, this spinner board shows various body parts displayed as erogenous zones."

I squinted at the card, recognizing an erect penis symbol, a woman's vulva, breast, and a few other familiar zones. But I shook my head when I noticed some unusual areas of the body highlighted.

"I didn't know that the *armpits* and the back of the *knee* were erogenous areas," I said.

"I suppose we're going to find out soon enough," Madison said, peering at me with a sly smile. "I'm going to spin the needle twice. The first person and body part that it points to will be the designated *receiver*, who will receive stimulation to the indicated body part. Then I'll spin it a second time, and the person it points to that time will be the *giver*, using only the new body part shown. Pretty simple, yes?"

"What's the hourglass for?" Laura asked.

"We've got a fairly large group, so in order to spread the loving around, we'll have to limit the duration of each round to ensure everybody has a turn before the night is over."

"And we'll be doing all this fully *clothed*?" Dylan said with a raised eyebrow.

"What would be the fun in *that*?" Madison said, lowering her head as she peered at Dylan with a Cheshire Cat grin.

"What's the purpose of the oddly-shaped *pillow*?" Brad enquired.

"As you'll see, a few of these body parts are in some hard-to-reach places. The pillow will offer some extra support to make it easier for your partner to caress you in the various nooks and crannies."

"Is the rubber sheet there for the reason?" Ryan asked.

"What reason were you imagining?" Madison teased.

"Well, if things get heated up enough, there could be some unexpected emissions..."

"There could indeed," Madison smirked, holding up a spray bottle of Lysol and a roll of paper towels. "But I've anticipated such a possibility, so we can clean up quickly in preparation for the following round."

"Exactly how long will each round last?" Bonnie asked.

"Ten minutes, give or take," Madison said, lifting up the hourglass and turning it over as the grains of sand began to spill from one side to the other.

"And you think that will be enough time for each of us to, um, mess up the sheets?" Emma said.

"Well, they say it only takes the average person two minutes to get off while having sex. I think we'll find this is a little more titillating that the average erotic encounter. Especially with everybody watching. Something tells me that ten minutes will be more than enough time to get everyone's juices flowing."

"What if..." Amy said, crossing her arms over her chest defensively. "We're not *comfortable* being touched in the designated area?"

"No worries," Madison said, taking a more solemn tone. "If at any time you feel uncomfortable participating, you can simply pass your turn or just say no if you think your partner is going too far. The whole point of this game is to have fun and open ourselves up to new experiences. You'll always be in control of who and what is done to you."

After Amy nodded to signal her consent, Madison peered around the group and smiled.

"So if everybody's ready to begin, shall we get *naked*?"

Everybody peered at one another for a moment, then a few people slowly began peeling off their clothes until everyone sat naked around the mattress, awkwardly trying to cover up their exposed body parts. But it was obvious from the hardening nipples of many of the women and the slowly expanding penises between the men's legs that they were already becoming excited about what was about to happen next.

3

Madison spun the game needle and when it finished turning, it pointed toward Lucas, pausing on the image of an erect cock. A few people hummed teasingly as they peered at the handsome hunk while his girlfriend simply glared at him. Then Madison spun the needle a second time and it landed on a picture of a foot, pointing toward Laura. The group ooohed aloud, taunting the two partners, then Maddy smiled as she peered at the selected couple.

"Alright then," she said. "Our first pairing will be between Laura and Lucas, with Lucas receiving stimulation to his penis from Laura's foot." She nodded toward the mattress in the middle of the circle and smiled. "Assume the position, you two."

The two partners crawled onto the mattress on their hands and knees toward one another, and when they came face-to-face, Lucas paused, peering at Laura inquisitively.

"How do you want to do this exactly?" he asked. "What position would you like me to be in?"

Laura glanced at the large triangle-shaped pillow and smiled.

"Why don't you sit up using the pillow to support your back and spread your legs while I sit in front of you?" she said. "That way, I'll have direct access to your cock and you can watch me while I stimulate you."

"Works for me," Lucas said, positioning the pillow behind him and leaning back with his arms spread out over the top edge.

Laura positioned herself between his legs then propped her arms on the floor behind her, slowly lifting her right foot to flap Lucas's pecker from side to side. He was already half-erect, and as she tapped her toes against his manhood, it slapped against the inside of his thighs while their other partners looked on with tight lips.

Lucas's cock was uncircumcised, but nicely proportioned, about eight inches in length and six inches in circumference. His phallus had a pleasing caramel color that matched his tanned skin, and as his penis began to expand and rise to its full length, many of the women around the group gasped.

"Mmm," Laura moaned, watching his cock slowly elevate as she teased it with her toes. "I haven't tried something like this in a long time."

"Neither have *I*," Lucas panted, clearly enjoying Laura's ministrations.

"That's a nice flagpole you have there, Lucas," Laura purred, admiring his package now standing fully erect and perfectly straight above his belly. "Let's see if we can unfurl the colors, in a matter of speaking."

She placed the soles of both feet on opposite sides of Lucas's erection, pulling them down toward his balls. The hood of his cock slid down over his purple crown, revealing his glistening bulb coated with precum. The women and a few of the men took a deep gulp when they saw his engorged glans, and a few of them shifted position on the floor, clearly becoming aroused watching the action.

"Do you like that?" Laura said. "Do you like it when I pull your foreskin over your dripping head with my feet?"

"Um-hmm," Lucas groaned, staring between Laura's legs at her parted labia while she angled her knees outward to gain a better grip on his dick.

"Are you looking at my pussy while I stroke your big cock with my feet?"

"Mmm," Lucas hummed, trying not to make his girlfriend any more jealous than she already was watching another woman stroke his dick while she looked on a short distance away.

I peered over at Laura's husband and noticed his dick was *also* standing straight up between his crossed legs while he looked on. Whether he was becoming excited imagining his wife doing the same thing to him, or he was simply getting turned on watching her with another man, I wasn't sure. But from the looks of the bouncing erections around the circle, it was obvious he wasn't the *only* one getting turned on watching the show.

"Are you wishing it was my *cunny* stroking your cock instead of my feet?" Laura teased, watching a dribble of precum falling over Lucas's crown and sliding down the side of his prick.

"Uhnn," Lucas grunted, not wanting to reveal what he was *really* thinking.

"Or perhaps you'd prefer my *mouth*?" Laura said, tilting her body forward while blowing gently on his throbbing organ.

"One body part at a time," Madison interjected. "Those are the rules."

"But I'm not *touching* him with my mouth!" Laura huffed. "I was just *blowing* on him."

"Yes, well," Maddy said, watching Lucas's cum beginning to spill down both sides of his pole like an overflowing volcano. "From the look of things, it appears to be having a similar effect. The point of this game is to see how far we can stimulate our partners using only *one* body part."

Laura reluctantly backed away from Lucas as his hard-on bounced against his belly.

"I thought the point was to excite each other using our *imagination*?" she frowned.

"I'm sure you can use your imagination to stimulate your partner in plenty of other ways just using your *feet*," Madison smiled. "As far as I can tell, Lucas seems to be enjoying what you're doing just fine."

"Is that true, Lucas?" Laura said, peering at his flushed face. "Do you like the feel of my feet on your burning pecker?"

"Yes," Lucas panted, no longer trying to conceal his mounting enjoyment of Laura's attention.

"Do you want to cum all over my feet?"

"Yes," he groaned, lifting his hips off the floor as he thrust his hard-on between Laura's soles.

I peered over at Amy and noticed her hand beginning to move between her legs while she stared at her boyfriend's glistening pole rocking between Laura's feet. At the same time, Brad rolled his fingers over the tip of his erection while he watched the couple, equally mesmerized. In fact, by now just about everyone around the circle was stimulating themselves in one way or another while they took in the show. I smiled as I glanced over at Madison, who was nodding quietly watching the couple. I had to give it to her. She definitely knew how to break down people's inhibitions and get everyone in on the action.

Even the spouses and partners of those having sex in full view of the rest of the group.

Maybe it was the fact that a bunch of strangers were watching them while they caressed and probed each other's bodies. Or the fact that they were being forced to have sex with someone other than their usual partners. Or maybe it was the novel way she'd set it up for each of the partners to stimulate one another.

Either way, I was getting just as turned on as the rest of the group, and as Lucas began to open his mouth in rising pleasure while he pistoned his prick between Laura's feet, I couldn't resist pressing three fingers into my hole while I imagined it was his beautiful dick plowing me instead.

"Yes, baby," Laura moaned watching Lucas's purple head popping in and out of his hood as his balls pulled closer to the base of his pole. "Cum for me. Let me feel you soak my feet with your sweet spunk. Fuck, this is hot."

"Uhnnn," Lucas groaned, lifting his hips further off the mattress as he pumped his dick faster and faster between Laura's clamped feet.

But just before he was about to pop off, Madison interrupted again.

"Time's up!" she announced, holding up the hourglass to show that all the sand had spilled over to the other side.

"*What the-*" Brad groaned as Laura turned to look at Madison with fireballs in her eyes.

"You've got to be *kidding* me!" she said. "You're stopping us *now*? Can't you see how close he is to cumming?"

"So it would appear," Madison said, glancing at Lucas's bouncing cock with streams of precum falling down over his purple balls. "But what fun is a game if we don't play by the rules?

"Besides," she said, peering around the circle noticing half the men gripping their erections in their fists and the women holding their hands between their legs. "There's nothing stopping him or his girlfriend from *finishing* the job once he returns to the group. There weren't any rules about that."

"You're *evil!*" Laura hissed, retracting her feet from Lucas's burning organ while she shook her head and frowned at him apologetically.

"That's why you *love* me, right?" Madison said, winking at Laura as the two partners returned to their positions in the circle.

When they sat down next to their partners, I noticed Amy reach over to grip Lucas's tool tightly in her hand, squeezing it so hard it turned his glans a bright purple. Whether she was doing so because she was pissed that he'd gotten so aroused from another woman's touch or because she was eager to finish him off, was unclear.

All I knew was that you could cut the sexual tension in the room with a knife.

4

———

Madison took a short timeout to spray down the sheet with some Lysol, then she wiped up the wet stain Lucas had made in front of the pillow.

"Okay," she said, peering around the group. "Just so we're clear moving forward, each pairing will have a maximum of ten minutes together, as shown by the hourglass." She pulled a chair up beside her and placed the hourglass on the seat. "From now on I'll leave it prominently displayed for everyone to see how much time remains. Are we ready for the next round?"

"*Hmmpf!*" Laura grunted, still glaring at Maddy with her arms crossed.

"I'll take that as a yes," Madison smiled.

She spun the game needle and this time the pointer stopped on the image of an anus, aiming toward Mia. Everyone gasped as they peered at the pretty biracial girl, realizing she was about to be touched in a forbidden area. Then Maddy spun the needle again, and it landed on a picture of lips, pointing toward Alex, the pizza delivery boy. The group chuckled when they saw his wide eyes looking at the board with a mixture of fright and excitement. As a bead of sweat began to form on his forehead, I noticed his cock twitching between his legs.

"This should be interesting," Madison smiled. "This time we'll have Alex using his mouth to stimulate Mia's rosebud. Are you two ready?"

Alex and Mia peered at one another from across the circle, then they crawled onto the mat, pausing when they reached the triangle-shaped pillow.

"I've never done something like this before," Alex said nervously to Mia.

"Neither have I," Mia said, unsure exactly how to proceed.

"Someone once told me there are two kinds of people," Madison said, interrupting to ease the tension. "Those who *love* to have their assholes licked and those who pretend *not* to."

When everybody laughed, Mia peered into Alex's frightened eyes and smiled.

"I guess it's worth a try," she said. "We can always stop if either one of us feels uncomfortable."

"You better get started then before your time runs out," Maddy said, turning the hourglass over and setting it on the chair.

"How do you want me to do this?" Alex said, peering at Mia like a deer caught in headlights.

She looked at the pillow resting beside them then positioned herself in front of it.

"It might be easier if I bent over a little to give you easier access. Why don't I rest against the pillow while you kneel behind me?"

"Ok," Alex said, staring at her sexy ass as his penis began to rise.

Mia slowly spread her legs apart then leaned over the front of the pillow, resting her elbows on the mattress on the opposite side. She had a magnificent, tight round ass, and when she bent over in a forty-five-degree angle to match the shape of the pillow, everybody on my side of the circle could see her entire perineum exposed from her glistening pussy to her tight brown pucker.

By now, Alex was fully hard, as his cock bounced excitedly in front of him while he gawked at Mia's exposed snatch. For a moment,

I wondered if he'd even had sex with a woman at *all*, let alone used his tongue to stimulate one anywhere below her neck.

"Don't worry, she won't bite," Madison said, trying to egg him on. "I'm sure Mia washed herself thoroughly before coming to the party tonight. Give it a try, you might like it."

"Yes," Mia purred, turning her head to look back at Alex. "I scrubbed myself clean inside and out. Tell me if you can detect the scent of grapefruit and jasmine from the bodywash I used."

Alex leaned forward slightly, lowering his face closer to her dark crevasse as he wrinkled his nose, sniffing her ass.

"What do you think? Mia said. "Does it smell appetizing?"

"Mmm," Alex nodded as he stared at her dripping pussy mere inches away from his face.

"Why don't you start by kissing my cheeks," Amy purred. "Assuming Madison thinks that's not stretching the boundaries of our engagement."

"I think we'll give you a little extra latitude under the circumstances," Maddy smiled.

Alex paused for a moment then he lowered his face to Mia's ass, kissing her buttocks with soft pecks.

"Mmm," Mia groaned. "I like the feel of your breath on my ass. It feels sexy. Let me feel your tongue on my skin."

Alex extended his tongue, lapping one side of her ass like he was licking an ice cream cone, and Mia wiggled her hips to signal her approval.

"Yes, baby," she purred. "Lick my ass with your tongue. You're making me wet. Are you looking at my pussy while you stroke my butt?"

"Mmm-hmm," Alex nodded in a trance while he fixated on her exposed vulva as he swiped his tongue over her firm buttocks.

"Lick me at the top of my crack," Mia said, rolling her hips to encourage Alex to move closer to her butthole.

I smiled at her subtle way of coaching her reluctant partner to stretch the boundaries of his limited lovemaking experience. When he curled his tongue into the crease near the small of her back, I noticed a drop of precum fall from the tip of his cock onto the mattress. It was obvious that he was becoming increasingly excited touching the sexy African-Asian girl this closeup, and as he began to trace his tongue further down her cleft, Mia moaned in pleasure.

"Oh *God*, Alex," she panted. "That feels so good. Your tongue feels so warm and soft against my ass. Lick me lower–you're driving me crazy."

I shook my head as I watched the innocent adolescent explore Mia's body. Madison wasn't kidding when she suggested we might pick up a few new techniques from participating in this game. Not only was she introducing some unusual new procedures, but the feedback from the person receiving the stimulation was providing invaluable lessons for all of us.

As Alex lowered his tongue into her crease, Mia tilted her hips upward, encouraging him to go further.

"*Fuck*, that feels good," she groaned. "I've never been touched like this before. Suck my ass, Alex. You're making me tingle all over."

"Mmm," Alex hummed, beginning to lose himself in the feeling of burying his face in Mia's sexy ass.

As he continued inching lower, his tongue began probing the edge of her sphincter, and I saw it contracting excitedly in anticipation of Alex touching her private spot.

"Oh yes," she hissed. "Lick me right there. Let me feel your tongue on my rosebud. That feels incredible."

Alex paused for a moment, then began circling Mia's pucker with the tip of his tongue as he placed his hands on both sides of her cheeks.

"Uh-uh!" Madison chided from the opposite end of the mattress, and Alex quickly withdrew his hands, pressing his face harder into Mia's crack.

"Oh my God, Alex," Mia grunted, grinding her mound into the hard surface of the pillow. "That feels *insane!* Suck my ass with your tongue. You're going to make me come if you keep doing that."

"Mmm-hmm," Alex nodded excitedly, bobbing his head up and down as he slathered his tongue over her starfish.

"*Fuck, fuck, fuck,*" Mia panted. "Yes, baby. Keep sucking me there. Stick your tongue in my hole. I'm so close."

Alex paused for a second then he extended his tongue and pressed it slowly into her hole.

"Holy shit!" Amy squealed. "Yes! Fuck my ass with your tongue. You're an incredible lover, Alex. I'm going to come all over your face soon!"

"Mmm," Alex nodded, his dick dripping strings of cum onto the rubber mattress below his tightening balls.

It was an incredible sight watching the two lovers with their asses turned up in the air while their juices dripped onto the mat, pooling in a puddle beneath their gyrating hips. As they began to moan more loudly and shake their hips in unison, I peered around the circle noticing everybody jerking and jilling themselves unashamedly as they watched the erotic performance unfolding before them.

I turned to look at the hourglass and noticed only a sliver of sand remaining in the upper half.

Come on, Alex, I wanted to scream to make sure he took Mia over the edge before time ran out again. *You can do it. Suck her ass like your life depends on it.*

Alex also seemed to sense the urgency and as Mia began flapping her hips harder against his face, he buried his tongue deeper in her hole, crunching his jaw up and down like he was eating her ass. This seemed to drive Amy even crazier, and within seconds, the room was filled with the sound of her screaming as her hips shook against his face.

As I watched her buttocks quivering from the convulsions she was feeling inside, I noticed Alex's cock bobbing up and down as he began shooting long strings of cum toward his belly in the direction of Mia's pulsating pussy. Suddenly, the entire room was filled with the sound of moans and groans as one person after another began climaxing watching the erotic show. Up to this point, I'd been so focused on watching the couple in front of me, I hadn't even thought about touching myself. But when I saw everyone else shaking and convulsing around the room, I thrust my hand into my pussy and came hard as I pressed my wrist against my burning clit.

Mia's orgasm seemed to last forever as she writhed against Alex's face, and when he finally pulled his dripping face away from her vulva, I saw her anus clamping open and shut like a jellyfish as her orgasm began to peter out. By the time they collapsed on top of one another, the only noise you could hear in the room was the sound of everyone panting in blissful satisfaction.

5

———————

"Well, I'd say things are starting to heat up *now*," Madison smiled when Alex and Mia returned to their positions in the circle. "That was crazy hot! Are you guys ready for some more fun and games?"

As everyone nodded excitedly, Maddy crawled onto the rubber mattress to wipe down the huge puddle next to the pillow.

"Anybody else need some paper towel?" she said, holding up the roll. "Cause from the looks of things, Alex and Mia weren't the *only* ones enjoying that last episode."

After everybody cleaned up, Madison positioned the game spinner in front of her on the mattress for everyone to see.

"I hope you guys saved a little for the next round. Because if that *last* one is any indication of what's to come, there's going to be a lot more juices flowing before this night is over."

She flicked the needle with her middle finger and when it stopped spinning, it landed on a picture of a woman's breast, pointing toward Emma. The group hummed approvingly, then she spun it again and it stopped on a picture of a vulva, aiming toward Amy.

"This should be interesting," she nodded. "This time it will be Amy using her *pussy* to stimulate Emma's *breasts*."

Madison peered over at Amy, remembering her earlier hesitation about touching certain body parts.

"Are you guys up for this?" Maddy asked.

"*Damn straight*," Amy said, clamoring excitedly onto the mat without even bothering to glance at her boyfriend.

I smiled at how far she'd come from her initial reluctance to participate, to her current eagerness to gain payback for Lucas's earlier rendezvous with Laura.

When the two girls reached the center of the mattress, Emma peered at the triangle-shaped cushion and shook her head.

"I'm not sure how much help the pillow will be this time," she said. "Unless you want to stand over me while I press my breasts up for you to fondle."

"Fuck *that*," Amy said. "It'll be easier if you lie down on your back while I kneel over you. That way you can relax while I move freely over your body."

"I like the sound of that," Emma said, lying down and peering up at Amy's dripping pussy as she straddled her waist and lowered her crotch down onto Emma's quivering stomach.

"Mmm," Emma moaned. "You feel so warm against my skin."

"Only *warm*?" Amy grinned.

"And *wet*," Emma smiled.

"Have you ever had another woman do this to you before?"

"Once before," Emma said, turning her head to glance at me. "During an all-girls' camping trip. But we were more focused on rubbing certain *other* parts together than trying this."

"Well lie back and enjoy then," Amy panted as she slowly rocked her hips forward and back over Emma's tensing stomach muscles. "You've got some pretty tight abs there, girl."

"Do you like rubbing your pussy on my stomach?" Emma teased, glancing at Madison to make sure they weren't overstepping their bounds.

"She's moving in the right *direction*," Madison nodded, giving her assent for them to continue.

Amy pushed her hips a few inches higher on Emma's stomach, pausing when she reached the bottom of her ribcage.

"Uhnnn," she groaned, rubbing her twitching clit against the hard bone while she leaned forward, staring into Emma's eyes.

"Yes, baby," Emma purred. "Rub your clit on my chest. I can feel your nub rolling over my skin."

"This is almost as good as a man's *cock*," Amy smiled. "*Better*, actually. At least this way, I get some direct stimulation on my most sensitive area instead of him just ramming his tool inside me."

I peered over at Lucas who tilted his head while he peered at Amy with a sheepish grin. But that wasn't the *only* body part tilting, as his big dick began to rise between his legs while he watched his girlfriend fucking Emma.

Every man's dream, I smiled, shaking my head in dismay. *Watch closely, Lucas, and take some mental notes. You might learn a few things about how to satisfy your girlfriend watching her make love to another woman.*

While Amy rocked her hips against the bottom of Emma's ribcage growing more aroused from the direct stimulation to her clit, she lowered her torso onto Emma's chest, rubbing her tits softly against Emma's breasts.

"Uh-uh," Madison interrupted, reminding the girls of the rules of engagement. "Pussy to breasts only. Surely you can think of some *other* ways to tease Emma's pretty tits other than with your breasts?"

"Don't mind if I *do*," Amy said, sitting up straight and dragging her hips forward on top of Emma's compressed cleavage. Then she placed her arms on the floor beside Emma's shoulders for support and began rocking her wet pussy all over Emma's glistening tits.

"*Fuck*, that's hot," Emma said, tilting her head up to stare at Amy's shaved pussy rolling over her shiny globes. "Fuck my tits with your pretty pussy, Amy. This feels incredible."

"Almost as good as rubbing *other* body parts with another woman?" Amy grinned.

"Yes," Emma panted. "In a different sort of way. I've never tried it

this way before. I'm definitely going to be adding this to my repertoire, both ways."

"Oh?" Amy teased, spreading her legs further apart to press her
pussy down harder onto Emma's breasts. "You like the idea of fucking
a girl's *tits* with your pussy? Do you think you'd like it as much as
when your boyfriend rubs his *dick* between your breasts?"

"*Better*," Emma smiled, glancing over at Lucas who was pumping
his cock up and down in his fist. "This way there's some natural lubrication and I don't have to worry about getting squirted in the eye."

"We'll have to *see* about that," Amy grunted, shifting her hips a few
inches to the side to position her vulva directly over Emma's right
breast.

"Yes," Emma shuddered watching Amy's gaping slit roll over her
erect nipple as it disappeared in and out of her hole. "Fuck my breast
with your pussy. I can see your bulging clit while you rub it over my
nipple."

"That's not the *only* thing that's bulging," Amy smiled. "I'm going
to rub myself against your teat while your breast caresses my ass."

Emma glanced once again in Madison's direction to make sure
they weren't breaking the rules, but Maddy simply nodded as she
began to roll her fingers over her glistening pussy.

I was happy to see Madison had gotten naked with the rest of the
group when the game began, and as I watched her trill herself, I
wondered when my turn would come around and who I'd be paired
with. But for the moment, I was enjoying watching the two girls rub
their bodies together, and as Amy began to moan more loudly, I
pinched my own nipples imagining it was me she was tit-fucking
instead of Emma.

"This feels amazing," Amy panted, rocking her hips harder against
Emma's bouncing boob. "I'm going to come soon against your sweet
breast."

"Yes, baby," Emma hissed. "Come all over my tits. I want to watch
you coat me with your juices while you fuck me with your pretty
cunt."

"Nnngn," Amy grunted, beginning to approach the peak of her pleasure.

I glanced quickly at the hourglass, estimating they only had a minute or so left before time ran out.

Fuck her hard, Amy, I said to myself. *Show your boyfriend it takes more than a big cock to get you off.*

By now, Lucas was pumping his organ just as rapidly as Amy was humping Emma's breast, and I wondered who would pop off first. But just as his mouth began to gape open on the brink of climax, Amy howled as her body began shaking over Emma's chest while Emma pumped her pussy in the air behind her. I glanced between Amy's legs, noticing her squirting all over her partner's chest and neck, then Lucas groaned as he began to shoot one long rope of cum after another out of his dick clasped tightly between his two hands.

Fuck me, I thought, feeling my own orgasm wash over me while I tribbed my clit watching the three of them grunting and shaking, coming harder than any of them had in a long time.

That ought to make up for your ruined orgasm, I smiled at Lucas, feeling some spittle dripping out of the side of my mouth watching his giant pecker oozing all over his hands.

When the girls finally recovered from their orgasms, they crawled back exhausted to their previous positions in the circle. I noticed Amy glance down at her boyfriend's spent penis then grin up at him, staring him straight in the eyes.

Two can play this game, I saw her mouth the words while he looked back at her with a lopsided grin.

6

After Madison cleaned up the mattress again, she sat cross-legged in front of the spinner board and smiled.

"Are you guys enjoying the festivities so far?"

"Mmm," many people in the group hummed to signal their approval.

"Is everyone looking forward to having their *own* turn?"

"Mmm-hmm!" they grunted in excitement.

"Does anyone *else* think ten minutes is too short a time for each round?"

Maddy looked around the circle, and everyone shook their heads.

"That's good, because we've still got a fair amount of ground to cover, both in terms of who's still left to play, and which body parts to use. Are you ready to move on to the next round?"

When everyone nodded their heads, Maddy flicked the spinner and it landed once again on a picture of an erect penis, pointing toward Neil. Then she spun it again, and it rested on the penis picture again, this time pointing toward Shae, the pretty transgender girl.

"*Oooo!*" the group huffed, teasing the two participants while I peered over at Neil to gauge his reaction. As a dyed-in-the-wool heterosexual, I wondered how he'd feel about being asked to rub cocks with someone else. But as he glanced at Shae, I noticed him running his eyes over her sexy figure, lingering on her hefty cock slowly drifting up the side of her thigh.

Unlike most transgender women, Shae was a true hermaphrodite, equipped with both male and female parts. Instead of balls resting below her sizeable pecker, she had a regular woman's vulva, including all the usual internal anatomy. Although she had a fully-functioning penis, in all other respects she looked like a normal woman, with firm large breasts, a narrow waist, and a curvy round ass to die for. It didn't take long for Neil's cock to begin rising in lockstep with hers as they peered at one another from opposite sides of the mattress.

"Are you two just going to *stare* at one another the whole time?" Madison said. "Or were you thinking of actually *touching* those pretty peckers together?"

Neil and Shae stood up and walked onto the mattress, and when they met in the middle, he paused a few inches away from Shae, unsure how to proceed. Shae peered at his cock pointing straight up toward hers and stepped forward, slapping her dick against his like she was having a sword fight. Neil took one look at her big dick and began to swing his hips back and forth as the sound of hard flesh slapping together echoed across the room.

Shae was uncircumcised, and after a few seconds of playful slapping, she pressed the tip of her cock against Neil's, rubbing his dripping precum over her hanging skin. Then she peered at Madison, raising an eyebrow.

"Do you think I can use my *hand* for just a moment?" she asked. "If the objective is to touch our cocks together, I have an idea for how we might make this a little more interesting."

Madison peered at their dripping dicks, then looked around the circle, curling her lips into a smile.

"What do you think, gang?" she said. "Should we give these two a little extra latitude under the circumstances?"

"*Absolutely!*" Alex said, hypnotized by Shae's impressive girl-cock.

"Okay," Madison nodded, peering back at Shae. "But only for a couple of minutes. I want to see how creative you can be just using your penises. From the looks of it, you both seem to be enjoying it fine so far."

Shae pointed Neil's tip toward hers then she encircled the end of her erection with her hand, pulling her foreskin forward, overtop Neil's glans. Then she began rocking her hips forward while squeezing their joined crowns, creating a lubricated sleeve for them both to glide against. As he stared at Shae's tits, Neil groaned, thinking he'd died and gone to heaven.

Talk about stretching your sexual horizons, I thought. *I bet he never even dreamed of doing something like this before.*

As they rocked their hips together in rising pleasure, Shae cupped Neil's balls, squeezing them softly while she tightened her grip on the tip of his cock still buried in her foreskin.

"Fuck *me*," Neil groaned, obviously enjoying the experience far more than he imagined.

"Okay," Madison suddenly interrupted. "I think that's enough use of the *hands* for a while. We've got to be fair to everybody else. Let's try to keep it just cock-to-cock the rest of the way, shall we?"

Shae paused for a moment, then she pulled their dicks apart, rubbing Neil's gushing precum all over the side of his shaft with her flapping tip.

"I have another idea for how we can rub our cocks together," she said, peering into his hooded eyes.

"Whatever you want," he panted, completely at her mercy. "You seem to have more experience in these matters."

"Mmm," Shae nodded, positioning Neil in front of the triangle-shaped pillow, then pressing gently down on his shoulder, encouraging him to sit against it.

After he squatted down onto the mattress and leaned back against the pillow, Shae pulled his legs apart and bent his knees upward. Then she squatted down in front of him, pointing her cock up in the air, inches away from his. As she shimmied her hips forward, their shafts touched. Neil groaned when he felt his balls press against Shae's wet vulva, then she began to rock her hips forward and back, sliding her dick softly against Neil's.

"Holy shit!" he grunted, hardly believing his luck being paired with the sexy transgender girl.

"Do you like rubbing your dick against another cock?" Shae teased, watching his precum pour out of his slit and down the sides of their joined phalluses.

"I like rubbing *your* dick, that's for sure," he panted.

"What about my lady parts? Do you like them *too*?"

"Fuck yes," Neil grunted, ogling her bouncing tits.

"Would you like to fuck my pussy while you stroke my cock and watch me come all over your hairy chest?"

"*God* yes."

"It's too bad Madison has all these rules," she said. "Maybe we can get together later and touch a few *other* body parts together?"

"Absolutely," Neil panted, no longer worried about protecting his straight body image.

"I'd like that," Shae said, peering over at the hourglass. "But we better make the most of our limited time together. Madison's going to cut us off any moment now. Are you getting close?"

"I'm almost there," Neil grunted. "I just need a bit more friction..."

Shae wrapped her legs around Neil's hips, pulling their bodies closer together, then she leaned forward, pressing their cocks up against their bellies. As she rubbed her tits against his chest, their shiny dicks rolled over one another while they both began to pant more loudly. For a second, I thought Madison was going to tell them to separate since they were touching different body parts. But when she saw there was only a little bit of sand left in the hourglass, she hesitated.

As the two lovers grunted more loudly while they ground their hips together, I noticed quite a few other people around the circle jerking and jilling themselves as the watched the sexy couple. Apparently, Neil and Shae weren't the only *ones* turned on by the idea of a pretty transgender girl frotting her cock with a man. Having already experienced my *own* fling with Shae a few months earlier, I knew first-hand all the unique ways she could please her partner, and for a moment, I was a little envious of Neil having her for himself.

By now, the two lovers were locked in a passionate embrace as they wrapped their arms around one another, no longer concerned about Madison's restrictions. With one final thrust, they jerked their cocks hard against one another, grunting loudly as they began spurting over each other's chests. While I watched their bodies shaking and convulsing together, soft moans and sighs began emanating from around the room while other participants reached their own climax watching the erotic performance in the middle of the circle.

When the they finally separated, panting and exhausted, Neil and Shae peered into one another's eyes and smiled. In the space of ten short minutes, Neil had gone from being a dedicated straight man to a happy bisexual.

I wondered how *else* Madison was planning to stretch our sexual horizons this evening, watching her staring at my fingers deeply embedded in my throbbing cunt.

7

———

"Whew!" Madison sighed when Neil and Shae returned to the circle. "Is it getting hot in here or what?"

"Yeah," Ryan said, fanning his face with a floppy wrist. "That was crazy hot."

I smiled seeing his dick still standing at attention between his legs, knowing that as a gay man, he must have been doubly turned on by the sight of a straight guy hooking up with a transgender girl.

"Give me a second to clean up the mess these two made," Maddy said. "Then we'll get back to the action. Does anyone need a bio-break or some extra refreshments? Help yourself to beer or wine in the kitchen."

We all took a short break and when everyone reassembled around the circle, Madison sat down excitedly, placing the spinner board between her legs.

"I don't know about *you* guys," she grinned. "But I'm dying to find out whose turn it will be next and what body parts they'll have to use. Are you ready for some more tribbing and frotting?"

"Damn *straight*," Ryan panted, his dick still flapping excitedly between his legs.

"Maybe we can find another straight boy for you to play with, Ryan," Madison smiled, peering around the circle.

She spun the needle and when it stopped turning, it landed on the picture of a pussy, pointing toward herself.

"Oooo!" the group squealed, excited to see Madison finally getting in on the action.

"Hmm," she said, shifting unsteadily. "I'm not sure I qualify to participate, being the *host* and all–"

"Fuck *that*," Neil said. "We didn't have any choice when you forced us to pair up with our partners using the parts you selected. It's *your* turn to be the submissive one this time!"

"Alright," she said, winking toward Shae. "But I didn't exactly see you complaining when it was your turn in the last round."

She spun the needle again, and after a long pause, it landed on another picture of a pussy, pointing toward me.

"Woo-hoo!" some of my friends welped when they saw that I'd be the one providing stimulation to Madison.

Maddy glanced over at me and grinned.

"I *told* you to there was no telling who or how you'd be paired up this evening. Are you up for this?"

"Are you *kidding* me?" I said, running my eyes over her naked body. "I've been up for this since we all took off their clothes at the start of the game. Assume the position!"

Madison crawled out onto the mattress then paused as I stood over her, staring at her upturned ass.

"What position did you want me to be in, exactly?" she said, looking up at me.

"Hmm," I hummed, stroking my chin. "So much pussy, so little time."

Then I peered at the triangle-shaped pillow and smiled.

"Why don't you bend over the pillow with your ass pointing up? That way, I'll have clearer access to your pretty peachka."

"Mmm," she purred. "And what position will *you* be in?"

"You'll just have to leave that to me," I smirked. "I've got a *hundred* different ideas running through my head."

Madison turned to face the pillow then she leaned her hips against the front of it, bending over with her elbows resting on the floor.

"*That's* what I'm talking about," I said, widening my eyes when I saw her dripping cunt flaring open for the whole room to see.

I squatted down a few inches and grabbed the sides of her ass, rubbing my mound against her crack.

"That doesn't exactly feel like you're caressing my *pussy*," she said, peering back at me.

"Stop being so anal for a moment while I work up to it. I'm trying to get you in the mood."

"You're the one fixating on my *anus* at this moment," she joked. "I'm *already* in the mood. Rub your pretty cunt against my pussy. We don't have all day."

"Hey!" Laura said, suddenly turning toward Maddy's vacant spot in the circle. "Speaking of time, Madison forgot to turn the hourglass over before they got started. Can one of you guys do it for her? She put each one of *us* on the clock. Now I want to see how far *she* can go in ten minutes."

As Lucas turned the hourglass over, I peered at Maddy's slit between her parted legs and got down on all fours, pressing my buttocks against hers. When I tilted my hips upward, our vulvas touched, and Maddy groaned.

"Yes, Jade," she grunted. "Trib me with your wet pussy. I've missed feeling your sweet cunny against mine."

"We haven't tried it this way before," I panted, feeling our labia and juices intermingling.

"I like it," she said. "I like the feeling of your ass rubbing against mine while you trib me with your pussy."

"Oh?" I teased. "You don't think we're overstepping the rules by touching our *asses* in addition to our pussies?"

"I don't see how we *couldn't* in this position," she chuckled. "Besides, you're definitely rubbing your pussy against mine, so I don't think we're breaking any rules so far, what do you say group?"

"I don't *know*," Laura kidded, peering around the circle at the other participants. "What do you think, gang? Should we let them touch their asses while they're rubbing their pussies together?"

"Maybe just for a *couple* of minutes," Shae smiled, winking at Madison.

"You better make this count then, girl," Madison said, peering around the pillow to look at me while I stared at our dripping slits mashing together.

"I plan on it," I grunted, pressing my cheeks harder against her ass while I tilted my hips, sliding my wet pussy over hers.

But as I watched the sand spilling from one side of the half-empty hourglass to the other, I shook my head wondering if we had enough friction on our clits to get off in time. After slapping our butts together for another minute or so, I pulled away and stood up.

"What the *hell*?" Madison said, turning to look up at me. "I was just getting into it..."

"I was too," I said. "But we don't have much time left, and I'm thinking of a different position that might be even more fun."

"I'm all ears," Madison smiled. "Or rather, all *pussy* at this particular moment."

"Turn the other way around," I said. "With your back against the pillow."

Madison pulled herself up then turned to lie against the pillow with her butt resting on the mattress.

"No—with your ass facing *upward*," I smiled.

"How do you mean," she said, looking at me with a puzzled expression. "How—"

"Lie down with your shoulders resting on the mattress and with your back against the front of the pillow. That way, we'll be able to rub our pussies together more easily, and I'll have more room to maneuver."

"Got it," Madison nodded as she flipped herself upside down, pointing her pussy up in the air.

I bent her knees and spread her legs apart, then I positioned myself between her legs, slowly lowering myself down into a scissor position.

"Fuck, yes," Madison panted. "That's much better."

"And we're no longer breaking the rules," I grunted, feeling her vulva touching mine.

As I began to rock my hips forward and back, the sound of our wet pussies slapping together echoed around the circle while the rest of the group started playing with themselves watching the two of us moaning on the mattress.

"Oh *God*, Jade," Maddy rasped. "That feels incredible. Fuck me with your hot pussy. I can feel your hard clit rubbing against mine."

"Yeah?" I said, pulling her knee up against my chest while I pressed my pussy harder against hers. "Do you *like* this new position?

"Yes," Madison panted. "I'm going to have to incorporate this pillow more often in my lovemaking repertoire."

"Me too," I hissed, feeling the pangs of another orgasm welling up inside me.

"Fuck me, baby," Madison panted. "I'm going to come soon. Grind your pussy against my cunt while I watch your pretty tits jiggling overtop of me."

"Unghh," I groaned, starting to fall over the tipping point. "I'm coming Maddy! I'm coming hard against your sweet pussy..."

As I held her upturned knee tight against my chest, my pussy began convulsing against hers, spraying my juices all over her stomach, tits, and face. She blinked up at me with a sputtering mouth, digging her fingertips into the side of my ass while she shook and moaned in simultaneous climax. Within seconds, the entire room was filled with the sound of everybody jerking and squirting while they came along with us taking in the sexy show.

As I shuddered overtop of Madison peering up at me, I smiled.

"How's that for getting our juices flowing?" I whispered, remembering her promise to me in her email invitation earlier in the week.

She could only smile back at me as my river of pleasure poured over her pretty face and tits.

Ready for more erotic chills and thrills? Download the exciting first story in Victoria Rush's new erotic fantasy series, *The Enchanted Forest*:

Sometimes it's not just the grass that's greener on the other side...

FOLLOW VICTORIA RUSH:

Want to keep informed of my latest erotic book releases? Sign up for my newsletter and receive a FREE bonus book:

Spying on the neighbors just got a lot more interesting...